C

I
GET
ON
THE
BUS

I GET ON THE BUS

A Novel by
Reginald McKnight

Little, Brown and Company
Boston   Toronto   London

Library of Congress Cataloging-in-Publication Data

McKnight, Reginald, 1956–
    I get on the bus: a novel / by Reginald McKnight. — 1st ed.
        p.   cm.
    ISBN 0-316-56055-3
    I. Title.
    PS3563.C3833I18   1990
    813'.54 — dc20   90-30267
                                                                CIP

10 9 8 7 6 5 4 3 2 1

FG

Published simultaneously in Canada by
Little, Brown & Company (Canada) Limited

Printed in the United States of America

For Michele

I
GET
ON
THE
BUS

1 I Get on the Bus

The bus stops. I get on. It is crowded and hot. There is no air and the skin feels like chicken fat. I try to push my way toward the front in search of more air, but there are too many people so I remain in the middle. No one will make way for me. It is well past midday and everyone is tired and irritable; I cannot blame them. It is always hot here. The Senegalese sun has no mercy. It is colorless, cruel. I have been here only three months; a desert of twenty-one months stretches before me. Sometimes I get very tired. I think I am coming down with something.

I must admit the Peace Corps is not what I had hoped it would be. In fact, it is worthless. Or I am. I teach a little English, here and there, but mainly I do nothing. I sit in my bungalow, get high, and pretend I am Kurtz waiting for Marlow. I kill flies. I read books. I think about Wanda. I take walks. I sleep. Yet I will stay on here. What else am I to do? There is nothing for me in the U.S. Nothing I want or need, anyway. Memories suffice. I am here. I may not do my job — nobody cares or notices what you do here anyway — but I will not go home before those twenty-one months are up. I will let this hot sun and these strange people have their ineffable effect on me.

Someone taps me on the shoulder. I have forgotten to pay

my eighty francs. A young boy with peppercorn hair and a ragged, grayish boubou tells me so. I do not understand his words, but he is pointing at the ticket cage and holding out his hand for the money. He will pass it along to the cageman. The cageman gives me a nasty smile from behind his dark glasses. I do not like his face. He says something to me in Wolof, but I do not understand. He speaks to me in French. I shrug, point to my ear. "What section?" he says, shaking his head. "Section two," I tell him as I hand the money to the boy. The cageman says something in Wolof to the boy and the boy laughs and nods; he returns my change and gives me my ticket, smiling at me with sly eyes.

It is true. I speak neither French nor Wolof. I am, however, an excellent test-taker, and had no problem fooling the Peace Corps bureaucrats in Washington. I can read a little French, write a word or two of it, but have made no real effort to speak the language. I hate French. It is a language that is impossible to get one's teeth and tongue into. Its sounds are too subtle. It begs to be mispronounced. And as for Wolof? What is the use?

The bus stops, hisses, and squeals. Many more people get on. The boy with the peppercorn hair wedges himself into a small space in front of me. His head is under my chin. I must keep my own head tilted back because the top of his head is covered with sores. The sight of his sweaty head with its many dime-sized sores makes me queasy and hostile. I want to clout him on the ear with my free hand, but I am, in the same moment, fascinated by the ulcers. I stare at his head for a long time. Pus, blood, matted hair, a yellow, red, black, and brown mosaic.

The bus stops. One man gets off; several people get on. It seems impossible that more could get on. The boy is swallowed up into the invisible recesses of the crowd. I am pushed to the opposite side of the bus, stuffed behind a

4

young girl. She wears a simple wraparound skirt and a loose, white camisole. I can, with little effort, look over her shoulder and down her décolletage. I gaze into the soft slope of her breasts. I can almost, almost see her nipples. Whenever the bus bounces or brakes, her breasts sway. Her heavy, round buttocks push against my groin. The bus turns, rumbles, bounces, brakes, shifts, vibrates, grunts, rolls. With my free hand, I reach into my pocket to ease my penis into a more comfortable position. I have never done this sort of thing before, and I wonder whether the girl knows what I am trying not to do. She makes no indication that she does. The bus shudders.

The bus stops. A very young boy leads a blind man on. The bus fills with the sound of his alms-crying. It is less musical than impressionistic. The sounds do not touch the ear, but wring the stomach empty, shrink the testicles, scale the neck. I take twenty francs from my pocket and let them fall into his weathered hand. "Jerrejeff," he says. And he turns his face to me. It is misshappen and cicatrized on the left side. His eyes look like half-cooked egg whites and are brimming with tears. I turn away from him. Now that he has collected a few alms, his cry is shriller.

Though the sun is setting, the bus still swelters. Few people are talking. Some have fallen asleep. I think my underarms stink, and instead of holding the handgrips above I grasp the armrest of the seat next to me. My knuckles push against the yielding thigh of a truculent-looking woman of fifty or so. I do not like the sensation at all. She looks at me askance, or rather, in my general direction as if I were an irritating draft from a window. She is enormous. She is dressed in a bright pink boubou and wears heavy gold on both wrists, her neck, and ears. Abraxas. She is beautiful. She is royalty, and I imagine her reposing in some many-faceted obsidian hive with thousands of tiny

5

eunuchs clustered round her fat oiled thighs. Feeding her. Fighting and dying for her.

The bus stops and people continue to pack themselves on. Very few get off. I am squeezed into the corner near the rear window. I take a handkerchief from my shirt pocket and dab my neck and face to no avail. The perspiration slithers down me, soaks my shirt to transparency. I try to open the window, but it will not budge. I want to ask a policeman next to me for help, but as I have said, I speak no Wolof, and my French, I have discovered, is too pathetic for even such a simple request. I am too proud to mime and gesticulate for a little air. The policeman looks neither friendly nor kind. He stands here, sweating as I do, with malicious indifference shaping his face. He probably smells me too and would perhaps be hostile to me.

I stare out this window at all the swirling movement below. It is a liquid collage. Smears of color hardly subdued by the oncoming dusk. There is running, laughing, buying, thieving, limping, strutting, rolling. I smell an infinity of odors, all of them overpowering and unfamiliar. I hear vendors bark-chatter-grunt the virtues of countless items; the car rapide boys yell, "Dakah! Dakah! Dakah!" as if chanting to keep the world fluid. It gives me a headache. Nothing makes sense. Nothing stands still.

I am frustrated because the window will not open, because I stink and can do nothing about it. This world spills into me. I cannot stop it. I cannot open this window. I cannot open it. A thick bile gushes into my mouth. It is so bitter my neck muscles draw taut. My breathing stiffens. I look about myself, at all these faces that reveal nothing but what I put there, tell no stories, tell no lies, exhibit neither fear nor boredom. Nonfaces. Blaring African dress, cheap black-market watches, jewelry of pure gold, jutting shoulders and breasts, hips and knees, elbows, chins, skulls.

I am not here. I am missing.

I would scream, but I have no language for screaming. There is too much to see. I am blind. I am deaf. I cannot breathe. I cannot breathe. I cannot breathe. My head hurts.

The bus stops. I get off. I walk.

How odd that I can walk.

2 I Go to a Restaurant

My head hurts. It has been hurting for two weeks now, yet I have done nothing for it. No aspirin, no medicine of any sort. I do smoke marijuana, but it does nothing for the pain, really. It only makes it more interesting. It makes my head feel like a helium balloon. My head floats upward on my long string of a neck, and just before the string is stretched completely vertical, it is as if an invisible hand grabs the string and gives it a violent, downward jerk, causing an explosion of pain at the base of my skull.

When I am not high (which is rare), the pain is more constant, throbbing with the rhythm of my heartbeat. I now step down the sidewalk to the rhythm of my heart. My head beats like a drum. I am afraid to change my pace, fearing the pain will increase if I do not match footfall with heart rate. I am not sure where I am. I am simply walking, happy to be moving according to my own will.

It must be late because shops are closing. The buses that are heading north, away from Dakar, are full. Those that are heading south are empty. I hear the muezzin's cry. It sounds muffled, far-off. Hunger pulls at my stomach so I turn into the first place I see, a Vietnamese restaurant decorated in fading red and yellow dragons. I sit. The place smells of pork and soy sauce. It is too warm. I feel like leaving, but do not. A grave-looking man with a flat nose and a raspberry stain on his neck perfunctorily welcomes me, sets a clear red tumbler of water in front of me, and hands me a grease-spattered menu. My heart slows.

The proprietor and his wife snap at each other in their nasally Asian voices. I sip my water, slip my cigarettes from my shirt pocket, and take one from the pack. It is soggy, but I am able to light it. It tastes very bad. I smoke it anyway. The proprietor returns and I give him my order. All I want is a vegetable-and-rice dish.

"Le poulet est très bon aujourd'hui," he says.

"Non merci."

"Voulez-vous une brochette du porc?"

"Non merci. Riz et légume seulement."

He spins around and struts away, muttering to himself. Suddenly my vision blurs, a pain shoots through my head. I shut my eyes and clasp my hands over my scalp, clench my teeth. I imagine being clubbed on the back of the head by a gang of thick-wristed, baseball bat–toting rednecks. The pain subsides and I feel dizzy. Then the dizziness subsides and I feel numb — not everywhere, just my head, my back, my fingers and lips. I open my eyes and find myself back on the bus.

My first thought is that I am unconscious, dreaming. I am neither distressed nor surprised. Yes, I am unconscious, I think. I am dreaming. In reality, I am lying on the floor, or slumped over my table at the restaurant. The man with the flat nose will call a cab or an ambulance. I will be rushed to a hospital. I will be treated, released, and will be able to finish my weekend here in Dakar. I will go back to Ziguinchor refreshed, relaxed, ready to goldbrick and suffer the usual boredom. I am not really on the bus.

But because I can feel, actually feel the vibrations of the bus, feel the bodies around me, smell the couscous, goat

leather, incense, diesel fuel, pomade, ocean water, the familiar and the unfamiliar, I begin to suspect that I truly
am again on the bus. The experience is too arabesque, too
busy. Someone tugs at my sleeve. I turn and face the boy
with the peppercorn hair. He leers at me, looks me dead in
the eye, which is something the Senegalese usually do not
do. He pokes his upturned hand just inches from my nose.
"'Merican," he says. "Money." I reach into my pocket, grab
one hundred francs, slap it into his hand. I want to ask him
where and when I got on the bus, where the bus is going.
But, of course, I am unable to. But what does it matter? I
must be dreaming.

It is very dark. I cannot see out the windows because of
the interior lights. Only by working my way back to the
rear window, putting my nose up to the glass, and cupping
my hands around my eyes, will I be able to see where I am.
It is my thought to do precisely what I would do if I were
actually awake. I will get off at any familiar stop, treat
people respectfully. I will try to avoid snuggling up with
village girls.

I begin moving toward the rear of the bus. Blocking my
way are two very tall men, one in traditional garb, a beautiful green and gold boubou, the other in neatly pressed blue
jeans and a dark, short-sleeved shirt with "Tiburon" printed
across the front in red. "Pardonnez-moi," I say to the two
men. Neither of them so much as twitches. I turn my shoulder and wedge in between the two men. They are as impassive as turnstiles, neither giving way nor resisting. It is the
same with the others whom I pass on my way to the rear,
and by the time I get there it is clear to me that none of the
passengers is aware of my presence. None, it seems, but the
boy. I will talk to him, I say to myself. I will talk to him
after I find out where I am.

I press my nose against the rear window, using my hands

as blinders, and peer out the window. At first I can discern nothing. Vague blobs of light, unfocused shapes, are all I can see. And though it sounds and feels as though the bus is moving, I am unable to determine any visual proof of motion. I turn around, immediately finding myself face-to-face with the boy. He is holding my change between two fingers, grinning at me in the usual way. I wish to tell him to keep the change, but I do not remember the French word for "keep." He drops the change into my palm and turns away. "Hey," I say. He turns. And handing him the change, I say, "Where are we?"

"I don't speak English," says the boy; but he says this in perfect English. I *am* dreaming, I say to myself. I really am unconscious. Then I say to the boy, "Your pronunciation is sure good for someone who doesn't speak the language."

"I told you. I don't speak English."

"I'm sorry."

The boy grins, squints a bit, and curls his finger, beckoning me to come close to him. I lean over a bit, but am sure I am quite close enough. He cranes his long neck, breathes sour air into my ear, and says, "I don't have to tell, do I, américain noir? I really don't have to tell you. You must know it. You must." And then he pauses. A nice, long theatrical pause — two, three, four, five — "You're fucked," he says.

The bus stops. I get off.

3 I Murder

I find myself in the very same place where I got off before. Nothing seems surreal. Nothing seems dream-like. On the contrary, everything seems powerfully real. I smell the sour cooking charcoal from nearby houses. I hear reggae music thumping and rattling out of bad stereo speakers somewhere in the apartments above me. I step down broken sidewalk, each step marking the rhythm of my throbbing head. The air feels good on my neck, arms, and face. Marley sings, *Nooo, woman no cry. Noo — oh, woman no cry* . . . to the jump-pump of the reggae bass. I find I have to struggle a bit to maintain my walk's rhythm. Rather suddenly I smell bread. Saliva gushes under my tongue. Bread sounds good, I think to myself. Better than going back to that greasy-smelling Vietnamese restaurant where I am perhaps still unconscious, my pockets probably being rifled by the man with the raspberry-stained neck. I walk to where I think the smell of the bread is coming from. I see the place. It is about half a block away.

When I get to the doorway of the boulangerie, I see a small figure moving toward me down the dark sidewalk some twenty feet away. It appears to be a child, a small boy. His gait is very strange, a rocking side to side, like a metronome. Because it is late, I am concerned that the child is lost, ill, or injured, perhaps all three. I step forward with the intention of helping the child, but stop short as the small form totters from the darkness. It is a man walking on the stumps of his amputated legs. Had he legs, he would be a rather tall man. I would not have mistaken him for a child.

The man stops in front of me, looks me up and down, then asks me for a few francs.

"Je n'ai pas d'argent," I say. It rolls off my tongue. That is one of the first French phrases I learned. He asks me for the change. I am not really sure of this, but I hear the word *monnaie* and assume this is what he has said. "Attendez ici," I say, unsure whether I have said "Wait here" or "Listen here." But the man stands fast so I assume he understands me. I step into the boulangerie. The smell of yeasty bread makes me feel centered and solid. Bread is the only thing here that is identical to what I knew in the States. Here, chicken does not taste like chicken, air does not smell like air. But after three months in this place, I have discovered that bread is bread no matter where you are. The smell of it, anymore, gets me dizzily high.

I slap a hundred-franc piece onto the counter and ask the big-eyed, bald-headed baker for a loaf of bread. I exit, clutching the heady stick as if it were a great archaeological find. The man with no legs is still waiting for me. I slip the *monnaie,* or whatever, into his leathery hand and say, "Mah selamah." He follows me for a few steps, thanking me in Wolof, French, and very bad English. *Jerrejeff. Merci. Is nice. Is too nice.* "Is nothing," I say. I break off a piece of the bread and hand it to him. He begins mumbling things about Allah, says "Is nice" a dozen times or so, then thumps back into the darkness.

I forget him in no time. I think that it would be wise to find a place to rest, a hotel. After all, I am very tired. I have been through a lot today. I know I am supposed to be back in Ziguinchor (where I "teach" English) before morning, but it is not really important. My boss has grown accustomed to my unreliability. He does not care. My students do not care. Who cares? Nobody really cares. The boss has gotten used, I say to myself, to my disappearances. He used to "write me up" for my peculiar behavior, but now he does nothing. When I return, all he usually says to me is, "Thought you were gonna be back day before yesterday." And I usually reply, "Is that what I said? Sorry. I meant today." He does not care. Not really. But he does seem concerned about my health. "Malaria is nothing to fuck with," he says. "I thought you were going to Dakar to see a doctor."

"There're doctors here, Allen."

"Then see a doctor here, man."

"The truth is I really don't want to see a doctor."

"Then why do you keep going to Dakar?"

"I look for things."

"You always say that. What things?"

"Supplies."

"What supplies, goddamit? You bring back what you take. What the hell's the matter with you? I ask you whether you're happy here, whether you want to transfer — something you're really not supposed to do until the end of your second year — and you say no thanks, you love it here. Then you end up spending those goddam four-day weekends in Dakar. What's wrong with you, Evan? Do you need a doctor? A psychiatrist, I mean? Talk to me, guy."

"I guess it's culture shock. Hey, I'm sorry, Allen. Give me some time to adjust."

We go through variations of this dialogue at least twice a month. We will doubtless do it for the next twenty-one months. Allen really does not mind. In fact, I think he likes

14

it. It is so boring, what we do down there in Ziguinchor, that someone like me brings vitality to that place. They like it, the way I come and go as I please, the way I refuse to see a doctor for the malaria. (I am sure it is malaria because it is malaria season, and so far I have refused to take my quinine tablets.) They think I am nuts. But really, I am not. There is something enriching about this pain. There is something very, very intriguing about it. It is doing something to me. And I will not take my medicine until I find out precisely what it is. I will not leave Africa until I know what it is. I will keep ambling down to Dakar until I know what it is. But I hope it happens within the next year and nine months.

I shove the loaf under my mustache. My head again becomes a balloon floating above my body. I watch myself step down the unlit street. The night is a purring velvet black, and I watch myself, a shadow against a shadow. There is not a soul around me save a big black hound who undoubtedly smells my bread. He follows me, but keeps a distance of some twenty or twenty-five yards. I yank off a piece of the bread and toss it to the dog. It starts and runs away. "Mangy bastard," I mutter. I turn and continue to walk toward what I hope is the center of town, my head throbbing more than ever. The night seems to grow blacker with every step I take. I walk like a dead man, a blind man, a ghost, a whisper, a wisp. I walk into the thickening night as if it were a stiff wind. I have no idea where I am. Soon everything is black. I cannot see a thing. Neither can I hear any sound, not even my own footsteps. I cannot smell the bread. I no longer feel my body moving. It is as if I am floating. The pain is relatively dull. It rocks, rocks, rocks in small breakers, and I make ready to be smashed by a great wave of agony. But nothing happens, except that the pain subsides.

I float for an indeterminable length of time. Suddenly, I feel hands caressing my head, lightly tapping my face. I see a large, hideous face above my own, inches away. "Monsieur," it says. "Monsieur . . . du pain," it says. "Monnaie . . ." I am being mugged, I say to myself. I am being mugged. I start flailing my arms, swinging, striking out with all my might. I holler as loud as I can, but my voice rasps as if broadcast over a cheap crystal radio set. My victim, on the other hand, lies beneath me now, silent, absorbing every belt, poke, prod, stroke, submitting like dough. The pain in my head increases with every blow. I am mad with pain. I get to my feet, while my victim lies there on the sidewalk, silent and still. Something to finish him off, I think. Something to keep him down there. I bend down and rip up a piece of the broken sidewalk. It is the size of my chest. "Eat this," I rasp. "Taste this, you asshole." I lift the slab over my head and step toward my victim. "Here's some bread for you." I take aim. Suddenly, I notice the shape and size of my victim. The man with no legs, I say to myself. Goddamn it, and I bet he was trying to help me, too. Oh well. I smash his head so hard the cement slab breaks in two.

I straighten myself, square my shoulders, inhale and look right, then left. I sense a presence behind me. I turn. Nothing. No one. Silence. Nevertheless, I stare for a long moment, sensing the heat of someone's gaze. My heart lunges heavy, pushing my blood so hard my entire body jerks with soft spasms. I stare. I stare. And by increments, as if my eyes are clotting the very darkness into flesh, the shape of a dog — only a dog, perhaps the very dog I chased off only a moment ago — solidifies before me. I breathe. The dog stands motionless, except for its almost imperceptible tongue, which pumps back and forth as if on springs. I swallow hard, open my mouth to shoo it away, but I begin to tremble and can make no sound. As if my foot were anchored by roots, I struggle for one forward step. The dog turns and is swallowed up into the night's open mouth.

Yes, I say to myself. I need some rest. I need a good hotel.

4 I Go to a Hotel

When I am sick of Africa, I go to a hotel. I always try to find the most Western-looking hotel I can afford. No stewards, bellmen, or desk clerks in traditional dress. No traditional African art all over the walls. I go somewhere that serves hamburgers and fries (pitiful as they may be), where the staff speaks relatively decent English (pathetic as it may be). After checking in I buy copies of *Time, Newsweek, Playboy,* the *Herald Tribune.* I buy a pack of Winstons, Coke or Pepsi, chips, oatmeal cookies, anything American, junky, too salty, too sweet. Anything not African. I hole up for two or three days. I stink up my room with the cigarettes, the junk food, American sweat and vibes. "They'll know goddamn good and well," I tell myself, "a Yank's been here when I walk out this motherfucker." I try to Americanize the room so deeply they will have to seal it up forever. But tonight I buy only cigarettes. I lurch up to my room, lock the door behind me, and pace, stopping to stare out the window every now and then. It has begun to rain. I see nothing but streetlights, headlights, and the glimmer of the wet streets.

I pick up the phone and dial the front desk. It takes me a minute or two to make myself understood to the hotel operator. It takes me nearly as long to make myself clear to the Senegalese phone-company operator. She keeps saying, "Yes, go ahead," and for the longest time I think she is saying, "Yes, goyim? Yes. Goyim?" Finally I get through.

"Mrs. Josephine Norris? I'll give you three guesses who this is."

"Evan! Son! Your father and I were just talking about you. How you doing, darlin'?" My mother's voice always booms over the phone. I ordinarily hold the receiver a couple of inches from my ear when I speak with her. The moment I hear her voice tonight I realize that I am in no mood for talk. No mood, really, for food or sleep, breath or motion. "I don't know, Mom. I'm not sure."

"What do you mean? Are you in trouble?"

I tell her I am fine. "Maybe homesick, I guess." I light a Winston and kick off my shoes. I sit down on the floor. The stale breeze from the air conditioner dries my brow and neck. "Homesick, I guess."

"You sure that's all?"

That is all, I tell her. My head tightens and I hear nothing but hissing, though I feel my mouth shaping words.

"Oh, we're all fine," my mother says. "That brother of yours left school again, though."

I tell her I am not surprised.

"Your poor father's so disappointed. He just —"

He is always disappointed, I say. Then I add that Scott is twenty-four, I am nearly thirty, and our father's disappointment in Scott's education or my Peace Corps enlistment is neither my problem nor Scott's. It is his own problem.

"Daddy loves you both, darlin'. He just —"

"Funny how you've always said that, Mom. I've never heard him say it himself." I can scarcely hear myself. Is it possible I am shouting?

"Oh, he loves you all right. But you had better watch

your tone with me, boy, 'cause love or hate, I'm your mother and you will respect me. Now look here. You got two Bachelor degrees. You got a Master's. How can you expect your father and me to be happy about the fact you're in the Peace Corps? Evan, anybody with a two-cent sheepskin and a pair of brogans can do that. And if you really wanna get down to it, I don't believe you gave more'n two seconds thought to the whole idea in the first place. Your father thinks you spent all that time in school to put off getting out into the world. And when you think about it, it makes sense. You got your Master's, drew unemployment, smoked dope, slung hash at that sorry-ass Oxford Hotel, drew more unemployment, and signed up. Just like that. And you bet' not deny one word of it 'cause Wanda told me all about it and the girl's never lied to me. You have."

What is wrong with the Peace Corps? I ask her. It is better than the goddamned navy. (I have never spoken this way to my mother. It is not the catharsis I had imagined it would be. I would like to stop this tone of voice, this conversation as well, but I cannot. It is somehow holding my guts in. It is keeping the hemispheres of my skull from flying apart.) "What's so great about the goddamn navy? A goddamn — goddamn radio tech is more important than a teacher in the —"

"Don't you dare talk to me that way, boy. I don't care how grown you think you are. You will not talk to me that way."

Without hesitation, I apologize. I tell her I am very tired, that I have been on the road all day picking up supplies.

"You didn't have a wall full of degrees when you went into the navy, for one thing. And we weren't so happy about the navy so much as the fact you made it to manhood. Thought you did, anyway." Her voice jabs into the middle of my head. The throbbing kicks up. I try to squint the pain away, but squinting makes no difference. I feel very weak. My stomach twists and folds. A chill sweeps over me. My head bleeds perspiration more quickly than the air conditioner can blow it away. My room hazes into a yellow-gray absence, then congeals back into form.

"Evan? Are you still there? Are you OK?"

I apologize. I tell her I am very tired, that I have been on the road all day picking up supplies.

"I heard what you said, son. Are you all right?"

Someone, I tell her, was outside my door. I ordered some food, you see, Mother. I thought maybe that was it.

"What was that sound you were making?"

I remember no sound, so I say: "The fan, but I turned it down."

"What kind of food are they giving you? You're not eating them funny African foods, are you?"

"Oh, yeah. Strange things. Rice, okra, chicken, fish."

"I see you ain't too tired to be a smart ass."

The pain surges deep and steamroller hard through my head. But it subsides so quickly I do not even have time to react. Suddenly my head fills with water. It is heavy and unbalanced. I want nothing so much as to hang up the phone, slip into bed, and sleep for ten thousand years. "Sorry," I say. My mother grunts, asks me whether I have heard from Wanda, my girlfriend. I tell her that I have just received Wanda's first letter.

"What did she say?"

" 'Hello. I'm fine. Tucker's fine. Everything's fine.' "

"Um-hm." She pauses for a very, very long time. "Do you plan to marry her?"

I do not reply.

"I know you don't think it's any of my business, but Wan and I have gotten to be pretty close since you left. I see her almost every day. Evan, son, that girl is perfect for you.

She's right for you. It's just something I know. I just don't understand how you can run off and — and — do this to her."

I do not reply.

"What happened between you two?"

Wanda has problems I cannot deal with, I tell her.

"What kind of problems?" She says this mockingly, as if I have said the most stupid thing ever spoken.

"It's not for me to tell you."

"She drink?"

"It's not for me to tell you."

"Drugs?"

"Mom —"

"Well, I know it ain't drugs anyway. I know she's been working her heart out, get you off that dope."

"It's not drugs. Look, Mom —"

"It's her boy, isn't it?"

"No." But I add that I do not really like children. "It's not Tucker. Not really. He's kind of a brat, but he's OK."

"Sounds like you're the one with the problem."

"Maybe."

"And I think you're selfish."

"I know."

"You are. You're selfish as they come, son. It's hard for me to say, but it's true. I don't know. Maybe it's the way we brought you and your brother and sister up. Maybe we gave you too much."

"Maybe. Not your fault, really. It's me." I cannot go on, so I remind my mother that the call is costing me ten dollars every minute. She tells me she understands and that next time I should call collect. "I wanted to surprise you," I say.

"You always surprise me, boy."

We exchange brief good-byes. She tells me she loves me and that she prays for me every night. I gently hang up the phone, but then lift the receiver and slam it into the cradle. I lift it and slam it again, then kick the phone off the night-stand. My head shatters into a billion pieces in a red and pink flash. It is beautiful, in a way. For the first time in two weeks I wish for something to alleviate the pain. For it is so astonishingly keen that all I can do is gasp, close my eyes, wrap my arms around my head. When I open my eyes, I am again on the bus. I am the driver. My hands are on the wheel. My left foot rides the clutch. My right foot is poised over the brake. I must be doing forty or so, but the speedometer is metric so I cannot be sure. I am tumbling down some fogbound road. I cannot see the road very well, but it is as if I know where I am. It is a peculiar sensation. I am half-lost, half-bemused, half-terrified, half-aghast — half-clearheaded, half-placid, half-confident. This is my job, I hear myself say. Of course I know where I am, where I am going. Stop is coming. Yoff Village.

I stop the bus, pull open the door. On steps the boy with the peppercorn hair. "Now you're getting somewhere," he says.

5 I Quit

I finish my shift early in the morning. I park the bus in the lot and turn in my keys and my log. The air is almost cool, almost sweet. Mist curls from the damp ground. There is a flock of gulls near the fence next to the garage. They peck at a pile of sour-smelling garbage. Their screeches unnerve me. I pick up a piece of broken tarmac to fling at them, but my actions remind me of those of the previous night and I drop the clod. Gradually, I begin to feel less and less like a bus driver. The memory of my night's labors fade. All I can remember, with the exception of the murder, are parts of my conversation with my mother, my subsequent tantrum, the pink and red explosion, the dark, fogbound road, and the boy. I make my way back down to the hotel. Back in my room, I undress and shower, collect my things, and later I check out.

I amble down Lamine Gueye Avenue, watching my feet. This is not my usual style of walking, but I am weary, and the air is already becoming warm and heavy. I move as if through water. I stop at a kiosk, buy a copy of *Le Soleil* and a half pack of Winstons. I make my way to Place de l'Indépendance, "reading" the paper, hoping to find something about the murder, hoping not to find something about the murder. There is no news of it, but then official news travels relatively slowly here. I am much more likely to hear something about it on the street. I consider going to look for the scene of the crime, but I feel miserable in this cloying heat, my head pounding the way it is, and a long walk into a neighborhood I scarcely know is more than I can bear. But oddly, it is not the anxiety of discovering whether I actually did or did not kill the man. I am certain I did. Why else would my knuckles be bruised if not from slugging his brow and chin? Why else would my fingertips be abraded if not from having clawed up the chest-sized piece of sidewalk with which I flattened his head?

I know I killed the man, just as I know I passed out in the restaurant. These malarial parasites are boring psychological holes through my mind. These things, I believe, are actually happening to me. They are occurring on the very physical plane on which I now stride. The only thing I am not sure of is why I do not feel terror at what is happening to me. Normally, I fear illness. I am horrified by pain, mental confusion, anything that is not linear and clear, anything that even suggests that I am not in full command of my faculties.

When I was in the navy I was sent to Survival Evasion Resistance and Escape School on Coronado Island. The course was to prepare one for the rigors of POW camp. It entailed — if you were captured (and you were always captured) — all manner of barely endurable torture. Burly "enemy" sailors would bind you so tightly in ropes you would swear your veins would burst. You would be interrogated for hours. They would slap you till you were dizzy, till your face burned. The worst torture of all, as far as I was concerned, was their tying your hands behind your back, binding your legs together, and shoving you into an empty oil drum. They filled the drum with water till the water was just under your nose. Then they screwed a lid on

25

the drum. They kept you thus contained for what seemed
like half a day. The first hour is not so bad. You imagine
you are back in your mother's womb. You imagine you are
in a space capsule, sailing through deep space. You imagine
you are a herring in a glass jar. Then it gets worse.

My own experience of this torture was unbearable. I
went from womb to capsule to jar, and then my muscles
began to stiffen and contract. I was sore; my body itched,
burned, unscratchable. After several long hours I urinated
in the water, and whenever water would seep past my lips,
I felt like vomiting. I wanted desperately to sleep, but it
was impossible. Every time I let my head fall forward, I
would snort water. My eyes would burn. I would cough and
sneeze, and these violent spasms made my already pain-
wracked body feel like it was being split to pieces by meat
cleavers.

Worse than all this were the peculiar things that began
to happen to my mind. About halfway through the torture,
I began to feel my body dissolving. I saw myself as a sand-
stone statue being eroded by ocean water. I felt my feet, my
legs, my genitals, my belly, my back and shoulders fall
apart, grain by grain, granules slowly tumbling down to the
bottom of the drum, mixing with its rust. The image was so
terrifying, irrevocable, indelible that I began to scream.
Each time I screamed, a guard would pound on the barrel's
lid and order me to shut my "pussy ass" up. But the pounding would only make me feel as though the pace of my dis-
solution was being expedited, and I would scream louder,
longer, curse the guard, swear I would kill him. When I was
finally released from the drum, it was four days before I
could even acknowledge the fact that I had fingers, toes, and
limbs that could move. I was nearly discharged for mental
instability. From that day forward I had always thought of
myself as relatively weak, and until now have always gone

out of my way to avoid any sort of pain, discomfort, psychological ambiguity, danger.

Now I find that I am fascinated by this illness. I almost relish it. It is doing something to me. I am not prepared to say it is making me stronger, the fire that turns iron into steel, but I do, somewhere inside myself, know there is some element of that notion that I do faithfully carry. I do not doubt this illness is leading me some place literal, real. This is no death wish. It is not mere masochism. For some reason or another, I cannot imagine this journey occurring in any other way.

I come upon a group of women squatting on the curb. They are selling oranges, shelled peanuts, and boiled eggs. Though I am not hungry now, I buy something from each of them for my journey back to Ziguinchor. I stuff the things into my day sack and thank the women in Wolof. They seem very friendly. And one of them even gives me an extra orange. Perhaps I have been cheated. I do not know. The Senegalese are but three things to my mind: beautiful, dignified, unknowable. My father, who has participated in nearly every package tour his travel agent has to offer, has never been to West Africa, but he assured me, as we played a self-conscious, sloppy game of pool in my parents' recreation room on the day before I left, that people are people. "The same everywhere you go." Some of them, he said, are saints, "But most of 'em ain't worth a dog's goddamn. Don't ever forget that you're in this world to look out for number one. Num-ro uno." He tucked the pool cue under his arm, lit a cigarette, pensively regarded the table. "Number one. That's all you got. You take care of him and everything else falls into place, you understand? Everybody's got to eat and there ain't enough food in this world to go all the way around. You got to keep your good eye on the hungry ones. If there's one thing I've learned from thirty-five years in the

27

food-distribution business, it's that there's a lot of hungry people in this world, and a motherfucker'll split your ass wide open for a hot dog." He bent over the table, squinted, said, "Four in the corner," shot and sank the ball. "One in the side," he said, chalking the cue.

I do not like to listen to him when he speaks this way, but I am afraid his words have seeped into every corner of my subconscious. I do not, much to my discomfort, trust anyone. And I am less comfortable knowing that I am chained to a paranoia for which there is so much apparent justification. My father is right. There is not enough to go all the way around. You must watch the hungry ones. But though I am paranoid, I am also in some measure defenseless. For though I regard the world as my father does, I behave in it — at least try to, feel I should, anyway — as my mother taught me to be: kind, generous, adaptable, patient. This is the source of my discomfort.

I should not have said the things I said to my mother last night. And most especially I should not have suggested that Wanda has some unspeakable problem. She has none that I know of. But I will not marry her. At least let me say that I should not. It would be too easy. I cannot just leave a family with money, a big house, phones and televisions in every room — even the garage — only to marry a too-beautiful woman with a child, tons of money, and a house with books in every room. I want something of my own. I want something that I myself have created. But what is more, I cannot marry a woman who loves me for no reason I can perceive, who forgives and forgives and forgives. Who would actually tell me in the letter I received from her last Monday that the two-year separation will be good for us. I would tell her, if I had the courage, that life should be this way but it is not this way. I left not knowing, not particularly caring, what happens between Wanda and me. This bothers me because I love her.

She is older, smarter, more human. Not only do her big eyes look into the very core of my eyes, but unabashedly reveal the inner workings of her own character. But I cannot see why she loves me. It is like watching some subtle mechanism tick and shift behind smoked glass. My mother is right. Wanda does not lie. She is good for me, my spiritual, physical, and moral touchstone. When I run my hands over her almond-colored skin, smell the tight coils of her hair, press myself against her firm body, search her and probe her, I come away seeing the streaks of my unworthiness. She sees some "potential" in me, something worth all her work and patience. I am her Galatea. She sands and polishes me with her lovemaking and conversation. And she, herself, is finished, complete with or without me. But I need something of my own. Life is not as she and my mother would have it. It is not a gift. Life is hard. It is stupid. One must earn it.

At this moment, as I think of it, I am finding the Peace Corps too easy. It is too much like the military. It employs you, even if it finds you somewhat incompetent. It feeds you, houses you, though all you do is gripe and behave indolently. It pays you — though not much — even though there is little you can do to say you have earned the money. Nobody cares. If you work hard, fine. If you do not work at all, that is fine too. I exert more energy killing flies in my room than preparing classes. I sleepwalk, smokewalk, through each day as a teaching assistant for a fat heifer of a woman named Ruth Barron. She taught for twenty-one years in the Detroit public school system before they discovered how monumentally incompetent she was. They retired her, but, perhaps figuring that her level of incompetence was high enough for government work, wrote loquaciously gooey letters of recommendation to the Corps for her.

Ruth is cruel, megalomaniacal, insane, and despises children — particularly African children. She mocks them when they mispronounce words in either French or English. She forbids them to speak any language indigenous to Africa on the school grounds. She teases children who suffer speech impediments, limps, missing limbs, skin rashes, threadbare clothes. If a child happens to be slow at schoolwork, she thumbtacks his work to the bulletin board, or reads it to the class. She is a relatively skilled cartoonist and can reduce children to tears by drawing their caricatures on the chalkboard. Ruth is black, but she is cruelest to the children with the darkest skins. She teaches our students words like darky, coon, pickaninny, spook, and coal monkey. When I suggest to her that her epithets seem terribly racist to me, she often replies, in her slow-burning, indignant way, "I don't believe you have ever heard me call any one of these children nigger. That's the word that hurts, you know. Every one of these children knows I love them, Evan. They know I'm only teasing them. It's good for them. Keeps their little minds alert. Besides, if there's one thing I know, it's that if you grow up black and poor, you can't lose your sense of humor, don't you think?" She knows I know nothing about poverty. She implies with tone and gesture that being black without ever having been poor is somehow not black enough.

"Asking them to conjugate verbs seems to keep their minds alert, don't *you* think?"

"Now, Evan," she laughs, "you're forgetting that I'm black too. Just as black as they are, in my own way. Don't let this yellow skin fool you. I'm black and I'm proud. And

I have never, in all my twenty-one years in the Detroit system and my six years here seen a black hurt another black with any of these words. You see, with us they're just terms of endearment."

I usually back down when she throws her twenty-seven years in my face. Not that I think those years make her a better teacher than I, but they certainly make Allen, my boss, think so. She is older than he, has taught twice as long, and speaks better French. He respects her, and this confounds me no end. The only time Allen threatened to make me miserable was the time I spoke to him of Ruth's inadequacies. "That woman is the best we've got," he said, adjusting his glasses, fingering his beard, "and you're hardly qualified to judge her."

"Have you ever seen her teach?"

"Of course I have, Evan. Do you —"

"Lately?"

"Meaning?"

"Meaning lately. She's nuts."

"Only if it takes one to know one, guy. To me she's as sane as they come."

"She hates kids."

"Look." He stood up, walked to the front of his desk, sat on the desktop. He stroked his impeccably trimmed beard, adjusted his polished glasses, dovetailed his fingers with their perfect mother-of-pearl nails lined up like buttons on a double-breasted coat. "Look here, Ev. What looks like hatred to you looks like experience to me. It's you, Evan. I've seen your kind of response before. You're just flipping because she doesn't coddle these kids the way you do. She doesn't have to coddle them. She's not afraid of them."

"And you're saying —"

"I'm saying that what you're doing is no different from

31

what other new teachers do. You're bending over backward for these kids so they'll like you. But liking doesn't cut it with the Senegalese kids. They learn best from those they respect. Those kids respect Ruth 'cause she's sure of herself. She knows who she is. And she's tough." He unlocks his fingers, articulates with his hands as though conducting an orchestra. "Ruth's ease with them," he says, "makes her look like a regular bounder to you, OK?"

"She's walking bullshit, Allen."

"That'll do, Evan."

"Why don't you believe me, man?"

"I believe you think you're right. But it's not for me to believe or disbelieve you, guy. If you want to submit a formal complaint, you know I won't stop you."

And he would, indeed, not stop me. But he knows I know that my submitting a complaint whose content he does not agree with would imply to his superiors that not only Ruth, but he, too, is incompetent. He is not. Allen is compassionate, clearheaded, intelligent, judicious, and open-minded in every matter with the exception of Ruth's malfeasance. His superiors know what kind of person he is. Any complaint I would submit would make me look like a mere malcontent. "I'm too lazy to do the paperwork," I say.

"No, you're not exactly the most ambitious guy I ever met, Ev."

"Guess you just won't ever see it my way, huh?"

"I empathize with you, bud. I really do, but you'll see how different you are a year from now. Just watch and learn. Ruth's a pro. And let's face it, guy," he said, grasping for but missing a light tone, "you not only need to work on your classroom skills, but I hear the kids can barely understand your French."

"I thought it was getting better. I'm sorry. I guess it's culture shock or something. I'm tired all the time. Really, my French is pretty good. It's just I haven't caught on to the way they speak it here. It has a different sort of — sort of . . ."

"Just take it easy. Relax, bud. Enjoy your time here. Let it come slowly. The Senegalese say, 'N'danka n'danka, moi diappa golo tsinaye.' Slowly, slowly, you must stalk the monkey through the bush. Isn't that neat?" He stuck out his hand, twisted up a bright prep-school smile. "See you, Ev." And I walked from his office, feeling as though I had just dodged a bullet by the hair of my neck.

Plodding up Lamine Gueye, it occurs to me that I will be inextricably mired in this situation if I do not do something about it now, this easy, simple life. They want me to do nothing. They do not want me to teach. They do not want me to complain. I will endlessly sleepwalk through Africa, Denver — wherever I go — unless I change rhythm and course. I walk to the American Cultural Center, go up to the second floor, where there is a rarely occupied office with a seldom-used phone.

"Allen? Evan Norris here."

He asks me how I am.

"Not so good, actually. As a matter of fact I'm sick as hell. Think I'll be checking into a hospital up here."

He asks me how long I think I will be gone and whether I am well enough to travel back to the clinic at Ziguinchor.

"I'm really pretty sick. Way too sick to get down there."

He asks me what I think the illness is and I tell him I am sure it is malaria. He admonishes me for not taking my quinine tablets. Malaria is nothing to play with, he says. He has warned me about this more than once, he tells me.

"You're right, Allen. I know."

He tells me he will come see me as soon as he is free,

33

that I should take all the time I need, and that he will send all the insurance forms to the embassy. He tells me I should report to the embassy infirmary before I go anywhere else. "Take care," he says.

"Tell Ruthie I said yo," I say. I hang up. I leave the office, sure I will never see him again.

6 I Go to N'Gor

I get off the bus. I check into the Massata Samb
Hotel, just outside N'Gor Village, about ten miles from
Dakar. The only thing I know about N'Gor and its two sister
villages, Yoff and Ouakam, is that they are inhabited by
people known as the Lebou. The Lebou are said to be bril-
liant traders and expert fishermen. They speak Wolof. They
are excellent swimmers. That is all I know. Tall hedges of
bougainvillea block my view of the village, but I know I am
no more than twenty or thirty yards from it. I smell the
sharp odor of cooking charcoal, sun-dried fish, the feces of
mammal and fowl. The eastern border of the village is abut-
ted by a large hotel complex, the western border by the
ocean. This is a good place for me to bury myself for a few
weeks until I can figure out what to do and where to go. I
am close to Americanlike food and periodicals written in
English. I am close to the ocean. No one knows me here. No
one is likely to bother me.

As soon as I get to the front desk, I scribble a quick note
to my parents, telling them I need money for an upcoming
vacation. I ask them to send it to the Massata Samb. I clam-
ber up four long flights of stairs to my room, fumble with
the key, open the door, finally, and fall into bed. I sleep a
long apneic sleep. I dream of Wanda. She is naked and we

are in what appears to be my mother's laundry room, except that there are no doors and the walls are made of coarse cement instead of the smooth pinewood paneling. There is one small window, the bottom of which is three or four feet above my head. A weak yellow light bleeds through the window, but the room is very dark. It is a small room and Wanda is very close. Her large nipples brush against my left arm and chest.

It is warm and steamy, as both washer and drier are on, humming and tumbling. I wish to touch Wanda, but I do not. She moves closer to me, pushes her small breasts into my chest. Her pubic hair brushes against my knuckles. My penis stiffens. "I need you," she says. "I'm hungry," she says. She rests her perspiring forehead on my chest, then stretches her neck so that her lips are close to mine. She does not kiss me. She stretches her neck even more so that her lips and nose brush against my right ear. She stretches her neck still further and rubs her cheek against the back of my head. Finally her long, long neck coils around my own once, twice. Into my right ear she whispers, "First I make love to you . . ." And into my left ear she says in a flat, conversational tone, ". . . then I eat you."

I wake up fascinated, terrified, sickened. My head throbs. My stomach roils. I stumble from bed and into the bathroom. I kneel over the bidet, dry-heaving uncontrollably. A glaze of perspiration sweeps over my neck, face, and back, but I feel cold. I tremble, an unnerving tremor that suggests the parasitic life in my blood is taking full control of me. And, as if strong hands pull at me from within, I curl over the bidet, retching out bitter saliva.

"I guess I am pretty sick," I say in a coarse whisper, attempting to sound offhand. "See? That's why I can't marry Wanda, Momma." But try as I may, I cannot distract myself from my misery. *I gotta get help. Room service.* I crawl to the bedroom. With every move I make pain tears at my head. I imagine my head to be a wasp nest, scores of wasps boring, tunneling, burrowing, scraping through it. I dial room service.

"Allo."

"I'm sick."

"Comment?"

"J'ai mal à la tête. Très mal."

"Voulez-vous une médecine, monsieur?"

"Yes. Oui."

"Quelle chambre, monsieur?"

"Four-oh-eight."

"Eh?"

"I don't know the number in French, man. Help me. Four-oh-eight! Four-oh-eight!"

"Parlez-vous —"

"No, goddamn it. Je ne sais pas le numero."

I am on the bus. I am sitting, reading the Quoran. It is in Arabic. *I am reading the Quoran.* Wrapped round the knuckles of my right hand is a string of beautifully colored prayer beads. A dark tortoiseshell color. *I am reading Arabic.* My hands are blacker than I have ever seen them. I stop reading and look at them. Really, really look at them. Deep black skin, calloused palms, thick fingers ending in thick, yellow nails. *Not my hands.* I am dressed in a green boubou. *Not my clothes.* There is an odd pressure encircling the top of my head. I reach up and feel, with these strange hands of mine, a fez. *I am wearing a fez?* What is wrong with me? Of course I am wearing a fez. I always wear a fez. I would feel naked without one, in fact. What is wrong with me today? Someone taps me on the shoulder. It is a tall, bearded black American. What is he saying? His French is abominable. I hate French, but this man has no business speaking it at all. "What is this village to name?" he asks me. What is this village to name? What it is to *be* I might be able to guess. But what it is to name? "Could you repeat that?" I ask him. For a moment it seems to me that I know him. But then I haven't spoken to an American since the war, I think. He repeats his question. It takes him a couple of attempts to make clear that he is asking me the name of the village we are approaching. "N'Gor," I tell him. "Merci, monsieur," he says, looking at the village as if looking at a new planet, a new moon, new stars. What does he see? I wonder. From the look in his eyes, one would think that N'Gor is more than a place where people live, bear children, and die. The bus stops. The young man gets off. He plants his feet firmly in the fine red soil of N'Gor, and looks and looks and looks. It is very curious.

7 I Meet the Marabou's Daughter

The little insects bore through the skull and carry out chunks of brain to feed their young. The body temperature goes up then goes down, so that you shiver in your sweat. You cannot eat. You cannot sleep. It hurts to move and speak. Black shadows slip into your room, ask you questions you do not understand. The one who speaks English tells you that you are not that sick, that it is a mild case of "grippe." Quit moaning so. You are alive, aren't you? You like her voice. It is the only thing that seems even vaguely real. But then there is the old one, who frightens you. The one who never speaks except to say "Aam" when he brings you the red tea. He will lift the pounding head, fill the mouth with tea, let the head drop, then step back, sit in a chair, and watch you, sometimes for what seems like days. He only watches. He has but one eye. It will not blink. It will not falter. His gaze lies like a great sack of millet on your chest. It presses the body down so hard onto the foam mattress you cannot breathe. You try to return the gaze, but his single eye pushes your eyes so deep into your head that you are made blind. The eyes do not so much as close but clamp shut — twin fly traps. You are crushed by sleep. You dream of vortices — whirlwinds, funnels, dust devils, draining sinks, hurricanes. When you awaken he is gone. Always, he is gone, and you know he has left something in you, taken something away.

The room is hot and full of sun. The room is soft moon blue and hot. The room is hot and dark. The room is hot and full of sun. The room is soft moon blue and hot. The room is hot and dark. The room is hot and full of sun. Days are twisted from the head like fat turnips. The body melts into the sheets. The consciousness fills the room like a mist, condenses on the walls, crawls down them in thin rivulets, evaporates. Hands, some gentle, some rough. Hands always firm. Hands lift the lolling head, fill the mouth with liquids that cannot be tasted, wipe the overflow from the chest. The one who speaks English says you are sicker than she thought. It is only malaria, she says. Are you a whiteman who could die from a mosquito's sting? Color and heat. Light and heat. Darkness and heat. Heat and heat and heat. Mosquitoes raise nipples on the skin, scissor past the ears like miniature jets. The muezzin rasps, barks, screams horrors and damnation through something antique, wired, plugged in. The sound shakes, crumbles the brain to powder. Where is it coming from? you hear yourself say. Can they turn it down?

Are you Muslim? says the voice. If you are, the prayers can heal you.

The room is hot and black.

The room is hot and full of sun.

She slips into my room. She turns on the light. She carries a covered bowl between the curve of her hip and her wrist. In her other hand is a spoon. "You hungry?" she says.

"No."

"I think you should eat."

"Maybe later." I look her up and down. Smooth, clear complexion, almond-shaped eyes, long corn-rowed locks decorated with blue, red, yellow, and green beads. Long fingers,

40

long neck, black eyes, well-cushioned ass, aquiline nose, slightly bucked teeth, medium-large breasts, slightly bowed legs. She wears a green-and-yellow skirt, a white camisole. She is barefoot. She is pretty. I cannot care.

She steps toward me. "How long you gonna starve yourself?" She has an American accent.

"I'm too tired to eat." I want to ask her where she learned her English, but I am too tired for small talk as well. "How is your head?" she asks me, setting the bowl in a corner of the room.

"Hurts. This is N'Gor?"

"Um-hm. My cousin Mamadou brought you here. He works at Massata Samb. He didn't know what else to do."

"So I wasn't on the bus?"

"What bus?" She stands with her weight shifted to her right foot, her right arm akimbo. Her right cheek twitches twice, almost as if she were suppressing a smile.

"Never mind. How long have I been here?"

"Almost five days. My family has been taking care of you. My father's a marabou. His cures don't all the time work, but you'll be fine. You should eat, though. I'll be right back." She slips from the room, leaving the door ajar. The room is tiny, much smaller than I had thought. Pocked cement walls painted pale green. A small lizard, the color of a gum eraser, clings to the wall on the door side. There are two purplish Naugahyde chairs on either side of the door, pushed into the corners. A single shelf secured by L-brackets next to the window holds my day sack, my shoes, my clothes, a blue plastic coffee cup, and a small tin bowl. There is a single, naked bulb hanging out of a hole in the wall just above the shelf and to the left of the window. No electrician could have done the job, for there is no insulated lamp holder, just a ganglia of wires and a cheap aluminum socket. I try to sit up to inspect the floor, but my head hurts too much. I turn onto my right side, facing the door, and wait. She is back in less than two minutes, carrying a washcloth and another bowl identical to the one that contains my dinner. She sits on the bed, dabs my neck and face with the washcloth. Her touch is firm. "Did you forget to take your quinine?" she asks me. Her right cheek twitches again.

"No. I didn't forget. Just never took it."

She stops dabbing. "Why?" she says.

"Didn't really think I'd get sick."

"You Americans are crazy."

"I guess. You've been to the States?"

She wrings the cloth, lays it over the bedboard. "I'm on vacation from my studies at Georgetown University. Have you heard of it?" I say that I have and then she tells me she studies English, that she likes many things about the U.S., but would never, under any circumstances, emigrate there. She likes fried chicken and hamburgers, American movies, discos, basketball, highways, jazz, and parks. She hates American men, American clothes, shoes, ice cream, snow, football, pizza, and the way Americans party. "Drink, drink, drink, that's all they ever do."

"If you hate American men," I ask, "then why are you being so kind to me?"

"You speak native English. I can practice." She folds her hands together, sighs, crosses her legs. I can tell she is not joking.

Several days go by and I begin feeling better, although I still refuse to take any quinine. Aminata comes every day, usually accompanied by her reticent younger brother, Phillipe. She comes to feed me, practice her English, and tell me what a fool I am. But I can tell she is beginning to like me, in a grudging way. At least I amuse her. Doubtless she thinks I am tragically silly, a pampered américain noir who does not have the vaguest idea who he is, where he is, or what he is doing here. She teases me about everything I do or say, but I sense no real derision in her. "Your arms and legs are hairy like a white man's," she often says to me. "Were you born in the bush with baboons?" Whenever I try to eat African-style, without utensils, she laughs and says, "If you want more food for later, I'll give it to you. You don't have to store it in your beard." Once when I asked her to buy some toilet paper for me on her shopping trip to Dakar, she told me that using toilet paper was a filthy Western habit. "You people," she said. "I think you would save money and underwears if you washed yourselves instead of wiped."

And she tells me stories, beautiful, funny, strange, sad, or a combination of any of the four. They are stories for children, I suppose, and not terribly important, but I listen to them as if they were as vital to me as water and air. Perhaps it is the way her long fingers move and the way the beads in her hair clack and rattle when she says, "And he shook his fist in the air and cried, 'Give me back my teeth, you evil sorceress!'" Perhaps it is because of her fluent English. I do not really know. She tells me of Bouki the Hyena, Thile the Jackal, Kakatar the Chameleon, strange creatures such as jinni — "like genies," she says — and kousses — "you, know," she says, "like trolls or something."

My favorite story is about a beautiful young girl named Aida, so beautiful, Aminata said, "that flowers would open when she touched them, no mosquito would dare to sting her, and young boys and old men would moan and shed tears from their eyes when they would catch a view of her bathing in the ocean."

We were at the beach when she told me this story. It was

the first time I'd been out in days. The sun hurt my eyes, making my head tick with pain. But it was a beautiful day. The sun turned Aminata's flowered skirt into an explosion of pink and yellow. A breeze tucked it around her hips and legs. I wore, for the first and only time since coming to Africa, African clothing, an olive green khaftan and sandals. Phillipe was clad in trunks, and we watched him swim, his long, powerful arms muscling around and through the small breakers. "But Aida's father," said Aminata, gazing out to sea, "his name was Amadou. Amadou would refuse any offer of bride-price from any man who wanted to marry her. This made Aida sad because already she was sixteen and ripe for marriage. But Amadou always said no. He was not a greedy man. He didn't want rich, but he wanted his daughter to marry Medoune, the disciple of a marabou. He wanted to have a better time in Paradise, you see, because God smiles on marabous and their families.

"OK, this Medoune, he had great knowledge, even though he was only twenty. He was smart in the ways of books and God. But Medoune was conceited and talked a lot. He never listened. He ignored all the people who didn't have rich and possessions. Aida didn't like him."

I corrected Aminata's English and she waved her hand at me. "Later," she said, and continued.

"But there was a badolo's son, you know? This poor man's son? And he was called Moussa. He was tall and handsome and was a hard worker. Aida wanted him for marriage because he was kind to animals and children. But, you see, a girl in our culture must listen always to her father. OK, the father decides who she marries and when. That's the way it is. But Aida made so much complaining and noise about Moussa that her father decided to give him a chance."

So Amadou, she told me, called the young marriageable men together and told them that the man who could teach a hare to kill a lion could marry Aida. Most of the men threw up their hands, lamenting the impossibility of the task. But Moussa, the badolo's son, and Medoune, the marabou's disciple, took up Amadou's challenge. Each man went his separate way to think things through.

We were on the hotel beaches since they are cleaner and softer than the village beach just a few yards away. The sky slowly grew overcast, and the air cooled. Goose bumps stood up on her folded arms. I offered to return to the house and get my jacket for her. She gave me the oddest look, bemused, ironic. She smiled, looked me straight in the eye. "American men," she said, shrugging. "You're not always so bad." There was something about that look that reminded me of the unbending glare of her father, the old one who brought me the red tea. Something that pushed me inward, made me sense something about myself. But it was not hard, as is Monsieur Gueye's. The old man's eye seems brutal, forceful, but hers delved far into mine, rather than battered in. Her eyes stayed there for longer than I could bear. I looked at her throat and thought of kissing it, looked at her mouth, her ears, her hands. My heart swelled one hard time, and not knowing what else to do, I folded my arms across my chest and looked down at the sand. "Are you sure?" I said. She shook her head, causing her beads to rattle, and said, "You're making me forget my story." Her eyes were still on me. I could feel them. She continued.

"So, anyway, Medoune, the marabou's disciple, tried everything he could — starving the hares to make them mean. Sharpening their teeth with files to give them a sharper bite, beating them, sneak up behind and scaring them. He tried tere, you know, charms? Magical things? To make the hares grow big and grisly . . . 'grisly'? 'Fierce,' that's good. Thank you. To make them more fierce, but nothing worked. All the hares died.

45

"Then one day, Moussa appeared in the village. No one had seen him for a long, long time. Way, way, way long, you know? And he had with him a small, small hare on a string. The hare was hopping around and nibbling grasses and looked gentle as could be. Moussa took the hare to Amadou's house and said, 'Tomorrow this hare will bring you a lion,' and he walked away."

I wanted to sit closer to her, have her whisper the story into my ear. The sound of her voice made the inside of my head hum, and I thought for a moment that I might sleep. But the story would not let me. Her voice was a pillow, soft and deep, but her story was kola nut, keeping me alert. There was no way I could have drifted off. She sat there, cross-legged in her long skirt, barefoot. She pulled on her toes as she spoke, and rocked slowly back and forth.

"Amadou awoke the next day to a loud dragging sound outside his hut. He left the hut and almost fell down when he saw the little hare pulling the body of a dead lion across his compound. He said, 'Ayy! Ayy! He has done it! He has done it! Wyyy!' Oh, it was something, American man. There was this hare, pulling the dead lion on the ground. And Amadou was amazed. He ran to Moussa's home to see if there was some trick, but there was no trick. Moussa was asleep when Amadou got there. And Amadou noticed also that Moussa looked very weak, and he even had a long cut on his chest. Amadou said, 'How did you get that cut there?' And Moussa said, 'It is my wound from teaching the hare to fight.' Amadou said, 'You have done it, my son. You may have my daughter for a wife.'

"So, Moussa went to get his hare, and he left the lion's dead body for Amadou. Then Moussa went back to his hut and he had the hare under his arm. When he was inside his house, he took out his knife and killed the hare and took out the heart. Then he reached inside the cut on his chest and took out the heart in there. 'I must have my heart back, my friend,' he said. 'I need it to love Aida, who will be my wife.' "

She waved to Phillipe as he waded out of the water, hugging himself, shivering. "Well," she said without looking at me, "that's it."

I tried to tell Aminata how wonderful I thought the story was, but I am not much good at praise. I thought of putting my arms around her, breathing in her damp skin, nuzzling her neck and ear, but I would never really do a thing like that. "Nice," I said. She clasped her hands together, shrugged, and said, "It's not as good as real stories, not like the other ones I tell you. I just made it up."

The only time she does not joke with me, tell me stories, talk at all, really, is when her father is nearby. He is a frighteningly imposing man. In appearance he is a mixture of Mahatma Gandhi and a horror-picture ghoul. The old widower is tall, bald, and slightly stooped. He walks with a limp and struts around his compound, or through the rooms of his large house, austere and forbidding, with the aid of a heavy staff. He has only one eye. It is a piercing black and bloodshot yellow. It sees through, around, over, behind everyone and everything in its range. This eye seems to possess the clearest omniscience. It seems capable of catching every nuance of movement, interpreting the most minute shade of expression. A glance from that eye reaches like an arm, articulates like a tentacle. When he is anywhere nearby when I am with Aminata, she is perfunctory, curt, edgy. I think, sometimes, that she is as afraid of him as I am. And how he feels about me I cannot say. He still leaves me with the crushing, airless feeling he did in those first several days, only now he never enters my room. He no longer brings the tea. He has never attempted to speak to me beyond the usual Senegalese greetings: "Asalaam Aleikum," "Bonjour," "Nangadeff?" But Aminata tells me he likes me and asks about me often. I ask her about him, too, on occasion.

"Is your father a powerful marabou, Ami?"

We are sitting in the common room, directly adjacent to my room. She is braiding her sister Binta's hair. Her fingers seem to move by themselves, over and under, over and under, very quickly. When I ask my question her fingers slow up as if they were considering the question. Aminata smiles, tells me my question is stupid. "If your father were a dentist," she says, "what would you think if I asked you if he is a powerful dentist?"

"I mean, what's the extent of his power?"

"I don't know what you mean."

"Like, can he do things to you?"

She stops braiding, points to a brush on the coffee table, close to my knee. I hand it to her. She snatches it from me and vigorously brushes out a section of Binta's hair. She sighs heavily. "Man, you ask some stupid questions."

"Well, I —"

"A marabou — a true marabou, anyway — is like a doctor. He helps people. He heals people, gives them advice, helps them to understand the Quoran, OK? He doesn't do things to people. He does things for people." She plaits the section she has just brushed, her fingers moving at an aggressive speed. "You Americans make me sick with the way you always assume that Africa is full of witch doctors and voodoo priestesses. I am not saying that we don't have our mysterious things like jinni and demm —"

"Demm?"

"Soul-eaters. These crazy people who eat other people's souls — but anyway, you in the West have your vampires, werewolves, witches. . . . Why you always think we have these things and don't think of your own things? I have gone to school four years as an undergraduate and a year as a graduate student and not once did I ever ask my friends about all your Dracula and Halloween things, because I know it's ninety-nine percent fantasy. But you people, if you're not always asking me, a Senegalese, about South Africa, you're asking me about witch doctors and spells. People in your country are so bigoted, you're so backward. You think we live in trees and bushes, and when I tell people in your country I live in this big ten-room house, and that my father owns another one just like it in The Gambia, and that he earns enough money to support two families, one here and one there, either their eyes get big and they almost die from shock, or they . . . they smile at me and shake their heads because they think I lie. I have to tell you, Evan, I get very sick of the whole thing. And I hope you don't believe those little stories I tell you."

"Well, I'm sorry."

"Sorry. Wyy! Open a book. Look around yourself. Listen to people!"

"Well I am. I do. It's not like . . . Well, it's just that people tell me that marabous can do all this amazing stuff. They say they can fly, stop time, make love potions, invoke good or evil spirits and make them do all kinds of weird things. A guy down in Zig told me that marabous can make a gris-gris so powerful that it can protect you from bullets and knives. Now I didn't read these things in some Denver newspaper, Ami; African folks told me these things. All I'm asking is if your father can do any of this stuff. Or if he claims to."

Aminata picks up the brush then puts it down. She stops braiding, turns to me, rests her right hand on my arm. Her hand is warm. It makes my arm glow with feeling. It is as though her touch hollows me out, fills me with light. My face flushes, my nipples tickle against my shirt. It strikes

49

me that she is the first woman to touch me skin-to-skin since I first came to Africa, excepting Ruth Barron's perfunctory handshake, and the customary quotidian handshakes of the Senegalese. But it is more than just some hunger that causes my blood to rise this way. It has been only four and a half months since I made love to Wanda. I have gone much longer than that. No. I do not doubt my desire to swim between the heaviness of Aminata's breasts, to drink from her tongue, to submerge myself, without air or light into her very source. Any man would feel this way. But if I could take myself inside her, seep into her, membrane by membrane, coil myself vinelike around her nerves, fill up the empty spaces between her cells, I think I would feel I could do anything. Maybe teach a hare to kill a lion. I know I am being stupid. I have no idea why I feel this way. It has been both gradual and sudden.

"OK," Aminata says. "You're right. Many people think that these things can happen, I guess. But most of them are very old, uneducated, or very young. I never talked to my father about what he can do. If you notice, I don't talk to my father unless he talks to me first, and out of respect I don't talk *about* him. If I want to know something about him, I wait till he tells me, or my brother tells me. But there is one thing I know, man." Becoming self-conscious, she lifts her hand from my arm. The glow remains. I want to put my arm around her, hold her close. "My father," she says, "is not powerful. He is knowledgeable; that is real power. He is a very smart man. And if you are smart, you will not talk about him. Never talk about him."

I cough, phonily. "Sounds a little like you're afraid of him."

"I respect him. *You* are afraid of him."

"A little."

"Why?"

"I don't know. He never speaks to me. He just stares at me. It makes me crazy."

"Well, in the first place he's been quiet to almost everyone since my mother died. And in the second place he's just trying to get used to you. You're a little weird, Evan."

"It's like he doesn't trust me." I have the compulsion to place my hand on her arm, but the way she holds herself, thumbs tucked inside her fists, fists on lap, knees drawn together, head cocked toward me, I know I would be a fool to touch her. She says something in Wolof to Binta. Binta rises and heads toward the door, skittering across the floor on her toes. She is a very beautiful child, but will not grow to be as beautiful as her sister now is. I am desperate to touch Aminata, desperate to endear her to me in some way. I inhale deeply to refocus my thoughts, but my nerves fill with her fragrance and my thoughts scatter. She smells like rain, incense, ocean water, wheat. I swallow all the bones in my throat. I close my eyes. I cannot remember the words I spoke last. "A marabou," says Aminata, watching her little sister's exit, "doesn't seem to depend on trust. If you want him to understand you then try to make yourself get better. I think he doesn't like the way you enjoy your sickness." I cock my head to the side, unsure of what to say, unsure, for a moment or two, of what she has said to me. I wish I had not begun all this talk. Really I do not care about her father. Not now. I turn half-left and glance at the door to my room. We can go there, Ami. We can do this. Still facing away from her I say, "Enjoy my — Listen, I'm not that sick anymore. I'm feeling much better."

"Really?"

"I'm still having headaches, but I feel stronger. I'll be out of here in no time."

"Hmm."

"Just tell him I'm better. I don't plan to stay here forever.

51

And tell him I'll pay for everything he's given me. My parents are sending money soon."

"I won't lie to my father."

"I'm not lying. I got money back in the States."

"No, no, no. Not the money, your health. You might be feeling better, but you're not getting better."

"What in the world are you talking about? Listen, this isn't important. Sorry I brought it up. I just . . ."

She unfolds her hands and touches me on the arm again, but this time the touch is dispassionate, condescending. She stands and says, "Sometimes you make me very tired, American. See you later." She leaves the room. I sit for a long while and try to figure out what she has tried to tell me. But soon my thoughts descend to more carnal matters. I think of lying down with her on some secluded spot on N'Gor Beach. I nibble her breasts, explore her softness, investigate each mound and fold. Would she shriek or moan? Would she scratch my back or caress my face? I lose myself in her imaginary body. We heat up, pores open, genitals deepen in color, stiffen. Each and every time I come inside her, would my head beat with an exquisite, mad pain? Would bus engines roar in the background?

8 I Look for a Job

Each morning at about ten o'clock I take my toilet kit, a towel, and a roll of toilet paper and go to the bathroom. In order to get there I must walk from my room into the common room, where there may be as many as a dozen people sitting around talking, eating, smoking, or what have you. I find it embarrassing to traipse past them with my toilet articles. Everyone knows where I am going. Everyone knows that I practice the "filthy" habit of using toilet paper. Besides this, a good many of the closer neighbors know when I am going to the shango, too, as there is no internal entrance to it. One must walk outside, past the N'Doye family compound, between the N'Doye and the Faye family compounds till one gets, finally, to the rear of the marabou Gueye's house, where the shango is attached rather like a toolshed.

The bathroom has no mirror, no basin, no hot water, no electricity, and no roof. It consists of three cement stalls, one for showering, one for drying, and the last is a toilet. I do not particularly like the toilet. It is one of those squat-style affairs that confound most Americans. There is no seat. It is a ceramic hole in the ground, with footrests and a flush tank with a pull chain. For obvious reasons I hate using the bathroom at night.

On this morning, in any case, I make my way to the bathroom, greeting hosts and neighbors as I go. I open the door and step into the drying stall. I step on a fat blue-and-yellow lizard. It is dead. Its body is stiff, its head bent at a ninety-degree angle. I kneel, carefully perusing the lizard. It is large, a dozen inches long, perhaps. I open my toilet kit, dig through it. I remove a disposable razor, poke the lizard with it, roll the lizard over. As I manipulate the lizard this way, it occurs to me that whoever tossed this dead thing here probably used his or her bare hands. Africans, village people anyway, are not aghast at the feel and taste of nature. They are not afraid to touch their food, to touch each other, to let their children run out in the fields or explore the beaches. They know what to touch, how to touch it, what not to touch, how to use or avoid it. I admire this propensity, but as the pale yellow belly glows up at me, I consider how little I know about nature. I have never hunted, fished, or camped. I am ill at ease around stray animals, suspicious of wild vegetables, garden vegetables, and fearful of most insects. I keep my room in Ziguinchor, as well as my room here, perpetually stocked with pesticides. In my second week in N'Gor I discovered a mouse in my room. I asked Phillipe if he knew where I could find a mousetrap. "What is mouse trap?" he said. I told him. "It's a very small animal," said Phillipe. "It can't hurt you." "Yeah," I said, "but it doesn't pay rent." And I smiled. Phillipe raised one eyebrow, shifted in his chair. "That is very American joke, I guess," he said. I wrap the lizard in toilet paper and toss it over the wall.

After my shower, I return to my room and change clothes. For the first time in a month, my head feels almost normal. The pain is most intense when I stay in the sun too long, or when I do anything physically strenuous. The only sensation I feel at the moment is an intense itch at the top of my head.

Just as I button my jeans, there is a knock at my door. It is Aminata.

"Nangadeff?" she says.

"Mangifirek."

"Fodiem?"

"Mangidem Dakar. I'm gonna try to find a job."

"You told me you were in the Peace Corps."

"I told you I quit the Peace Corps."

"What kind of job?"

"Teaching."

"Where?"

"The American Cultural Center. Word is they always hire in late summer. Can't hurt to try."

"Then what will you do?"

"Hm?"

"Will you leave N'Gor?" She folds her arms, lowers her head. I am glad she does this because sometimes she is so beautiful I cannot look her in the eye. "Will you live back in Dakar?"

"Will I *go back to* Dakar, you mean. I never lived there."

"Will you?"

"That's up to your father, I guess."

She tells me she is sure I can stay if I want to.

"I'll stay for a while."

"At least till you get better," she says with a shrug. Then she tells me she will go with me to Dakar.

Aminata, Phillipe, whom I have come to realize is our chaperone, and I amble through the narrow village paths. N'Gor is a relatively suburban village in comparison to the villages around Ziguinchor. It is an odd agglomeration of two-story, five-bedroom, tile-floored homes with full kitchens and indoor plumbing, on the one hand, and, on the other, crumbling shanties of cast-off lumber and roofing tin. The village smells of fruit and fish, goatskin, chicken shit, and mutton, disintegrating under the obtrusive sun. It smells of tobacco, marijuana, palm wine, cheap perfume, incense, home cooking, coffee, tea, and charcoal. Odors twisting in the air, as visible as fiesta streamers. People in red, people in blue. Greens and yellows to make the mouth pucker. They sit on benches along the pathways, drinking, smoking, talking in warm or vigorously percussive tones. People in blue jeans, khaftans, boubous, pagnes, suits and ties, going to work, coming home from work. A young girl, broom in hand, chases a cat. A boy strolls toward the beach. He balances a Coke bottle on his head. His arms swing smooth as ropes in a breeze. On the red dirt esplanade near the bus stop, bird-legged boys play soccer with an airless grapefruit-sized ball. The market women sit on their big round asses, selling peanuts, boiled eggs, bananas, oranges, and a small green round fruit with pink insides called goyave. It is sweetly bitter and makes the mouth dry.

We get on the bus.

We get off the bus in Dakar.

We go to the American Cultural Center and, as Aminata and Phillipe wait in the open-air hallway, I speak with Calvin Whitaker, the director of the English school. He is a tall penny-colored man with a Vandyke and muttonchops. He wears glasses, the photo-gray type that makes even the occasional glance sinister. He eyes me suspiciously. "I think I've seen you before," he says. "As a matter of fact" — he fiddles with a cigarette and a box of Le Boxeur matches — "I saw you here with Allen Weitz. You in the Peace Corps?"

"No. I know Allen, but I'm not in the Corps. I met him in Ziguinchor, where I was a lay missionary. I used to work

with Father Perrin." I sound phony, even to myself. "Old
Father P.," says Whitaker. "Good man."

"You know him?"

"Sure. I know just about everybody in Senegal who's
worth knowing. Some who ain't."

"Well, yeah, the father and I had a falling out a couple
of months ago. We're not getting along these days."

"Um."

"See, I've left the church."

"I see." He pushes the matchbox open with his middle
finger, extracts a match, lights his cigarette. A thread of
blue-yellow smoke slips across his eye. He squints, rubs his
eye with a finger, leans back in his chair, then leans forward.

"And I'm looking for work," I say.

"I see. Can you teach?"

"Teach? Yeah. Sure."

"English?"

"Oh yeah."

"Where you living?"

"N'Gor."

His bony fingers drum the desk, twiddle pencils, scratch
his nose, fondle his stapler. They flex, fist, spread apart,
close together. Finally, two of them clasp the cigarette and
yank it from his mouth. "Out there, huh?" he says.

"Is anything open? A job, I mean?"

"Not now. Not right now, anyway. But I might be able
to work you in for the fall."

That would be fine, I tell him.

"You know, Dakar isn't all that expensive. You could live
cheap here if you know what you're doing."

"Oh, N'Gor's OK."

"You're not one of those bloods who've come out here to
become African, are you?"

"I don't get you."

He leans back in his chair, leans forward. "You know. Those space cadets who come out here thinking they're gonna get reunited with their long-lost kin and all that bullshit. Got a lot of that type coming out here after *Roots* came out. They try to come out here and be what they can't be.

"But let me tell you something, brother. The majority of these niggers out here don't give a walking fuck for you or me or any other black American. Shit, most of the ancestors of them niggers in N'Gor, Ouakam, Yoff, and so forth, the better-off ones, anyway, made a great deal of their money selling folks into slavery.

"Think about it, man. You might be shacking with some family that got fat off selling your great-great-grands to some European slavers. Can you relate to that? I mean they grin and smile at you and shit, but brother, let me tell. If slavery existed today they'd do the same goddamn thing to you in a heartbeat. They play a lot of mind games, try anything to take your money. I've lived here twelve years and have never even set foot in a village. Nothing but a bunch of trifling fools out there. I can't tell you what to do, man, but if I were you, I'd get my ass out of N'Gor. They got nothing for you there. You got a degree?"

"Master's in English."

"Um-hm. How's your French?"

"Not so hot."

"I see." He opens his desk drawer, removes a small pink pad and a pen, scribbles something, closes the drawer. "You get what I'm saying about living around them." He puts it declaratively, as though there is no doubt in his mind he has made an impression on me. I tell him I understand him, but that I am in N'Gor because I do not like cities. "As mellow as Dakar is, things like that crippled guy getting his head bashed in last month get to me. That kind of thing isn't real likely to happen in a village —"

"People get killed in villages just as easily as they do in Dakar or anywhere else. Dead is dead." He stands and crushes out his cigarette. "Listen," he says, "I might be able to use you. Come on down three weeks from today and we'll see what we can do." He jabs his hand at me, shakes without looking me in the eye.

"See you," I say.

"Right." He turns from me and starts rummaging through a stack of papers and books on a typing table behind his desk. "Wait up a second," he says. From the stack he pulls out a lime green textbook, hands it to me. "You might as well look this over. You'd be teaching level three." I thumb the book's pages then slip it into my day sack. My fingertips touch something soft and unfamiliar. I reach deeper into the pack. "What the fuck?" I say out loud.

"What," says Whitaker, lighting another cigarette.

"Somebody put a goddamn dead lizard in my pack." It is the same species as the one I had seen in the shower. Only this one has apparently been killed by strangulation. Several inches of twine are tightly tied round its neck. It has been freshly killed. No rigor mortis has set in. "That's what you get for living around them village niggers," Whitaker says. "That's just what I'm trying to tell you. That kind of thing won't happen in Dakar."

"What's this supposed to mean?"

"Means village niggers don't know how to act."

We get on the bus, Phillipe, Aminata, and I.

"What's this supposed to mean, Ami?" I hold the animal by its tail, look into Aminata's eyes. She gazes right back into mine, coolly, ironically. Then she looks away.

"Someone's playing a joke on you." She stares out at the hustle and swarm of the Grand Marché. She laughs and points out to Phillipe and me a vendor who is bullwhipping a raggedly dressed man who has apparently tried to steal something. A throng of people quickly collects around the two. A policeman stands on tiptoe at the periphery of the throng, grinning at the fracas. I try to smile but am too preoccupied with the dead reptiles. I tap Aminata on the arm. "I don't think it's very funny."

"Eh? Oh, the policeman will stop them before anyone is seriously hurt."

"I mean the joke. The lizard. I don't think it's funny." I drop the lizard back into the sack.

"Is no important," says Phillipe.

"It's not funny either. Do you know who's doing it?"

"How should I know?" says Aminata.

"Yes, don' worry about him, Eva'."

We get off the bus and wind our way home. My head feels tight and the itch at the top of it burns as if it has been sprinkled with lye. Internally, I feel much worse. I feel, strangely, exposed, the way a liar feels when he realizes he has confounded the details of a lie, and his listener does nothing but smile and nod. It is odd, but I can describe it no other way. The lizard means something. I do not doubt this, but I cannot begin to guess what it is. A dull panic twists through my gut, and for a brief time I tremble. I look at Aminata, then at Phillipe, but there is nothing in either of them that suggests intrigue. The trembling subsides. Aminata asks me if I want to go for a swim later. "Maybe," I say. Then I pause and tell her that maybe I will not go, that I need to lie down for an hour or two.

"I forgot to ask you if you got the job," she says.

"Maybe. Maybe not. I'm supposed to go back and check with him on the third." As we step into the foyer, I tell my hosts I am tired and wish to lie down, that I will not take my midday meal. I step into the common room and find Monsieur Gueye and his neighbor, Monsieur N'Doye, sitting on the wicker and black Naugahyde sofa that is just outside the door to my room. Both men greet me, N'Doye grinning, Gueye focusing his black and amber gaze on my chest. I feel a peculiar pressure there. "Come speak English with me," says N'Doye. "I am practice English with you." I shake hands with each man. "How are you?" says N'Doye, intoning the phrase with parrotlike detachment.

"I'm fine."

"How your fam'ly?"

"Fine."

"How your job?"

"Good. I think I may have found a job in Dakar."

"Comment?"

"Fine. Fine. It's fine."

"How your wife?"

"No wife."

N'Doye turns to Gueye and speaks to him in Wolof. Gueye tersely replies. "Why you are no marry?" says N'Doye.

"I don't know. I just — I don't know."

N'Doye speaks to Gueye. Gueye replies. "Are you Muslim?" says N'Doye.

"No."

"Chrétien?"

"Christian? No. I don't have a religion?"

"Eh?"

"I don't believe in God."

N'Doye chuckles and tells Gueye my answer. Both men laugh, N'Doye till tears come to his eyes. Finally, N'Doye says, "Where is your mother? Is she die?"

"No. She's alive."

"Go back to her. She don't finish you." N'Doye is laughing so hard he can scarcely tell Gueye what we have been talking about. Gueye merely smiles, more to himself, it seems, than to either N'Doye or me. One of Gueye's younger daughters enters the room, carrying a bowl of tjebujin and three spoons. "Doh lek?" says Gueye, keeping his eye on his daughter. He is still smiling. I tell him in Wolof that I am not hungry. He expresses surprise that I have used his language. "Come an' chop," says N'Doye. "Fish and rice make you speak more Wolof, make you Senegaleseman."

"Je suis très malade toujours," I say, holding my hand over my stomach. "Je vais dormir."

"Sleep is good for sick," says N'Doye. "Sleep is too good. Too fine. Maybe you hear Allah speak to you. Maybe you mother come you home."

I shut my door behind me, rub the top of my head, unbutton my shirt. I am asleep before I close my eyes.

9   I Take a Walk

I wake up with the sensation of being stabbed on the very top of my skull. It is steady, piercing, firm, like an ice pick. My room is black, my blankets damp. It smells like rain. I am alarmed that I have slept so long. I am unaccustomed to napping for such a long time. Frogs, bats, and crickets whir, trill, bleat outside. The village is sleeping. I rise from bed and dress. The air is still very warm and my clothes are damp. They smell musty.

I step out of the house into the half-moon night. The air feels thick, like a series of sheer curtains. The ground is spotted with puddles and streams. I consider going back into the house, but the air is sweet, and besides, I am restless. It is a good night for a walk. I feel content, mainly, but the pain at the top of my head is disquieting. I think of the lizards, and wonder if there is some connection between them and the pain. Then I wonder if the pain is a result of the malaria. After perhaps five minutes of trundling these questions over and round and round, I decide there is no way I can know the reason for my current malady. I must accept it as I accept the bus.

I think about my conversation with Whitaker. More specifically, I consider his response to my comment about the murder. His reply neither confirms nor denies whether the murder actually took place. I might have said more, asked a question or two, but did not want to fixate on the murder. He already seems to be an expressly suspecting sort as it is. The way he questioned me this morning, the way he diddled with the things on his desk, perused me from behind the gray gaze of his glasses, makes me wonder whether he plans to speak with or has already spoken to Allen. It would not surprise me at all if he did.

I take my wallet from my pocket and find a half-smoked joint I had tucked into it several weeks ago. I am running low on marijuana. I am most content when I smoke once or twice a day. I must ask Phillipe about where I can find a good source. I light the joint and the smoke rasps my throat. I am enclosed in a good high before I have taken half a dozen paces. I like to get high. I like a sleepy, slack-jawed walk when I get high. It helps me think. Wanda does not like me to get high. She disapproves of anything that is purported to be mind-altering. A little wine with dinner is all she approves of. Approve is her favorite word in regard to me. She does not approve of my cigarette smoking. She does not approve of my using the word *fuck* when I mean "make love." She disapproves of the fact that I often walk in public with my hair uncombed and my shirt untucked. When I whisper to her when we screw, when my kisses are too wet, when I watch too much TV, or watch programs she refers to as lowbrow, when I burn incense, when I eat junk food, when I drive too fast — "It's not really something I approve of, Evan," she says. Most of all, she does not like, let alone approve of, my friends.

"When you spend time with those creeps you change. You act different."

"Like I keep telling you, you're jealous."

What on earth does she have to be jealous about, she will ask me.

"You were my shrink. You think you're the only one who's supposed to have some kind of influence on me. You don't like the idea of me hanging out with Chuck and those guys, because they're older. You think they're leading me around by the nose. You'd like —"

"The fact I was your counselor has nothing to do with it."

It does, but she will never talk about it. Instead, she rants about Chuck's two voluntary tours to Vietnam. *Don't you think that indicates some sort of mental imbalance?* She points out Tom's several arrests for drug peddling. *I can see why he's so well-read. No better way to spend your time in the slammer than read.* "Nobody uses the word 'slammer,' babe." *Don't change the subject!* As for Bebe? *She seems so nice. What on earth could she see in Tom?* As for Star? *Can't you see the vicarious thrill that bitch got out of setting you up with all those white chicks? She wanted you. If you can't see that, you're blind.*

Wanda is, she puts it, a "recovering hippie," and is therefore intolerant of all the underpinnings, extenuations, implications, suggestions, and accoutrements of what she perceives to be the dark side of the Aquarian Age. She despises, as I said, drugs. She despises "free" love. She despises unkemptness; free-floating, grab-bag spiritualism; loud music, Indian music, long hair, hip language, paisley, ben-wa balls, love beads, dashikis, holistic medicine, any sort of hedonistic excess. She knows full well that none of these things was originated in the sixties and seventies, and not all of them are intrinsically harmful, but they were endemic to a time from which she was one of the earliest escapees. She hates all her generational peers who still hang on to the symbols and/or practices of that period, namely, Chuck, Star, Alice, Tom, and Bebe. She hates their VW buses and graying beards, their graying middle-parted long long hair. She hates their low-slung jeans, their pot smoking, their talk of dharma, karma, Che, and Mao. But of all these Aquarianisms, her greatest hatred is for interracial love. *That's a contradiction in terms if I ever heard one. Do you think those women ever liked you? Can't you see you only tickled some exposed psychosexual nerve in them?* " 'Exposed psychosexual nerve,' " I say. "You should be a writer." *Don't change the —* "the subject. I know. I'm avoiding."

Before I left, she did not seem nearly as optimistic as her last letter indicates, and she said two or three times, I recall, "At least you'll be around black people. At least you won't end up with some white chick."

"I told you I'm coming back to you."

"Two years is a long time, Evan. Don't patronize me."

"And you can come see me like we talked about."

And then she would pause, staring into space for a long moment. She would shrug, stir the vegetables, rinse the dish, wipe Tucker's face, whatever, and say, "At least you'll be around black people."

My high begins to dissipate. I am thinking too much. I stop, turn, and face west. I peer into the black, glistening water, the powdery black sky. The stars near the horizon are sparse, but as the eyes travel upward, they thicken, a scatter of pearls, salt, sand, chalk smudges, broken glass. The ocean tongues the sand, hisses, inhales. The high closes itself around my head like a web. Wanda. I do not like the name. The name of good witches, hairdressers, flaccid soap-opera addicts. What kind of name is this for a woman with a powerful intellect? What kind of name is this for a tight-bodied, clear-eyed, Shiva-dancing woman? Aminata. Now there is a name. It flows like her seamless body, surges like her speech. Would Wanda approve of Aminata? *Not really, but at least she's black.* Does Aminata approve of me? *I do not approve. I do not disapprove.* Why does she spend so much time with me? *So I can practice,* she would say. So she can practice. So she can speak perfect English. So she can find a good job. So she can travel the wide world. *So I can travel the wide world, and find a good job. So I can live anywhere I want to. You speak good English.* When I want to I do. *I do not approve. I do not disapprove.* This is what she would say. But I do not know, really. She knows I smoke. She says nothing. She does not smoke, but her cousin Mamadou and Phillipe do. She says nothing of this. "Did you ever get high?" I once asked Wanda. "I don't think you get high," she said. "I think people just think they're high. And what do people mean when they say 'high,' anyhow? All that stuff really does is make you so self-centered that nothing and no one else matters. You shut out the world and mentally masturbate. When I smoked I didn't feel anything at all."

"How much did you smoke?"

"I don't know. Few puffs each time."

"Did you inhale?"

"Tried to."

"Well you probably didn't smoke enough."

"How much was I supposed to smoke?"

"I don't prescribe the shit, I just smoke it."

"Well, what was I supposed to do, develop a dependency before I could see the virtue in it? You smoke that trash because you're bored. If you'd get a good job, work out, maybe, stop hanging out with those throwback creeps and —"

The next thing you know, I told her, you will be asking me to take cold showers and toss a medicine ball around like some earnest Victorian. My friends have nothing to do with my habit. I picked it up long before I met them. And as for the job, I told her, I would get one, but would continue to get stoned even if I were elected president. I do work out, I told her, it is just that I do not like to go to that funny-smelling health club of hers. And I told her that people like to alter their reality a bit. You of all people should know. Animals like eating fermented fruit. Little children like to whirl around till they get dizzy. Cats like catnip. Joggers run farther and longer than they need to, nodding to the beat of their own endorphins. She inexplicably dropped the entire matter. Said, "Dinner's ready." And vegetarianism being the only thread from her college days she ever found worthy of weaving into her present life, she served up the finest eggplant Parmesan I ever tasted. "Let's take a walk before you go home," she said. Then asked me if I liked the meal. Perhaps my last remark, reminding her of our earlier relationship, caused her to change gears that way. You of all people, I said. But she would, of course, never say so. She never talks about it.

Though I hear nothing but the suspiration of the ocean, I have the feeling I am being followed. I feel an odd pressure at my back, a prickly sensation on my neck. I decide to head back to the house. The ice-pick pressure at the top of my skull increases with each step. As I near the village, I hear the most peculiar high-pitched squeal. It sounds like a dental drill. If I am not mistaken, it is coming from me. It is as if there is a tiny hole in the top of my head through which air is leaking. I do not panic. I am fascinated. Here I am, squealing away like a punctured balloon and walking nervously away from something I can neither hear nor see. It makes me smile. I stop and listen for the engines, inhale anticipating the oily stink of diesel cloud. I close my eyes, expecting that when I open them I will find myself on the bus. But when I do open them, I discover that I am still in N'Gor, standing in a puddle, muddy water filling my shoes. I come very close to laughing.

In my room again, I strip and get into bed. The night is full of the sounds I awoke to. Whirring. Trilling. Bleating. Croaking. But underneath it all, first softly then expanding in volume as though someone were turning up a radio, come footsteps. Back and forth. Back and forth, right outside my window. I rise, kneel on my mattress, peer out the window. There is a junglelike tangle of foliage in the back of the house. I have always thought this unusual, given the fact that the land in these parts is mainly savannah, baobab trees interrupting the flow of grass here and there. But right outside my window there is this eruption of trees, bushes, vines, grass. I asked Aminata about it once and she told me that before the hotels came, before the Sahara burned so far south, there may have been more jungle than grassland here. But she was not sure.

I consider going outside, climbing the wall that runs along the back of the compound and confronting whoever it is treading around this way. I cannot do this, though, without a flashlight. And the black profusion of branches, stems, and vines most surely squirms with all sorts of fauna. I must be honest. I do not think a flashlight or even daylight would give me the courage to go back there. I listen. Perspiration creeps warm from my armpits, cool down my rib cage. I listen. It is a goat. No. It is a two-legged gait. I listen. The bats are knocking fruit to the ground. No. It is regular, left right left right left right. I listen. It is N'Doye. He has a garden somewhere at the edge of the little jungle. No. It is too close. Why would he be so close? Pacing. Not working. I lie down, swallowing my Adam's apple, and listen. The pacing continues, hour after hour, till the muezzin makes his call just before daybreak. Now there is a streak of orange light against the wall opposite my bed. As I fall asleep I hear my thoughts ask me, "What now? What next?" I hear my thoughts reply, "Do not ask."

10 I Find a Chicken

Two weeks have passed since my meeting with Calvin Whitaker. I begin to find the lizards everywhere: in the shower, under my bed, on my windowsill. When I see them my skin prickles, my breath stops. That odd feeling of nakedness, of feeling exposed, opened up, comes over me. I have given up asking Aminata about them. She is no help at all. She looks at me with those black eyes squinting in concern and tells me she will ask her father. So far she has not done so because he is busy or away. "I'm sure it's nothing to even worry about, Evan," she says, and she carries on preparing our meal or washing clothes or whatever. One afternoon, when Aminata was in town and I was giving her brother Phillipe lessons in American idioms in the common room, Monsieur Gueye stepped into the house, greeting us both but turning directly toward the stairs to his room rather than shaking our hands and exchanging the customary salutations. He had taken his midday meal at the N'Doyes' house and looked as though nothing else was on his mind but rushing up to bed and taking a long nap. Before he had mounted the second step I called out to him. "Monsieur Gueye," I said, "un moment, s'il vous plaît." And then I paused, looking at Phillipe to see both whether I had violated decorum and got my French right. Phillipe looked surprised but said nothing. He simply retucked his shirt into his jeans, smoothed his short Afro and folded his arms. "Phillipe," I said, "I need you to help me talk to your father." Phillipe nodded but said nothing. I approached Old Gueye and shook his hand. I asked him to please wait there till I could go to my room for something. "What do you get?" said Phillipe, but I ignored him, went to my room, and came back with the lizard I had most recently discovered. It had been in my toilet kit, and rather than throw it away, I kept it, planning this event from the moment I found it.

I clasped the animal's tail between thumb and index finger, held it away from me as if it radiated death. I stepped toward father and son. I said, "Phillipe, ask your father why these things've been in my room." I looked into the eyes of both men, reading nothing. Phillipe turned to his father and spoke to him in Wolof. Old Gueye shrugged and turned toward the staircase. "Wait a second," I said. "What'd he say?" "Nothing," said Phillipe. "He don't say nothing."

"Ask him again," I said.

"Eva' —"

"Ask him again, Phillipe."

"He don't —"

I dropped the lizard to the ground. "Like fuck!" I said. I did not yell it, but spoke with sufficient force as to make my emotion known, something I had not intended to do. All three of us stood still for a moment, looking down at the lizard. Everything was still, quiet. It was as though we were all locked in silent prayer over the body of the lizard. Then Old Gueye slowly lifted his staff, pointed to the lizard, and said something to Phillipe. Phillipe crouched down, scooped up the beast, stepped to the door, and tossed it outside. I looked back at Old Gueye. He pointed the staff at me and spoke to me in French, but I could not follow him. "Phillipe —"

"He say you look too tired. He say you need sleep."

"But —"

"He will tell you if he learn something, Eva'. He don't know nothing."

Old Gueye ascended the stairs and suddenly I felt as spent as he looked. I forgot all about the lizards, my anger, my fear. I turned from Phillipe without a word, fumbled with the latch on my door, staggered into my room, fell to bed, and slept a long burdensome sleep. I dreamt of dust devils, hurricanes and whirlwinds, and nothing else.

Whitaker's words do not leave my mind. I do not doubt that someone in the house is responsible for the lizards. I am almost certain it is Old Gueye. He has become inexplicably friendlier toward me since that last encounter. He asks about my family, my health, makes sure his daughters have properly cleaned my room and washed my clothes. He even, on occasion, asks me whether I have found any more "strange things" in my room. I always lie to him. I tell him no. He is being kind, either because I have given him two of the fifteen hundred dollars my parents sent me, or because he pities me in the same way an experienced hunter pities his prey. The pacing continues, too, night after night. but I do not know who is responsible for this. Gueye's gait is so distinctive I would know it in my sleep. It cannot be he. Aminata would not do this sort of thing, neither would any of her sisters. As for Phillipe? All I can say is that if it were not for him, I would think I am losing my mind. Or I would believe/disbelieve it as I do the bus. Phillipe, anyway, has heard the footsteps.

Last week, Phillipe and I sat in this stuffy room, smoking a spliff rolled with a six-by-six-inch square of *Le Soleil*. We talked for hours about everything Phillipe finds fascinating — the U.S., reggae and the genius of Bunny Wailer, sex, politics, and Pele. He is only around nineteen but speaks with the cool of a man twice his age. And I marvel at how quickly he picks up English. "Where did you learn that?" I will ask him about some expression or another. "What," he will say, "you mean Don' Bogart that jointmyfriend?" And he will tell me that he knew exactly what I meant when I had used the phrase. "I see Bogart on the television," he will say, "and I ask myself, 'Hey, why this guy hold that cigarette in his lips for the whole cinema and don' light?' And when you say me, Don' Bogart that joint, I know what you mean." I am invariably amazed at how quickly he makes these connections. With my Wolof and French, it takes me at least a week to learn a phrase well enough to use it in conversation. But then, I really do not try hard.

Though I could not stand the wheat straw—petroleum—sulfur taste of the spliff, I got very high. Phillipe had told me that Senegalese pot is relatively weak, so we smoked nearly half an ounce. It is not that weak, really. I was so high I could not understand much of Phillipe's conversation. But he was high, too, and his English cannot bear the weight of deep intoxication. "Uh-huh," I said, half-listening.

"He say, 'Them belly full but we hun-gree. A hungry man is a h'angry man —'"

"Marley."

"Eh?"

"That's Bob Marley."

"OK."

"And it's 'mob,' not —"

He raised his hand, and I thought for a second that he was angry with me. "Just a minute," I said, but he shushed me and shut out the light. "What?" I said.

"Denga."

"You mean —"

"Harra minyo! Denga! Denga!"

I did as he told me, and listened. Phillipe moved across the room, knelt on my bed, peered out the window. I could scarcely see him; the moonlight shone softly on his skin, a beetle-shell glow. He rested his long fingers on the sill as though he were playing piano. He listened for what seemed a long while. It is hard to say how long, for the pot splintered my perception in a dozen different directions. I found myself gazing at the quarter-moon; then watching Phillipe, admiring the way he stays so natty, in spite of the plentiful sand and soil through which one must tread to get around the village; then I would listen to the brazen footfall; then feel for my matches; then scratch the mosquito bites on my arms; then think of being in my dark room with Aminata rather than her brother. I did each of these things as though nothing else in the world were on my mind at the time, as though nothing existed before or after each action or thought. Finally Phillipe stepped across the room, flipped on the light, lit a cigarette, and said, "I think you should be careful, Eva'."

"Be careful of what?"

He shrugged. "Be careful of whatever you do."

"What is it? What's out there?"

He shrugged, drew on his cigarette. "I think you should be careful whatever you do. That's all."

He would not tell me, but deftly drew me away from the subject with talk of reggae and sex, the U.S., a new pair of shoes he had had his eyes on at the Bata store. "They are white on top and black on sides. Maaan, I will be styling, n'est-ce pas, Eva'?" Had I been straight I might have been able to negotiate his evasion, but before I could raise the subject of the footsteps again, he began an impromptu French lesson, a dozen or so phrases, for making passes at "femme difficile." Two days later I bought a flashlight, and spent three consecutive nights traipsing about the rear of the compound to no avail. I could not muster the courage to search as thoroughly as I had planned. I did, however, discover that there are no pens back there. The only animals I could detect were bats. All I know is that, first, the pacing keeps me awake until cock crow, so I have taken to sleeping from noon till around four P.M., and second, Phillipe, when he wants to, can be as silent as dust. I do not like this in Phillipe, and sometimes I am not sure whether I like Phillipe at all.

I do not like his yellowish eyes. I do not like the arrogant curve of his mouth, or the way he silently studies me. I cannot stand the way he (seemingly) unconsciously imitates me. I thread my fingers, he threads his fingers. I whistle, he whistles. Maybe it is because he is only nineteen. Maybe it is because, as he once told me, he admires and respects Americans. Who can tell? He is rather obsessive about things. "Do you know Bob Dylan?" he will ask. "Do you know Jackson Five?" and Do-I-know Santana? Miles Davis? Ralph Ellison? Kool and the Gang? Earth, Wind, and Fire? E. A. Poe? Jesse Jackson? Andrew Young? He quotes them, analyzes them, studies them. He does not really think I know them personally, of course, but of them, and this sort of pestering I do not mind. The imitation makes me want to batter his eyes out.

And then there are times when his imitation is discomfortingly purposeful. He has the uncanny ability to say anything you say, as you say it. Say anything, in any language, at any speed, with any trick of the tongue — lisp, croak, scat, holler, whisper, and Phillipe will check you, note for note. "Do you know what I was saying?" I may ask him. "Some," he will reply. Unlike his sister, he is no storyteller. Sit with him in a room for an hour, and three quarters of it will pass before he says a word, then suddenly words will whirl from his mouth for ten or twenty unbroken minutes. It is commentary. It is opinion. It is review. It is reportage, but never story. And everything sounds mannered and rehearsed. It may be that he is weaker in English than he appears to be. Perhaps he does rehearse everything before he speaks. I cannot be sure.

So that night I kept trying to get him to talk about the footsteps, and he kept putting me off, until finally I threw up my hands, interrupting a dissertation on John Wayne movies, and said, "Well just tell me this. Does it sound like two feet or four?" He scratched the top of his head with his middle finger, rubbed the back of his hand across his handsome chin, and said, "Four, I think."

"Sounds like two to me."

He giggled. "Then why you ask?"

I spend most of my time in my room these days. I do not like going out among the village people anymore. I feel conspicuous, exposed. Every smile seems to be a suppressed laugh. All the children I meet, with the exception of Gueye's children, call me "toubob," which means either whiteman or stranger, and ask me for money. I generally leave my room only to take my evening meal with Phillipe and Aminata, or walk N'Gor Beach in search of one of the two local pot dealers, or to go into town to buy toilet supplies.

This afternoon I wake to, of all things, the clucking of a chicken. It sounds very near. It is in my room. I tumble from bed, fall to my knees, and look underneath my bed. I see nothing. I turn to the pair of Naugahyde chairs on the other side of the room. One of them is in relatively good repair. The other is beat up, all springs and cotton held together by tenuous strips of the phony leather. I check under the good one and find nothing. The chicken clucks again. The

sound comes from the bad chair, but I look under it and still
find nothing. The chicken clucks once more. It is most certainly coming from the older chair. I pull the chair away
from the wall and turn it around. There is a long slit in the
back of it. I reach into it and pull out the bird. Its legs are
bound by coarse twine. I do not know the meaning of this,
but I immediately become enraged. I can actually hear the
blood pound through my eardrums. My teeth are clenched
so tight that they hurt. The high-pitched squeal screams so
that if it were audible to anyone other than me it would
break glass. It would shatter skulls. Gripping the bird by
its legs, I march upstairs to Aminata's room. She is sitting
on her bed, reading. She looks at me with big eyes. I have
never before had the effrontery to enter her room. It is a
tacit household rule that a male who is not a member of the
family does not enter, without a chaperone, a female's room.
Before she can speak, I dash the chicken to the floor and
say, "What the fuck's this supposed to be?" I am surprised
to note that the bird makes no noise. I think I have killed
it. Aminata's face twitches once, twice. "I don't know. I have
no idea."

"Don't bullshit me, woman, goddamn it. This is your
house. You know what's going on here. You practically run
this place. I'm goddamn sick and tired of this crap with
these lizards and this . . . What the hell's going on? Do you
have any idea how this makes me feel?"

"Do you think I did this?" She looks terrified, indignant.
She sits straight, holds her body stiff, holds the book to her
breast between her crossed arms.

"Fuck what I think. Tell me." I step toward her and she
starts back, throwing her right arm up to protect her face.
I am shocked that she would think that I would actually do
her harm, but at the same time, perhaps because I have felt
so powerless for so long, I feel a momentary urge to strike

her, or worse. A sick, hot sensation surges from my groin
to my chest. I feel myself shaking, and then against all my
efforts to stop myself I begin to cry. I fall to my knees, lean
toward Aminata, try to take her hands in mine, but she will
not let me. I spring to my feet. "Bitch!" I begin pacing in
front of her. *"You're* afraid of *me? You're* afraid of *me?* You
people do all this ... goddamn voodoo or whatever" — I
sweep my arm in a wide arc — "and you're afraid of me?" I
pace in front of her, back and forth, saying goddamn, goddamn in a half-whisper, over and over. I feel my pockets for
my cigarettes, but find none. I pirouette and sit cross-legged
at her feet, wipe tears from my eyes. I fold my hands in my
lap. "You people bring me here," I say, "feed me, try to give
me medicine, and then you do all this? And don't you try to
tell me it's all some joke, because you know it's not. You
know what's going on. You're the only person I can really
talk to here. Goddamn, Ami, tell me something." She kneels
beside me, lays an arm around my shoulders. Her body is
soft, nothing at all like Wanda's muscular tautness. My underarms leak. My face grows hot. I feel my pulse beat in my
temples, my throat, my groin. I draw her close to me and
kiss her neck. She tenses. "No," she says.

I release her, sit on the floor. Neither of us speaks for a
long time. Then she rises and sits on the bed. "I am your
friend," she says, "but —"

"Don't explain. That's one thing you don't have to do."

Another long silence spreads between us. Aminata splays
the fingers of both hands, rubs her palms together. I find
my cigarettes tucked into my sock. I slip them out, light up.
I look around at her room. There are photos of family members on the wall, Old Gueye in black and white. He wears
a fez, a khaftan. The picture must have been taken a long
time ago, for Gueye has both eyes. They are the same intense, penetrating marabou eyes, but strangely incongruent

to the smooth, fortyish, almost smiling face that surrounds them. I roll my eyes across the room to her bureau. Its top is littered with perfume bottles, makeup, candles in saucers, a small can of bug spray, a decorative whiskey decanter. It is an eagle in tacky red, white, and blue. It rests on a pedestal that reads "1776–1976 Bicentennial Commemorative Special Blend." In the center of these articles, like an icon amid garbage, sits a picture of a woman I am sure is Aminata's mother. The frame is oval, the perfect penumbra for Madame Gueye's face. She has the same black eyes, the same aquiline nose, the same superior demeanor, the same, the very same suchness of Aminata. I stare for what must be an embarrassingly long time. "You know," Aminata says, leaning away from the cigarette smoke. "I do like you. I do want to be your friend, but I can't be maybe everything you want."

"You engaged?"

"Hm?"

"I know sometimes that Senegalese people get engaged early. I thought maybe you were promised to someone or something."

"I was, but it was my father and his father's choice. My fiancé and — my ex-fiancé and I are friends, but we don't want to be married this way. It's old-fashioned. Anyway, it's not that."

"You don't like American men."

"I like you. I like some American men. I don't like all, anyway."

"Well, I'm crazy about you."

She folds her arms, says nothing for a while.

"I am, Ami," I say.

"I don't know who's doing these things to you, Evan. If I knew, I would tell you. But you're right. It's probably someone in this house. And it isn't a joke. I don't know. All I know is that the chicken tied like this is kind of a gris-gris. It is supposed to make a person weak in the mind so he will give you whatever you ask him for."

"Terrific. Very nice. You know how it works."

"It works on you if you believe it, I guess. I don't know."

"You think maybe your father did it?"

"Why do you say these things about my father? He is trying to help you."

"He hates my guts."

"If this is true then why does he take you in his house?"

"You tell me. I'm sure he's got reasons. Maybe he's frustrated that I'm not getting much better and he wants me out of here. Maybe he doesn't like this guy in his house who makes everybody speak a language he doesn't understand. I can't tell you. All I know is the guy doesn't like me. I can feel it. It's nothing logical or anything I could explain." I lie back on my elbows and cross my legs. I consider, for a moment, telling her about the odd dreams I associate with her father — the vortices, but I change my mind. I can only imagine her laughing at me. "What about the lizards," I say. "Tell me about the lizards."

"I don't know about them."

"Come on."

"I don't."

"Right." I stand, walk to the window, and toss out my cigarette butt. I spot Old Gueye, apparently leaving the N'Doye place, walking toward the house. He looks up and sees me. He stops, stares, raises his staff and points it at me. "Here comes your dad, Ami. He's pointing his cane thing at me." Aminata springs up, wringing her hands together. She moves toward me then hesitates at the foot of the bed, perhaps not wanting to be seen with me at the window. I turn back toward the window. Gueye is no longer in view.

"Go," Ami says.

"We haven't done anything."

"Leave."

"But we haven't —"

"Go!'

"Fine. See you." I leave the room, leave the house, the village. I walk down N'Gor Beach, to the Meridien Hotel beach. I sit and watch the half-naked Europeans sunbathe, wade, preen, windsurf, converse. They glisten like steamed sausages. The men are refrigerator shaped and hairy, the women like streamlined hood ornaments. These people are neither beautiful nor ugly, but I watch them almost lustfully. I am embarrassed as I realize that I miss being around them, white people. I miss their impassiveness, their arrogant blindness. They leave one alone.

It is so strange for a black person to leave America where one is looked through, yet feels conspicuous, then come to Africa where one is most assuredly conspicuous and feels seen through. Africans are skilled in the way of people. They do not spend hours a day watching television, hiding from even their own family members in their own rooms, or compartmentalized in their cars, blasting down highways at invisible speeds, or eating TV dinners prepared by strangers. Most Africans have nothing to do in their "leisure" hours but spend time with one another. They are more literate in the tao of humans than any people I have ever seen. This angers me, frightens me.

I want to be at Tom's Place, Thomasville, Dominoe Junction, The Boneyard. I want to sit on that beanbag chair, smell Tom's pine-paneled walls, smoke, talk, hold some huggable long-haired woman in my arms and on my lap. I will hold her close, smell her marigold-flavored hair, furtively squeeze her breasts. It is OK. We are at Tom's Place, Thomasville, Dominoe Junction, The Boneyard. The room is powdered with cigarette-pot-fireplace smoke. Asleep at the Wheel is on the turntable doing "It's Only a Paper Moon." Plants hang down like dreadlocks from blond-braided macramé. Plants shoot stiff from pots, like Mohawks. Across the room, Chuck slaps a bone down. "You guys are sleeping tonight. Gimme some comp, boys and girls."

"Fuck you," says Tom.

"That's my job," says Star.

Bebe sings, ". . . but it wouldn't be make believe, if you believed in me."

I holler from across the room, *"Day of the Locust."*

"What?" says Bebe.

"This song," I say. "It reminds me of *Day of the Locust.*"

"Never heard of it," says Alice.

"A movie," says Chuck. "Come on. Play."

"It was a book first," says Tom. "And don't forget to gimme my points."

"Don't start getting literary on us, boys," says Chuck.

"Especially you, Evan," says Star. "It's Friday. No shop-talk." Then she smiles, winks. "You guys look so cute together."

"You guys look so cute together," says Chuck, in falsetto, making a face. He strokes his big beard. "Come on," he says, "leave those non-hackers alone. Slap them bones."

And Bebe sings, "It's a Barnum and Bailey world, just as phony as it can be . . . but it wouldn't be make believe, if you believed in me."

I sit for too long a time, till the sun draws out my headache as a poultice draws out pus. I hear the high-pitched squeal. Pressure builds in my head. The ice pick bores into my skull. The most ineffable sadness lies over me, sinks into

my skin. "I'm alone," I whisper. I stand and walk toward
the hotel complex and am accosted by four peddlers. One of
them, a tall man, all neck, teeth, and forehead, tugs at my
sleeve, implores me to buy his trash. Quite to my surprise,
I wheel about and grab him by the collar of his khaftan.
"Motherfucker. Leave me the goddamn fuck alone!" All four
peddlers back away, apparently too shocked and frightened
to apply the usual persistence. I continue treading across
the sand. It is so quiet my footsteps sound like cymbals.
I make my way to the bus stop. I wait. The bus stops. I
get on.

11 I Go to Gorée

I take the bus to the end of the line, all the way to the wharf near Place Leclerc. It is my intention to walk from here to Place de l'Indépendance, the center of town. I simply want to walk in a place I am not known, where people do not greet me, ask me where I am going, how I am doing. I will perhaps go to the expensive boulangerie just off the square, where mainly white and Lebanese teenagers congregate. They will leave me alone. They will not even see me. Then I will go to a good hotel. But suddenly I spot the Gorée Island ferry ticket cage and decide that Gorée would be the perfect place to steep in my loneliness. Gorée was a slave depot many many years ago. Each time I go there I can smell taste touch the very fibers of slavery. The old holding-pen walls, the pebbles on the strand, the air, all vibrate with atoms of dried blood, evaporated sweat, desiccated vomit. It is unlike any other place I know. It is the perfect place for self-pity. There is pain there, but it is not my pain. It is like a chorus for my solo. Perhaps too many years have passed since what, for lack of a better term, I could call my ancestral leave-taking. Perhaps I am no longer African, or African only in the vestigial sense. My senses register the waterless horrors of the island's past as if they were photocopied pictures of paintings. I go there not because of some overpowering emotion that takes hold of me but because the ancient emotion does not overwhelm my own.

I get on the boat. The boat goes to Gorée. I get off the boat. The weather is beautiful, eye-splitting blue sky, deep green cut-glass water. The sunlight is almost audible. Many people, mostly Africans, are swimming, sunbathing. My head starts throbbing. My vision blurs. I see the world as if through water. Wiry African boys, rubbery African girls, move like stop-action figures, jabbering, squealing. I walk past them, to the village, past the village, and up the rocky trail that leads to the cliffs. I always feel nervous when I go to the cliffs alone. There is a legend of an old woman who lives up here. She is a powerful sorceress named Koumba Castelle. They say she rides a white horse around the island at night. They say her power is so sinister and fierce that if you were to meet her while walking in these hills, if you were to see her face, look her in the eye, the bottom half of your face will twist to the left, the top will twist right, and you will spend the rest of your days this way. They say that Koumba owns the island, that she jealously guards every inch. Once, after World War II, they tried to build a bridge connecting Gorée to Dakar. The sorceress did not like this, so she called up a tremendous squall, which tore the bridge like so many matchsticks. They rebuilt the bridge and again she tore it down, this time before it was ever completed. I have seen the remnant of the bridge many times, though I am afraid to approach it. It hangs out a hundred feet or so over the sea. Rays of rusted cable jut from the crumbling cement and asphalt like ribs. They say the bridge is cursed — no doubt it is — and birds, lizards, even weeds, neither thrive nor feed there.

Keeping a good distance from the bridge, I approach the edge of the cliff. I stare down into the water. It is astoundingly beautiful, clear. It shifts from blue to blue: indigo, cobalt, azure, robin's egg. The sunlight cuts into it, glassy blades scraping yellow lines onto the black volcanic rock on the ocean floor. I stare for a long time. I wait for tears. I wait for a great surge of self-pity to storm across the ocean and knock me flat. But nothing comes. Not a thing. Then, slowly as time in hellfire, a dull shame fills my gut. *Oh well is what you said that night, Evan. Oh well. What were you thinking? And who do you think you are? Here. Now. Trying to conjure up tears for yourself. Oh well? What did you mean? Oh well, it is only a dream? Oh well, since I have gone through the trouble of lifting this slab? Oh well, he is only a legless African?* He caressed my face. *So you killed him?* He was poor. *So you killed him?* He was grateful for the two brass coins I gave him. *So you killed him?* I broke bread with him. *So you killed him?* I did not know him. *So you killed him?* I think perhaps I did, but besides the dull shame I feel nothing. It is as though my nerves were spun in webs, wrapped in gauze, sealed in wax. I stand here and gnash my teeth, squeeze my fists, but can call up no real emotion. Instead, my head rocks; the pressure builds at the top of my skull. The high-pitched squeal builds and I hold my head in my hands for fear that my skull will literally explode. I inhale deeply in order to calm myself, and I smell diesel fumes. I hear footsteps behind me, a slow, unsteady gait. I open my eyes but do not turn around. Instead I try to focus on the water. The closer the steps, the deeper I stare into the water. But I can scarcely concentrate. The two pains, the one deep inside my brain, the other boring into the top of my head, alternately become one, then separate. The rhythms are like heartbeat and breath, working to keep something alive.

There is a man standing next to me. I find something familiar about him even before I look up at his face. Worn-out, point-toed sandals, gray khaftan, maroon fez, a bald head. There is nothing remarkable about him at first. Then he turns full face to me. It is the man with the teary egg-white eyes, the blind man to whom I gave alms when on the bus. Perhaps by reflex, I reach into my pocket and pull out a five-hundred-franc note. "Aam," I say to him. "Jerre-jeff, jerrejeff, jerrejeff," he says in a flat mumble. He slips the franc note into his pocket, spreads his arms, bends over as if looking for something on the ground, throws his arms forward, and dives off the cliff. He tumbles through the air, head over heels, head over heels, head over heels. My eyes widen, then I close them, and for the briefest moment I feel weightless, as though I, myself, am careening through the air. I hear him hit the water.

I turn and walk back toward the trail, but I become dizzy and sit down on a small boulder. My head is spinning. I am hyperventilating. *I gotta get out of here.* I shut my eyes and turn my face to the sky, breathing in deeply, exhaling, breathing, exhaling. I consider prayer. I consider jumping off the cliff myself. I consider, for a long long time, going back to the U.S. I think of *King Lear,* and what would have happened if Edgar had led Gloucester to the brink of a real cliff. Would Gloucester simply say, "Jerrejeff, jerrejeff, jerre-jeff," as he tumbled down? I think about many things, some of them quite stupid, but I keep these thoughts turning to assess my mind's lucidity. Again I hear footsteps. Again I am afraid to look. In fact I put my hands over my face.

"There you are, you asshole."

I open my eyes. It is Allen. He stands before me, red-faced, knuckles on hips, and slightly out of breath.

"Al. What are you doing here?" For a moment, I think I am hallucinating him.

"You remember Cal Whitaker? The guy who runs the —"

"You know him?"

"Yeah, and I guess you know him too. He happens to keep a place here on Gorée and it just so happens Evalyn and I were up here visiting the guy. He's a friend of mine. In fact, if you'll check that basket of fruit you call a brain, you might just remember you and Evalyn and Ruth and I met him at the Embassy for lunch when you first got here."

"I remember. He was probably too drunk to even see me."

"Oh. You think so? Well, guy, it just so happens he saw you just . . . just . . . strolling! Fucking strolling through the village like some goddamn tourist. 'Hey,' he says to me, 'I just saw that weirdo space cadet you been looking for.' And here you are. Goddamn. Son of a bitch. Do you have any idea what you've put us through? You got the cops, the gendarmes, the United-fucking-States State Department —"

"Allen?"

"What!"

"Shut up, man. Ain't it obvious I've quit the Peace Corps? I couldn't care less who's looking for me. And quit calling me names. I might be sick, but I'm still big enough to knock you down."

"Well, shit, Evan, if you wanted to quit, why didn't you just come talk to me?" As he speaks he repeatedly throws his arms into the air and drops them loosely so that his hands smack against his thighs. "You have any idea how many times I've come up here to look for you? I do have other things to do, guy. Everybody was sure you were dead, you big . . . Well, everybody thought you were dead or something."

"I really am sick, Allen."

"You got that right, dude."

"You can't tell by looking at me?"

Allen sits next to me on the boulder. "You know," he says, "maybe if you'd checked into that hospital you wouldn't be so damned sick." He pulls off his glasses and wipes his forehead with the back of his arm. Even though he perspires heavily, his shirt is perfectly creased. "I think you really ought to go back to the States," he says, "get some rest, maybe see a shrink. I think you know that, guy." He holds his glasses by one of the ear pieces, twirls them round and round. "I just don't think you're ready for Africa, Evan."

"May just be that none of us is, but I'm staying for a while."

He tells me that it is my business, but as far as the Peace Corps is concerned I am through.

"Fine," I say.

He tells me that I should go back to Ziguinchor to get my things and pick up my mail. I have received four letters from someone named Wanda Wright.

"My girlfriend, sort of. Could you just send my stuff up here? I'll mail you the postage. I really don't think I could go back down there."

He tells me he understands that. He asks me if I have seen a doctor yet.

"Oh yeah. A pretty good one. An African, no less. Name's Gueye. Hell of a guy."

He tells me he and Ruth, Evalyn, Carol, Bruce, Mike, Claire, and David will miss me. They all agree that, aside from my peculiarities, I had always been a great guy, an interesting person and very fun to talk to.

"Thanks. I'll miss everyone except Ruth. I really don't care for her."

Then I ask him if he would recommend me for a job at the Cultural Center. He laughs, slaps me on the knee, speaks for a minute or so about my chutzpah, and says, what the hell, he will talk to Whitaker. Something will work out.

"I appreciate that, Allen."

He puts on his glasses, stands, shakes my hand. Then, for reasons that I truly cannot understand, bends over and hugs me. It is a long and firm hug. I try to reciprocate, but really I am very tired. I am also embarrassed. "Take care," he says. He stands straight. He pats my shoulder. He walks away.

12 I Meet Ford

I feel like a schoolboy on the eve of summer vacation. I feel like a sailor making his final about-face on his discharge day. I feel no remorse. I am happy to be free from the Peace Corps. I am happy to be, at least momentarily, free from everything. I change my mind about going to the boulangerie and the hotel. Instead I decide to go to the Blue Marlin, a bar at the Meridien Hotel near N'Gor.

It begins to rain as I step onto the bus. The rain falls in large drops, hard and sharp. The bus is not crowded and I find a seat near the front. I look out the windows, people scatter under awnings, into doorways. The people the driver picks up at the earlier stops are merely spotted with rain. The ones at the later stops are soaking. A heavyset man in a beautiful sky blue boubou and a maroon fez sits down next to me. He sits too close and gets my right side wet. He immediately scoots right, apologizing in peculiar-sounding Wolof. I feel his eyes on me. He stares for too long a time. I try to piece together a French phrase that would be the equivalent of "Take a picture, it lasts longer," but I cannot. Then he taps me on the arm. I notice his boubou is a little soiled around the cuffs. "Where you from, homes?" he says to me. His eyes look as if they were made by an overzealous glassblower. Perfectly round, big as fists. "Denver," I tell him.

"What kinda nigger come from Denver?" he says. I shrug. He introduces himself as Africa Mamadou Ford. He is an American expatriate from Oakland. He seems reasonably nice, but for some reason I do not trust him. He is well stocked with the usual cool-jerk nonchalance. As Afro-American as he is overweight. "You in the Peace Corps, ain't you?" he says, and I tell him I am not. I tell him I am an African history graduate student from the University of Colorado, studying African sea lore for my dissertation. "Deep," he says. "What you trying to find out, my man?"

"Well, I think there's a connection between the maritime lore of South America and West Africa. It's my guess that black African sailors once traveled from the Gold Coast to the east coast of South America. There's a lot of physical evidence that points all that out, and I'm here looking for cultural evidence." I speak with animation, and almost begin to believe my own words as I go on. I have no idea why I am telling him all this or why I am so carefully detailing my story. Ford seems very interested, nodding at my every word and saying, "Right on. Right on. Right on." Unable to extemporize further, I stop, and Ford asks me how far up the line I am going. I take it he would like to talk to me some more. "The Meridien Hotel," I say.

"You ain't staying up there, is you? That motherfucka's ex-pin-sive." I tell him no, that I live in one of the cheap bungalows at the Meridien.

"Fuck that shit. You wanna know Africa like I know Africa, you gotta get amongst the people."

"Yeah?"

"Wouldn't lie to you, blood. You gots to force yourself on 'em. Make 'em feed you. Make 'em take care of you. It ain't about getting over, it's about getting African. It's the only way. Man, don't be like them folks who come out here and soak their lettuce in Clorox and drink bottled water. What you gotta do, see, is walk through these villages out here. Get with the real folks. Just go in they house and shake they hands and say, 'Asalaam Aleikum.' Black and nappy. Tell 'em you hungry. Don't be shy. It don't make no difference if you don't speak the language. Just put y' hand up to y' mouth. They'll understand. These the friendliest niggers in the world, bruddah. They think it's a honor to feed a stranger, man. A honor." The rain slackens, then stops. In no time the sun burns the clouds away and the countryside glows yellow-gold and green. The baobab trees throw their rootlike branches into the sky. The red soil shimmers and steams. In the distance the ocean blazes like a field of mirrors. I stare at it for a long while, but the glare sets my head to thumping. I look away and ask Ford where his stop is. "Heading up to the airport, man. Got this friend up there who holding a little package for me. Make my money out here selling printed Tee-shirts from the States. These niggers love anything with English printed on it." He pauses, lifts his fez from his close-cropped scalp, wipes his brow, and puts the fez back on. "One thing you gotta understand about being an American out here, homeboy: you number one amongst these niggers." He thrusts one thick finger into the air. "Number one, man."

The bus pulls up to the airport stop. Ford rises. I shake his hand, telling him I am going to the Blue Marlin for a beer or two, and that he is welcome to join me, since the airport and the hotel are only ten minutes apart by bus, and the trip is inexpensive. He thanks me and says he will join me there. He adjusts his fez, slips on a pair of shades, and descends the steps.

Though the sun is in its downward descent, it is very hot now. I get off the bus at the hotel. The lobby at first feels

cool, but, as if the heat is following me, it begins to feel very
warm in here too. Few patrons are in the Blue Marlin, as
it is still rather early. There are three loud-talking Englishmen sitting at the bar, two Frenchwomen and two Senegalese men sharing a table in the corner, and what I take
to be a black American couple sitting in the center of the
room. I take a seat in the corner opposite the French and
Senegalese contingent. I order a Heineken, sit and watch
the other patrons. The beer is more expensive than I had
expected, so I slowly nurse it. I am still drinking it when
Ford sits down heavily in the chair next to me thirty minutes later. "Hotter than a motherfucka out there, man," he
says. He dabs his glistening forehead with an oily white
handkerchief. "Rain didn't do shit for the cool. How you like
it here so far, homes?"

"It's OK."

"It's better'n OK out here, homeboy. I can see you ain't
dug deep enough into the place yet." He pauses to order a
drink. "One thing you gotta do out here is get you a woman.
A dude won't take you deep off into the culture the way a
sister will. A dude take you just so far and then leave you
hanging like a lynch mob. Yeah, bruddah, grab onto one a
these African wide-hines and you be rock steady. Co-pa-
cetic. You hear what I'm saying? Co-pa-ce-tic. Marry the
broad, homeboy. Marry a couple of 'em. You a Muslim?"

"I'm a nothing," I say.

"That shit won't fly out here, m' fella. You want a wife
out here you gotta get with Allah." He reaches into the
sleeve of his boubou and slides out a pack of Marlboros,
drops them on the table. He offers me one with a nod. I
think of asking him why on earth he thinks I want a wife,
but drop the idea. I do not want to antagonize. "Yes indeed,"
he says, lighting his cigarette, "these women'll take care a

you. Just remember one thing: You an American. That mean you number one with these niggers."

"I know. You told me."

"Never hurts to repeat it. 'Cause what it mean is that these bitches won't stop at nothing to make you they husband. 'Specially if you get ridda them American rags you got on there, learn some Wolof. Fuck the French, homes; I been out here three years and don't speak word one a French. Don't need it. And convert. You got to convert. Allah's what's happening. Allah, bruh, Allah."

His words fly rapid-fire fast. No periods, no commas between clauses. At no moment can I slip in a question. My attention drifts as he recounts a dozen or so of his sexual encounters with the "African wide-hines." I am reminded of the last time Wanda and I made love. It was not lovemaking at all, really. Whatever it was left me vaguely feeling as though I had committed rape. Vague feeling. Vague rape. She asked me if I had rubbers, so I went down to my car to seek one out. When I returned, she called out from the bathroom that she was having a little trouble with the diaphragm. "But I found a rubber," I said.

"No sense taking any chances," she said. "Chances," I said to myself. "Now there's a word for you." We took few chances in our relationship. I am a perpetual student, a perpetual wanderer, an habitual quitter. She is terminally middle-class, hopelessly careful and controlled, professional. A professional human being. She loves me (should I say loved?) and I love her in my offhand, irresponsible way. She would marry me, I am sure. But only if I would find a good job, commit myself to regularity, uniformity — stop being, as she puts it, "an overeducated street nigger."

Lemme remind you, homes. You an American. A-mer-i-ca-no. That mean one thing and one thing only: You number one amongst these bitches. All these niggers, to tell you the truth. To them, we don't come from a country. We come from a dream. We dream niggers, Jim.

She is, though she will not admit it, ashamed of me. She is ashamed for two reasons. The first reason is because I do not fit into her social sphere: the sharp-edged, well-oiled black middle class of Denver. I am, to make the matter short, a slob. I do not like creases, manicures, shined shoes, well-coiffed hair. She blames this on the fact that I have never lived, for long periods of time, among black people. I never learned to appreciate classiness, style, the hip. The second reason is that I am her former patient. We met when I was in graduate school. I was depressed about everything. I could not study or teach. I had passed zombielike through three trimesters of classes and had accrued five incompletes. I sat for hours in my bedroom and blasted away at my books with a pellet gun. Every weekend I would drive to Thomasville to play dominoes, smoke pot till my eyes would feel like baked clams, drink beer till it lost its flavor. We would sit around the rickety card table listening to Bob Wills and his Texas Playboys, Willie and Waylon and the Boys, Asleep at the Wheel. Tom and Bebe would talk about their Peace Corps tour in Colombia, filling my mind with images of fat-leaved jungles and milk white waterfalls. As much as I enjoyed these Friday nights, I realized none of it was helping me get my schoolwork done, and went to get help.

Ford talks on and on, but I hear Wanda now. Ford hammers the table to emphasize some point. *It's a dream here too . . .* I hear him say, but Wanda, tapping one perfect pearl-colored fingernail on her notepad, overrules him. "They don't love you," she says. "You're dreaming if you think they love you. They love themselves. They love their liberalism. They love themselves for tolerating you." Ford chuckles about the firmness of some woman's breasts, but I can only image the conviction in Wanda's eyes, the firmness of her gaze.

My sessions with Wanda from the very beginning were love talk. By our seventh session we were lovers. But it was a guilty love. She always told me the relationship was unfair to me. "This is wrong," she would say. "It goes against everything I've been trained to do. There's so much you've got to work out." Very little did work out. But neither of us paid that any mind at first. Things were good between us, mainly because we ignored all the potential problems. We never went out in public for our first year together. We would meet in her office for what came to be our pseudo-sessions. We thought we were in control because we never touched while there, in fact, we never even talked about touching. We met at her house for touching. We met at my place too, sometimes, but my threadbare carpets, rust-stained ceilings, and drafty bedroom made her uncomfortable. We never went out to movies, restaurants, nightclubs (which I could not stand anyway), walks in the parks, her friends' places, my friends' places. But by and by the daytime taboos began to bleed into our evenings, and our nighttime indulgences began to oppress our days. It got so that I could not meet her at the office without wanting to touch her.

Not here, Evan.

Why not here? Nobody can see us. I'm not asking to ball you. I just want a kiss. It's not like you're my shrink anymore.

I hate that word. Don't call me a shrink.

At night we became clumsy, hesitant, struggled for conversation.

Why not? What's wrong?

REGINALD McKNIGHT

The mood has to be spontaneous. I can't leap into bed just like that.

Even though we eventually stopped meeting at her office, things never quite balanced. Our relationship hobbled with all the unsteadiness of an old Chinese woman who'd been freed from her footbindings. Earlier warping left us permanently damaged. We were always strangers to one another.

Careful.

. . . careful, homeboy, don't let 'em dick you down. They got ways. They got ways.

She had been in the bathroom twenty minutes. I lay on her bed, regretting my suggestion: "Wanda, we won't be able to do this for at least a year, till you get to take your vacation and come visit me. That's too long, babe." Some suggestion. Really, I understand her reluctance. How could she trust me to care for her a year from then if I could not keep a job for more than six months, or finish a trimester's worth of classes? So we undressed, fumbled. We kissed, no tongue. Numb fingers. Stiff limbs. Comatose foreplay. Loose-fitting condom. Smell of contraceptive jelly. Phlegmatic motion. Not a word. Not a whisper. Not a moan. No afterglow.

". . . careful with these bitches, bruddah. They'll put some juju on you blow your mind. . . . Alright, you can look all cockeyed if you want to, but you be here awhile, you'll see. Woman'll put some juju on your ass that make you go to her every night." Ford pulls up his boubou a bit, crosses his legs, leans forward. "Happened to me a couple a years ago," he says. "Bitch put some juju on me, maaan, an' I had to go to her every night. I said, 'Sheeit, why I'm always going to this broad?' Didn't love the broad or nothing. Every night, every night, every night." He punctuates his words

98

with jutting little thankyouma'ams. "If I'm lying I dying. Finally had to go see this marabou at M'Bour. He gimme this shit to rub on my body every night for three nights. Then for seven days, every morning, I had to go to the ocean and bathe just before sunrise. Shit was col' too, man." He offers me another cigarette. I decline. "Yes indeed, homeboy, you not too careful, these bitches leave you baying at the moon. Ain't nothing in the world like 'em."

Liquor loosens tongues, lips, sinks ships. I am by no means an old man, but I have been around long enough to see liquor whip to death the most resilient of nervous systems. I have seen it rouse the sleaziest civilianhood in a Marine Corps sergeant major, raise up the red in a civil rights lawyer's neck, conjure up anti-Semitism in a Hassidic rabbi. But I cannot say I have ever seen liquor bring out the Cotton Mather in a Muslim. It is not that Ford's many drinks are merely Protestantizing him; that is to be expected. He is most likely a born and bred Baptist. And after all, it is liquor's role in our lives to reduce us to our ABC's. What intrigues me about Ford's drunk is that it seems to move him, not only from pretense, but from ego and motive as well. As the evening wears on he gradually abandons what I assume was his initial intent in speaking to me — "to freak me out" — and delves into an arena I had not expected. It occurs to me that Africa Mamadou Ford means to save my soul.

"Yeah, bruddah," he says, "that juju or gris-gris, whatever you wanna call it, some heavy shit. Powerful. You just thank Allah you come to Senegal. Allah still strong here, man. But like in Nigeria, them niggers don't play. In Nigeria they give you this stuff make you cough up money.

And like there these people in Nigeria, Ghana, Liberia, who, soon's you get off the plane, be all cool with you. Take you to dinner, give you money, weed, women, liquor. Take you anywhere you wanna go. Don't let you pay f' nothing.

"They do you like this for about a week. Let you get fat, black, and nappy. Then they take you to some cat's house, and he cool just like them. Then he shake your hand with this special ring he got on. Got a needle with this powerful herb on it. Dude squeeze this shit off into y' hand and you won't be able to talk, move, nothing. You his slave. Then he take y' ass out to the bush and make you lay down. Then he take out his machete, and when you see this, you start struggling and fighting to move, but you cain't. It's just like you in a dream. Then he laughing at you 'cause he know it ain't shit you can do."

Though his story captivates me, I interrupt him to ask him whether he wants another drink. He looks irritated, but nods. I flag the waiter, who promptly brings another Pernod and water for Ford and a 7-Up for me. I sip my drink with care. It is nearly as expensive as everything else in the Blue Marlin. "So they kill you, huh?" I say, as the waiter walks away. "Kill. Sheeit," says Ford. He looks behind his shoulder at the loud-talking Englishmen. "He don't just kill you, homes. He cut off y' head, y' legs, and y' arms. Then he bury the head to the north, legs to the south, and arms east and west. Then he come back two, three months later, and maaan, your mouth be full of diamonds. Diamonds, bruddah, diamonds!"

I cannot help it. I laugh.

"Go ahead and laugh, man," Ford says, setting his half-empty glass on the table and grinning. "Mama Africa loves her children to have a good sense of humor." He pulls his smile in, sits back in his chair, regards me as the learned regard the stupid. "Look, Africa," I say, looking as amused and smug as I think is my right, "I'm a dyed-in-the-skin nonbeliever. Hey. I'm not saying you're a liar. I'm just —"

"You lost, bruddah. You lost."

"You might be right, but I still don't believe you." I feel my anger rise. My head begins to tighten with pain. After a pause I say, "Can you tell me something? Can you tell me why it is that whenever a black person, especially a black American, doesn't believe every shred of occult bamboo that's spat his way he's lost? What difference does it make whether I believe it or not? No skin off your teeth, right? See, that kind of stuff don't scare me at all. What scares me is that I could be shot to pieces in a coup or something. That kind of stuff I know is real." I lean forward and punctuate my words by stabbing my finger onto the table top. "And I'm willing to bet my last dime . . . that you don't believe in all that European junk like vampires and werewolves, even though there're people out in the world somewhere who swear by that stuff."

"Spoken like a true toubob."

"Oh, so now I'm kicked out the club."

"Cain't lose what you never had."

"So behold! I am cut off from the people. So I'm not your hometown, homeboy, home-james-home no more. Think I'll go commit suicide."

Ford's eyes darken. His skin darkens. "Ain't but a matter a time before you do, man," he says. He makes to leave. Only then does it dawn on me that I am being utterly disrespectful to him. Furthermore, I suddenly recall that he is familiar with N'Gor Village, that he knows a marabou there. Could the marabou be Gueye? I wonder. The chances are good. There are only two marabous in N'Gor. If he leaves now I may not learn something important that will help me learn what the lizards mean. What the nightly pacing means. There is much he could tell me. "Yo, Ford," I say. "Wait up. Have another drink. I didn't mean to piss you off, man. Day's been real funny. My head's not right." He stands, slides his seat under the table, moving as deliberately as a sumo wrestler, and says, "Come on, homeboy. Let's go do some reefer. We gon' get that head right."

13 I Get High with Ford

"Nigerian?"

"Um-hm. Senegalese don't get a fly high."

I pull hard on the joint, try to hold the cloud in my lungs, but it forces itself out, leaves me coughing till my lungs crack. My head begins hurting, but it is bearable. It almost feels comfortable. It is the usual pain. "Smoke like a toubob too," says Ford. We amble up the beach from the hotel toward N'Gor Village. The strand becomes markedly trashier with bottles, cartons, fish heads, and seaweed. I consider commenting on all the filth, but say nothing, figuring it would only draw another "toubob" remark from Ford. I would be content to let no more words pass between us, even though I would like to ask him several questions. He pats me on the shoulder. I do not know whether it is out of affection, or whether he wants the joint. "So you home now," he says.

I pause, consider the irony of his remark. "I guess you could say that."

"Yeah. Had a lot a toubob in me too when I first got here three years ago. Didn't believe in jack shit. Wasn't no Muslim, no Christian. Not a good one anyway. Just like you." He passes me the joint; I take it, heave. "Yes, yes, yes, indeed," he says, "come here just like a baby on one a them two-week tourist things. Freaked me outta my natural mind. I did everything I could, went everywhere I could. But when them two weeks was up ol' Alvin Ford wasn't ready to go back to Oakland with all that madness and evil. I cashed in my return ticket and slept right on this beach f' three nights. During the days I went up to the village to grub with the people and whatnot. Um-um-um. N'Dyaye family there finally took me in. Then I moved over with a family name N'Doye. Good people. Solid people. I taught old man N'Doye an' his boys how to speak fluent English. Clean people over there, them N'Doyes. Real clean."

"You don't live there anymore?"

"Naw, man. Left." He bends down, snuffs out the joint. We stand, looking out at the ocean for quite some time. Ford hands me the roach. "For breakfast," he says. I thank him and put it in my wallet. I turn to him in order to ask him why he left the village, but before I can, he says, "Dark out here tonight, man. One a them nights when you don't know what gonna happen to you. Heavy . . . Heavy. Yeah, I used to be just like you, bruddah. But I'm a tell you something. There be some funny shit happen to you out here. There be days when you find yourself strumping some woman you don't know. Then another day when you feel something strong an' cold as death gnawing at your soul. And then there be a day when you'll wanna love somebody so bad you could die, but won't nobody be there for you, and you'll just plain die."

"Wait a second."

"Naw, naw, naw, I'm telling you. You in Africa now, bruddah. I'd advise you to take everything you ever learned in school, everything your mama taught you, everything the preacher taught you, everything you know, understand, believe in, remember, just stick 'em in your suitcase and toss 'em in that ocean. I'm not lying to you, bruddah. You better get y'self some black, an' you better get with Allah, 'cause, man, I'm telling you right now, this place is *baaaad*. Baddest bitch you ever likely to run into." He fires up another joint. "Don't matter. You'll find all that out if you take your mind out them books that the University of Whiteness done shoved into your head. All I'm trying to tell you is you can have anything in the world you want once you learn what it mean to be a black man."

It is quiet. I feel strangely peaceful. The sea rolls up, rolls out. I am as high as I have ever been, really feeling it, feeling ridiculously sublime. I almost feel like laughing at Ford and all his Don Juan nonsense. But that will do me no good. I do not want to alienate him again. There is much he can help me understand. I tap him on the arm with the back of my hand. "Tell me something, Africa," I say, refusing the joint he offers me.

"Um."

"Why'd you leave the village?"

"Had to, home. Got tangled up with demm. Soul-eaters."

"Soul-eaters."

"Um-hm. Family name Gueye over there live next to the N'Doyes. Very unclean folks. I left 'cause their shit was on me. Couldn't find no gris strong enough to protect me so I split."

My face becomes hot. My head thunders. "I know that family," I say. "I met Aminata Gueye here on the beach a while ago." I have the compulsion to tell Ford I have been lying to him, that I am not a history major from the University of Colorado, that I have been living in N'Gor for over a month, that I am now more frightened than I have ever been in my life. I begin perspiring. I am dizzy and I believe that if I do not sit down I will vomit. My head becomes light. It floats up on my long, string neck. It rocks and bounces like a balloon. I can barely keep my eyes focused on the top of Ford's head. My lips, face, and fingers tingle. The sensation is very pleasurable. Ford looks at me as though nothing peculiar is happening to me. I speak to him in a calm voice as if nothing is happening to me. "What exactly does a demm do to you?" My voice sounds to me as if it were channeled through a garden hose and directly into my ear.

"Cain't be sure, man," he says. "They just like everybody else on the outside. But they live on people's souls. They eat food, but only for show. Only when strangers is around. Most a the time they just kinda draw off your life force. You might think this is bullshit, bruddah, but I seen this happen with my own eyes."

He tells me about a young woman he knew, a woman named Penda, who lived in the village two and a half years ago. He said that she knew her soul was being eaten, but could do nothing about it. "Her stomach swole all up like she was knocked up, but she wasn't knocked up. Her legs and arms looked like string beans. Now, I know you gonna say it sound like I'm talking about malnutrition, but I ain't. I seen the chick eat all kinds a grub, but she just kept getting skinnier in her arms and legs. Died November last year. And don't think her people just tried to heal her with African remedies. Uh-uh, home, she died in a hospital. Them French doctors was tripping. Ran every kinda test they knew how on the chick. Didn't do no good. They some kinds a gris that can stop demm if you get it before they eat too deep, but the best way to avoid it is to stay the fuck away from 'em and never share food with 'em. Don't exactly know why, but that's what folks tell me. And don't let 'em, like, breathe the breath you inhale. They'll suck up y' soul like reefer smoke. You ever see how some a them village babes always be covering their mouth when they talk to you? Well, you'll notice shit like that if you keep y' eyes open. Anyway, they do it, see, to keep the soul in."

"Must be hard for 'em to eat sandwiches."

He chuckles. "Wouldn't surprise me," he says. I had been expecting him to give me one of his hard looks, to castigate me, but he must be high, for his laughter hoots out his throat, buzzes under his tongue. "Sandwiches," he says. "Naw, man, I'm not joking. Dag, sandwiches. Look. I don't know how they do it, or even if these motherfuckas is even human. All I know is that the soul is in the breath, in the body heat. It's the life force, man. And when a demm eat your soul, he nibble, nibble, nibble at it, and for a long time you feel all right, OK?" He pauses. "Now everything *feel* normal. But after a while you notice you cain't breath as deep, you lose weight, y' mind starts to get all fucked up and unfocused, cain't keep y'self warm on a hot July after-noon, night sweats, dream wild dreams, headaches, back-aches, stomach aches, all kinds a shit. Next thing you know . . . you gone."

"The Gueye family?"

"They demm; don't eat with 'em, don't drink nothing they give you, don't do nothing that got nothing to do with them people. Yeah, they demm, all right, but I don't know who ate Penda."

"They seem like good people."

"Aminata's cool. She and maybe . . . maybe Phillipe the only clean ones in the whole family, but the rest — Oh shit, man." He turns and starts up the beach. "Gotdamn, man, I left my motherfucking package back at the bar. Come on."

"I'm gonna stay out here awhile. Too stoned to be around a bunch of people. You coming back?"

He does not answer me. He just scurries up the beach, saying, "Gotdamn. Gotdamn. If that shit's gone I don't eat for a month. Motherfuck."

He disappears into the darkness, and I am on the bus. I am in the very front, in one of the lateral seats, sitting directly across from the boy with the peppercorn hair. With the exception of the driver and the cageman in dark glasses, we are the only ones on the bus. He is eating a bowl of rice, fish, and okra, a dish called supa-kanja. It smells delicious. The boy eats as though he has not eaten in days. He does not look up at me. His fingers and chin shine with oil, are speckled with rice. He eats for a long, intense time. He stops suddenly, looks back at the cageman, who smiles and waves. The boy places the bowl on the floor, directly between his feet and mine. Holding the bowl by the lip, he spins it round like a top. It is as clean and white on the inside as a skull polished by wind and sand. I look into the spinning bowl, astonished that the boy could eat every grain of rice, every dab of the fish and okra gravy. He belches loud and long. Looks at me as I look at him. He smiles, and says, "Bon appétit, toubobie."

14 I Steal a Kiss

I get off the bus at N'Gor. It is early morning. Pink and orange clouds striate the sky. I cannot cross the road to get to the path because a herdsman and three of his sons are leading their brahma across it. The herdsman waves to me with his switch. He smiles and greets me. "Mangifirek," I say. It is an appropriate response. It does not mean, "I'm fine." Rather, it means, "I'm still here." When the cattle, the man, and the boys pass, I walk to the Gueye compound. There I find the three youngest Gueye daughters pounding couscous with a huge mortar and pestle. They smile and greet me. I smile. "Eat my shorts, you little bimbos," I say. They carry on pounding, beating out a rhythm that sounds like Elvin Jones playing the solo to "Seven Steps to Heaven." I step into the house and find Aminata sitting in the common room. She is wearing a blue and yellow pagne, a brassiere, and flip-flops. She is mending a blouse. When she sees me she stops her work, stands up. "What happened to you?" she says, staring at me wide-eyed. She looks very agitated. Her face twitches.

"You know, you really ought to do something about that nervous tic of yours. Spoils your looks." I walk past her and into my room. Leaving the door open, I begin stuffing my things into my day sack. I hear Aminata enter my room.

"Where did you go?" she says. "We were worried about you. I was going to go to the hotel and call the police."

"Guess I would too if my dinner up and walked out the door."

"Huh?"

I turn and look at her face, then look at her breasts, her belly button, her hips, her feet. "Let's get married," I say.

"What's wrong with you?"

I turn back around and continue packing. "Get the fuck outta here, girl," I say.

"Why do you talk to me this way?"

I turn around again and sit on my bed. "Sit down," I say. "Close the door."

"I'm not supposed —"

"Close the fucking door or get out and let me finish packing."

She puts on her blouse, but does not button it. She merely pulls the front together as if it were a robe. She shuts the door and sits in the good chair. Her face twitches. Her fingers grip the armrests of the chair, and she holds her knees together. "Is something the matter?" she asks me, a dead serious, dead innocent look in her eyes. I smack my hands together and convulse with laughter. I fall back onto the bed, cradling my head in my arms. "Unreal," I say. "Ungoddamnmotherfuckingreal. You know, if I weren't so tired right now, I'd leap across this little room and kiss you right on your lovely African lips. Good God a'mighty, you're all right, woman. You're all right." I sit up, lean forward and thread my fingers together. It occurs to me I am behaving exactly as my father used to when he would catch me in a lie. The next thing I should do, in order to stay in character, is stand and pace around the room, rub my hands together like a villain in a Dickens novel. Rather than do this, I study Aminata's beautiful face. She looks at me with an impassive, almost angelic expression. "When are you heading back to the States?" I ask her.

"September ninth."

"Two weeks, I guess, huh?"

She nods.

"You think I'd be welcome here when you leave?"

"You can stay if you want to."

"Right. Good ol' Senegalese terenga, hospitality. Will you miss me?"

"Why all these questions? What do you —"

"Will you miss me?"

She swallows hard, then nods several times, very rapidly.

"How will you feel if I'm not here when . . . Are you coming back during winter break?"

Again she nods.

"How will you feel if I'm not here when you come back this coming winter?"

"You can stay if you want to."

"No, no darlin'. What I asked you is how you'd feel?" It sounds like one of Wanda's questions. *Yes, but how do you feeeel?* I feel like an idiot.

"I hope you will always stay in contact with me. I would miss you if you just disappear. I would miss you."

"That's real nice, Ami. Can't tell you how touched I am to hear that." As much as I want not to, I unclasp my hands and rub my palms together. "You know a guy named Ford, an American?" I say. I expect her to panic, moan, start and run. She does none of these things. She maintains the impassive, angelic expression. Her face does not even twitch. "I know him," she says. "He lived here a couple of years ago."

"I talked to him yesterday. He says your family's a pack of demm. I know it sounds crazy, but something tells me

111

he's not joking. He seems to like you, though. Says you're 'clean.' "

"Ford is crazy. Insane!"

"So am I. So is that cyclops daddy of yours, and so are you if you think I'm staying here one more day." I lean back on my elbows and watch Aminata. Her breathing seems markedly heavier, but perhaps it had been before and I had not noticed it. Her chest rises and falls. She seems on the verge of saying something. Then she squints, bends over slowly at the waist as if melting. She starts to cry, her fingers digging into the armrests. I feel my face flush. I stand and cross the room with the single step it takes to do so. "Ami? Hey, kid. Hey, hey, hey." She reaches up and squeezes my left hand, her body convulsing. Her grip is very strong. I kneel, place my arm over her back, and hold her close. "Hey, it's OK. I don't hate you. I'm confused. I wasn't kidding when I said that I'm crazy. I really am. I really am, and I care about you more than I can say. But I'm scared here. Too many crazy things happen at this joint. I probably would have left whether I'd run into Ford or not. Your dad scares me. You know yourself he hates me." She continues to sob, shaking her head. "You know he does. I know you love him, probably, but you can't sit here and pretend he's some kind of saint. I'm not as dumb as I act. Really, I'm not dumb at all. And the only reason I've stayed here so long is you."

She shakes her head and mumbles something.

"What?"

"I shouldn't be in this room, I said."

"Never mind that. Understand what I'm saying to you. I'm not saying I'm staying in this house because of you. I say I'm staying in this country for you. Look at me. Look at me. Please."

She will not look at me.

"All right, then, listen to me. Will you listen to me?"
She nods.

"Ami, you know Ford might be crazy, but . . . but he says some things that are really true. Like . . . like he says that no one in this whole continent can take you deeper into this place than a woman. And it's true. Look at all those stories you tell me. I've learned more about this place in the last few weeks than I've learned in the first three months. I mean, I've learned stuff like, 'Fi keckula nun dufa bohnde,' eh? I say it pretty good, right? Fi keck-keck-keckulaah! 'This place is so hard an egg don't bounce!'"

I think she is smiling.

"Right?" I say. "It was that story you told me about that little boy, the lazy boy, Dodo, right?"

She giggles. "Dudu," she says.

"Yeah, yeah, and he's so lazy he won't work for so much as a grain of rice. And he pretends that he's sick. Syphilis, right?"

"No!" she says, sitting up. She is smiling. She catches herself. Her smile fades. "I know what you are trying to do, American man."

"And it almost worked." Perhaps I am being too smug. I look into her eyes to gauge myself, but one moment she is skeptical, then indignant, then delighted, then calm, then removed. "Almost," she says. I release my embrace. I sit back, wrapping my arms around my knees. She sits back in her chair and brushes her beaded hair from her face. She folds her arms. I clear my throat. "A guy will put up with just about anything to be with the right woman. Ford's right when he — You know, I dated this white woman for three and a half years. When I was in college, an undergraduate. You know, I've had white friends all my life, and in a sense it was no big deal, dating a white woman. I mean . . . you know. But there were always these kinds of

113

white folk floating around that I never thought I'd ever deal with. Not intimately anyway. I don't know if you'd know the type I mean. The kind who wear tractor caps and big boots, and carry buck knives in their belts? They have long hair, and listen to country music and get into bar fights, and you always have the impression they hate blacks. Maybe you don't much see that type in Washington, but they run in herds in Colorado.

"Well, anyway, I was in love with this woman named Pauline, and all her friends were this type. Old hippies, I guess you could call them. I never imagined that I'd ever get close to folks like this, but, well, Pauline's been out of my life for over three years, but these people, Alice, Tom, Star, Bebe, they're still my friends to this day. That's how deep Pauline took me into her culture. That's what you're doing for me now. If it hadn't been for you I don't know what I'd do. You tell me stories; you interpret for me, make me laugh, make me laugh at myself."

I cannot read her face. She looks at me and I return her gaze. She leans toward me, tucking her hands between her knees. She looks at the floor. It is very quiet, but just outside these walls, just outside our silence I hear goats, chickens, turkeys, women, children, gulls, buses. A fly zips past my ear and I swipe at it. Aminata glances at me, then again looks at the floor. "Aminata, I didn't mean to hurt you," I say. "But I don't trust anyone but you, and if I don't get the story from you I don't get anywhere, or learn anything. You've got to tell me what's going on. I'm blind here without you." I rise up to my knees and place my hand on her arm.

"Hey," I say. "Can we get out of here? Come on, let's get out of here, go somewhere and talk." I pull away from her, stand up and grab my day sack. I pull out a T-shirt that Ami and her sister have scrubbed to a thin uselessness. "Here," I say, handing her the T-shirt. "Clean up. Let's go into town and get some lunch. Just me and you. No Phillipe this time. Let's talk. We gotta talk, Ami." I lean back as she sits up. She wipes her eyes, blows her nose. "I'm sorry," she says.

"Don't apologize."

"I'm not apologizing. I just don't like to cry."

She folds the shirt and lays it carefully on the armrest. She sniffs, and looks up at the ceiling, then at me. I offer her my hand. She takes it and stands. I place my hands around her waist and draw her close to me. She does not push away. Her breasts push against my chest. She is trembling. I am trembling. We kiss.

Two, three, perhaps four, perhaps five minutes later, I say to her, "Go get yourself ready. But don't dress too nice; I won't be able to match you. Then we'll go."

15 I Order Fish and Rice

We go to a little place on Place Leclerc called Le Café Lyon. It is run by a blurred-looking Chinese couple who greet us with smiles and half bows. Smiling waiters are rather rare in Dakar. The Chinese gentleman gives us free sodas because, he says, he likes Americans. As we wave flies away from our table, Aminata asks me if I have ever been to Gorée, and whether I would like to go there. I tell her I was on the island yesterday, but would not mind going back. Then after a long silence I tell her about the blind man's suicide. "How did the man find his way, do you think?" she asks me. I tell her I do not know, and suggest that I may have hallucinated it. I place my elbow on the table, rest my cheek in the palm of my hand. "I'm afraid maybe I've been doing a lot of that lately, Ami." I tell her about several of the odd and frightening things I have seen. But I do not tell her about the murder. Of all the things I have seen and done in these peculiar states of consciousness, the murder is the only one of them that still seems preponderantly real. "You think it could be the malaria?" I ask her.

She places her hand on my arm. The warm feeling springs through my arm, into my chest, my stomach. I place my hand on hers. It is nice to be touched by someone. Sen-

egalese women, with the exception of hookers and franco-
philes, do not ordinarily touch their men in public. I feel
honored. For even though we are in Le Café Lyon because
it is one place that no one from N'Gor is likely to find us,
she is still taking a great social risk. "I'm not a doctor, you
understand," she says, "but I have never heard of malaria
doing this to anyone."

"Well then what —"

"But things like this do happen. At least, this is what
some people say."

The waiter approaches and asks us whether we are ready
to order. I tell him we are not. He smiles and backs away.
We look over our menus. Ami lays hers down, says, "But
please take your quinine. For me. Papa and I have worked
very hard to help you get well. It's like you don't care about
the things my family has done for you. I care about you,
Evan. I want you to be strong and I want you to feel good.
You are not use' to this enviro'ment. You probably don't
even have the sickle cell to protect your blood. How do you
think I will feel if you die?"

"All right," I say, fiddling with my fork. "I'll take it. I
don't know what I've been trying to prove anyway." I sip
my drink. I look up at Aminata. "You say you've heard of
this kind of thing before? The hallucinations, I mean?"

"Yeah, but I don't know anything about it. I mean I don't
know very much. And if you think my father has something
to do with it, you're wrong. He doesn't do this kind of thing.
I don't even know if he knows how to do it."

"OK, OK. Calm down. He might be snacking on my soul,
but this stuff that's going on in my head started happening
before I even knew there was an N'Gor Village. What is
this thing? What do you call it?"

"I don't know the name. And will you quit accusing my
father of eating..." — her eyes dart left and right. She

117

looks at me. Her eyes are an impenetrable black — ". . . eating your soul," she says in a whisper.

"Is he what Ford says he is?"

"He has done nothing but good for you, and all you do is criticize him."

"He is, isn't he?"

Aminata leans back in her chair and sighs, her bottom lip quivers, but she controls it. "Many people say he is, Evan. But it's not true. Many people are jealous of him because he is the only true marabou in the entire village. You don't understand village life, do you? Strangers, toubobs, think that it is one big happy family all the time, but it's not. People say and think and do terrible things to each other sometimes. When my . . . mother died three years ago, do you know what some people said? They said . . ." She pauses, inhales deeply. She is on the verge of tears, but none fall. I would take her hand but am afraid if I do she *will* cry. "They said my father did it. Some said he took her soul, some said he poisoned her. How can they say these things I don't know, man. I don't believe in that sort of thing anyway, soul-eating and like that."

"Did you know of a girl named Penda? One who died at the hospital in November last year?"

"Yeah. Everybody said her soul was eaten. A lot of people say this about a lot of people. Maybe it's true, maybe it's not. But my father had nothing to do with it. I know that he believes that one person may eat the soul of another, but as far as I am concerned, this is just an ancient way of diagnosing an illness. Western medicine doesn't know of every disease in Africa. They don't really care about the diseases that kill mainly Africans. But if it happened that white people began to die of this disease, tomorrow they would 'discover' the virus and kill themselves trying to find the medicine to cure it.

"Evan, don't you see? Every day people in Africa die from things that white men haven't 'discovered' yet. But we Africans have known of these things for years. And we call them names that are many years old, names we maybe would not call them if we had the technology they have in the West."

She looks away from me, seemingly taking deep interest in the yellow, red, and blue fly strips hanging in the doorway. She rubs an eye with the back of her hand as though she is sleepy. The waiter returns and we both order fish and rice. I ask for a beer and Aminata orders iced tea. When the waiter leaves, I touch her on the arm. "I don't mean to be disrespectful, and I'm sorry about the stuff I said about your dad. But you said you'd heard about this thing that's happening to me. Do you think it's some kind of disease too?"

"No."

"Do you think I'm crazy?"

"Yes." She smiles a little, then lets the smile fade. "But this thing that's happening to you is not because you're crazy. But I can't tell you about it. Maybe we should talk to Papa. He knows about these things. I only know a little. Not anything at all compared to Papa."

"What about the dead lizards? What about the bound chicken? Does he know anything about that?"

She lowers her eyes. "Yeah, he knows."

"I *knew* it!"

"It's not what you think."

"Yeah, I'll bet."

"My father has been trying to protect his home, Evan. And maybe protect you too."

"With dead lizards and a chicken? Sorry to tell you, but all he's done is messed up my sleep and scared the hell out of me. And let me tell you something else while I'm on the subject of sleep. Your dad . . . does this thing to me . . . looks

119

at me, all right? And he, like, puts me to sleep, makes me dream about swirling things. Vortices, hurricanes. It's the deepest sleep I've ever felt. Like I'm pinned down in my bed, everything swirls like — like I don't know what. All I know is that this kind of thing isn't supposed to happen. It's scary. It's — What do you mean he's been trying to protect me? Protect me from what? Sanity?"

"He didn't put the chicken in your room. My sister Binta did that."

"Little Binta?"

"She thinks that because you are American that you're rich. She was hoping to get money from you, or get you to buy her things. Don't be angry. It's a child's thing to do. I would have told you Tuesday, but I thought you might hurt her."

"I wouldn't have."

She shrugs doubtfully, sips her drink, says nothing. Perhaps I would have.

"So what's your father been trying to protect me from? Why does he make me sleep that way? How does he do it?"

"Evan, I can't answer all these things. All I know is that he's been trying to protect you from a jinn. It is the thing that has been causing your troubles. It is a thing like a ghost or a demon. In the West you call it genie — I knew you would laugh, but it's not like the cinema or the stories that they tell children — Listen to me carefully, Evan. Don't think I am a hypocrite because one minute I say I don't believe in the old things, and the next I believe in them. These are two different, very different, things. Anyway, I tell you about the difference later. But listen to me good, American man. Someone, I don't know who or why, has sent a jinn on you. Jinni are dangerous. They are called up from hell with the parts of dead people, blood, herbs. There are many kinds, but the kind that follows you means to kill you, or drive you crazy. Both maybe. It follows you everywhere you go unless you are protected by one of the lizards." She folds her arms, scratches a mosquito bite on the back of her left arm. She is silent for perhaps half a minute. She stares at her glass, clears her throat.

"Once, when I was a little girl, my father took in this Frenchman who had been trying to sail around Africa in this little boat. It was a very little boat, not good for even fishing. It broke to pieces on the rocks behind Yoff Island. Yoff is a bad place, they say. Most people don't go there night or day because it belongs to — well — spirits. That's what they say, anyway.

"The Frenchman stayed there for three or four nights until, it seems, he couldn't take it anymore. You see, no one who lives around here, not Europeans or scientists or anyone can stay there even overnight. Very bad things happen there. But this Frenchman stayed there so long because he couldn't get off. Some fisherman from N'Gor found him there. He was screaming and trying to swim away from the island, but he was swimming in the wrong direction, west. It took them a long time to get him in the boat because he was fighting them and trying to get away.

"Well they brought him back to the village, you see. They didn't know what else to do with him. They brought him to my father, and as soon as my father saw him he send . . . sent my uncle to get him some things, and said to the fisherman, 'He can't go in my house. He has jinni with him.' But there was this empty house on the outside of the village where a Peace Corps man used to live many years ago before we had water and electricity. So they put him in there and tied him down in a bed with ropes."

"And the Frenchman was insane-mad," she tells me. He would tear at his own flesh whenever his hands were loose. He refused to wear clothes. He would try to eat his own

121

feces and drink his own urine. Whenever Old Gueye would go to visit him, he would shriek, howl, try to back away in fear. She tells me he spoke in "pure" Wolof, Mandinke, Pular, Serere, Fulani, Toucouleur, and other languages that none of them had ever heard. Old Gueye knew that the Frenchman had never learned the languages, but that the jinni spoke through him. They said horrible things. They spoke of Gueye's death, the death of his wife, the end of the world, the end of time. "My father did everything he could do for the man. He gave him herbs, he said prayer, he used everything he could to save the man, but he could do nothing. And then Papa found out that, one by one, the jinn were beginning to attach themselves to him. He began to get so sick and insane that he even cut out his own eye with a knife. What could he do? There was only one thing to do. He had to kill the Frenchman, and he did."

Aminata finishes her drink, then swirls the ice around in the bottom of the glass. She looks me straight in the eye, and it is not until then that my head begins to thump and my mouth goes dry. I look about myself, at the other patrons in the room. They are laughing, talking, eating, drinking. This seems strange to me. It seems wrong. A hot breeze tumbles through the room and I feel perspiration peel down the back of my neck. "So —"

"So I'm saying that my father is not God. I don't know anything about these hurricane dreams, but if he's making you dream them it's probably because he's trying to protect himself, and us. So a marabou can make you sleep. Is this such a bad thing? A Western doctor can make you sleep too, but do you fear this? How does he do it? I tell you right now I don't know. Papa has studied for years to learn these things. If your father were a brain surgeon do you think I'd ask you how he operates on a brain? OK. Now listen to me. You see, Papa can help you stop this thing, but you must do most of it yourself, and you must go to the source. You have to go to the one who sent it to you and make him stop it. And . . ." She will not look at me as she speaks. She keeps looking over my shoulder to the kitchen as if impatient for lunch. But I know this is not the case. Finally, she does look at me, her brow wrinkled, her nostrils flaring. "And if you can't make this man call back the jinn, Evan, you may have to kill him. That is our ancient science."

Our meal is finally served. We eat in relative silence.

16 We Go to Gorée

We carry our silence from the restaurant to the Gorée ferry. Aminata sits on one of the benches that encircle the cabin. She sits with folded arms, squinting down at her feet. I stand at the rail on the port side, watching her. Then I turn and look at the island, a green brush stroke on the horizon. I stare down into the water. The waves undulate beneath the ferry like a boil of black-skinned eels. Nothing holds my attention for long. I walk over to Aminata and sit. She looks at me, clearly trying to estimate the cant of my emotions. Something tells me not to reveal my feelings to her. I do not want to talk about our conversation at lunch. I do not really want to talk about anything, neither do I want her studying me so. So I smile. It is phony, but effective — she returns the smile and looks away.

We get off the boat and walk across the beach in slow steps. It is warm, but overcast; therefore, there are few white people on the beach. In fact, the only whites I see are a French couple trying by fits and spurts to introduce their infant son to the water. A foamy tongue of water sprawls forward to lap at his toes. He screams as though the wave has caused him horrendous pain. Aminata stops to watch the boy and his parents, as I gaze at the Africans on the beach. The Senegalese have the odd practice of rolling around on the sand in order to dry themselves after a swim. Whenever I see them lying on the beach in this fashion, I am reminded of a plateful of my mother's fried catfish. Soul food. Aminata sees my smile, probably supposing I have enjoyed watching the little boy and his parents.

Soul food. Not the castoffs of Master's kitchen: greens, red beans, hog maws, and chit'lins, but the siphoning off of one's life force, one's *suchness*. Do the eyes lose their glimmer? Do the cheeks draw in? Does the body harden like a drying sponge? Does slow squealing air rush from a hole in the top of one's head? How is the soul digested? Solid? Liquid? Heat and breath? It all seems so stupid. Why am I so afraid of such wild nonsense?

As Aminata and I begin the path that leads to the cliffs, I try to take her hand. "I'm OK," she says. She, too, I see, is practicing her own sort of evasion. We make our way to the cliffs, to the place I saw the suicide. Rather than recount the event, I tap Aminata on the arm and ask her why she had permitted me to kiss her this morning. She blushes a little, folds her arms, and shrugs. "I wanted you to," she says.

"I just thought I'd ask." She shrugs again and says nothing. I try to take her hand again. This time she lets me. She stares out at the water. It is dark blue today. Then she squats and wraps her arms around her knees. "Don't ask me to marry you," she says, "I can't."

"I didn't ask you —"

"We're too different."

"OK."

"And there's a bride-price here in Senegal, you know. You can't afford it."

"It's only money," I say. She does not reply. I pick up a smooth, flat stone and fling it, trying to skip it across the water, but the angle is wrong and the stone claps the water once, bounces up, and sinks. The cliffs do not look so high today. A leap from them would perhaps be lethal, but not inevitably lethal. I sit down, lotus-style, facing Aminata. "You ever been in love?" I say.

"No . . . but that's not really important. I'll love someone someday. I don't have time now." She places her hand on my knee. "You're a good man, Evan, but we're too different."

"You make it sound like I'm from a different planet."

"I didn't say that."

I place my hand on hers. "So what's wrong with me?"

She sighs. "I like you, American man. You make me think about things. You make me laugh —"

"You mean you laugh at me."

"I do, sometimes. But when I do, I feel like your friend, not like someone who is just laughing at your back." She pauses. I squeeze her hand, untangle my legs, and, kneeling, I kiss her on the cheek. "Behind my back," I say. "One laughs behind another's back." She does not look displeased by the kiss, but I sense that I should leave it at the one. She arches her eyebrows, smiles a little. "You say 'ain't' all the time," she says, "Do you know that?"

"I know, but you can still trust me."

"I know you don't believe one word I've told you today."

"I believe you," I say without conviction. I stare out at the blue-eyed-blue water and say nothing. I do not believe her and I do believe her. How does one assimilate such things?

Since my very first day here I have been at the mercy of every microbe, every blade of grass, every snotty-nosed two-year-old who holds out his hand for a few francs. But most of all, I have been at the mercy of everything everyone has said to me. When I first got here I tried to ignore everything just about everyone said to me about Africa. I received volumes of unasked-for advice, unasked-for dissertations on the current state of the continent. One fellow told me I could avoid getting any sort of African disease if I could find some American dirt in my suitcase, mix it with water, and drink it down. Another man told me I could render myself invisible if I kept peanuts in my mouth all day. One Peace Corps volunteer, a blade-faced man by the name of Ira Butterfield, used to come by my bungalow nearly every day to discuss direct escape routes to Mali in case "The Coup" came down. "Two three months, Evan," he used to say, "and this place is gonna pop wide-the-fuck-open." He quit coming by when I told him I had once worked as a mercenary in Namibia. "Killing's fun," I told him.

I remember the only time Ruth Barron and I ever really conversed. It was my very first week in Africa and our conversation began by my mentioning that there is not nearly as much laughter, music, and dancing here as I thought there would be. I admit it was a silly remark, one that came, most likely, as a result of all the Tarzan movies and PBS specials on Africa I had seen. Ruth and I were sitting in the classroom, eating lunch and trying to keep cool under the slow-turning fan over her desk. "These people," she said between bites of her sandwich, "are the most unhappy people in the world, Evan. There's no happy hunger. No happy poverty. What did you expect?"

"Well, I know they're poor, most of them, but I guess I haven't seen much starvation."

"There's not much now, because the rains have been OK the last couple of years. But it's here. You just don't know it when you see it. Don't have to see skinny dead people all over the place like they show you on the news. Anyway, the real reason these people are unhappy is because they know they have no future. They'll never build a city like New York. They'll never see the inside of an airplane, most of them — let alone build their own planes. Africa, I hate to tell you, is doomed. And these people know it."

"Now wait a second —"

"Just let me finish." She raised her right hand, looked me dead in the eye.

"Doomed?"

"Will you let me finish?"

"Finish." I shrugged.

She stood up, pulling at her tight-fitting blouse, sliding her tongue over her teeth, brushing crumbs from the front of her maroon pants, clearing her throat. She lumbered to the water barrel we kept in the room, ladled herself a cup, lumbered back, and sat down. "Quite simply, Evan," she said, slightly out of breath, "Africa won't make it for three reasons: One is that Africa is just too poor. The West is just too far ahead in the game to let poor little baggy-pants Africa even set foot on the court. Two. The African people have been colonialized, and some of them wouldn't mind being re-colonialized. They've gotten used to being someone's child, I'm afraid. Now, the third reason is that Africans are generally stupid."

"You gotta be —"

"I'm not finished." She pulled open her desk and began shoving its contents left and right. She found a pack of gum. "You want some?" she said. I declined. She slid out a stick, unwrapped it, shoved it in her mouth, chewed furiously. "Just about ruining my teeth on this stuff, trying to quit them cigarettes." Though she waited for a reply, I made none. Then she said, "I say they are stupid, Evan, because they don't really understand other people's cultures. They tend to warp the products of other cultures to their own . . . own misshapen worldview."

I held up my hands. "Wait a second," I said, "Just hold up a second. Let me ask you. Who doesn't do that? Why is it stupid? And what makes their worldview so particularly misshapen? You haven't said a thing —"

"When I say that their worldview is misshapen," she said, focusing on the cup of pencils on her desk and shaking her head, "I don't necessarily exclude the misshapen world-views of other cultures. But we're talking about Africans and their special kind of stupidity.

"Now, I say they're stupid because they try to Africanize every little thing they receive from the West. Now, I'm not talking about your typical cultural translation such as calquing, or driving on the wrong side of the road, or sing-ing a Chuck Berry tune in Japanese. What I'm implying instead, Evan, is that these people bend Western culture till it screams. Till it ceases to serve its intended function."

"So —"

"If you'll let me talk I'll tell you what I mean. See, your problem right here is that you've never thought about any of this. You keep trying to interrupt me in order to buy yourself some time to think. But you can't be so smart as to know what I'm gonna say before I *say* what I'm going to say, can you?"

I made no answer. "Now," she said. "Now, I say that they're stupid because they don't know how to *do* other cul-tures. You know, I have been on this continent for six years. I have seen these people . . . Evan, I was in Zaire several years ago. I had been trying to vacation there, but the place was just terrible. They put us, Valerie and I — You don't know Val, sweet girl. She died from hepatitis three years ago. Well anyway, they tried to put us in one of the most god-awful hotels you'd ever want to see. Now, didn't a damned thing work in this hotel. The refrigerator didn't work — not a damned refrigerator on this entire continent will work right — not one piddly ice cube for the liquor. The air-conditioning didn't work, and you couldn't get one of those lazy jigaboos to clean your room, bring you toilet paper, or give you the correct change for anything.

"I called room service one afternoon. And all I asked for was a glass of milk and some cookies. And after waiting forty-five minutes, comes this baldhead, rubberneck boy, standing at my door with powdered milk, a pitcher of water, and dog biscuits."

I could not keep from laughing.

"I'm serious," she said. " 'Rrrhoom suhveece,' this fool said, standing in front of me with powdered milk and *dog*, I said *dog* biscuits, now. I said to that —"

"Ruth, these people are some of the most intelligent, inventive people I've ever met. How does what you say even begin to prove that Africans are stupid?"

"Dog biscuits?"

I laughed harder.

"And you know what happened, Evan?" she said, wiping tears from her eyes. "You know what happened? I asked the boy if he thought the 'cookies' were good. 'Yas, they veery good, mahm. Veery good.' So I asked him could he try one for me just so's I'd know for sure. I told him they looked a little funny to me, you see. The boy plucks one off the tray, takes a chomp out of it, and says, 'Ees veery good, mahm. Not too sweet.' "

I could not stop laughing. Besides, what good would it have done to argue with her? "You see, Evan?" she said. "You see what I'm saying? These people got to be doomed. Without our help, anyhow."

How could I not have ignored what people said to me? How could I have believed any of it? And how could it not have affected all that I do and see here? There are just too many ways to read a book.

Aminata and I are now sitting close to one another, staring out at the ocean. My arm is around her waist. She is the most touchable woman I have ever known. Holding her is like holding breezes, soft grass, heat, light, blossoms, smoke, rich black earth. My hand and arm burn, grow damp where I touch her. I feel her pulse thump beneath her rib cage. It is a bass note — Mingus, Carter, Heath, Clarke, Freeman, Garrison, Heard. I know that she will never make love with me. Well educated as she is, she has not been debauched. She is a good Muslima. She is a good daughter, a good human being. I would love to sleep with her. I know I never will. But as long as she lets me touch her this way I will not complain much. As long as she tells me a story or two, I will not complain.

After a long time gazing, I say, "You sure it's not the malaria, Ami?"

She sighs, lets her head rest against the curve between my shoulder and chest. "Probably not," she says. "Maybe some, American man, but probably not."

17 The Marabou's Daughter and I

We kiss. She bites my lip, my tongue. This surprises me. And even though it is at least seventy degrees out here, I start to shiver. I am frightened by her energy, and my muscles jitter from deep within. I move tentatively. I expect to feel her muscles relax. I expect her to catch herself, but instead she eases from the position in which she sits and pulls me toward the ground. We uncurl ourselves onto the sand and grass as slowly as blooming flowers. She is supine, and I am on my side, touching her face, her neck, her breasts. She coos. She purrs. She does not complain. This too surprises me. I rub her stomach, run my hands into the curves and folds between her legs. She arches her back, presses herself into the palm of my hand. This astonishes me. I am almost afraid. I want to tell her that we are outdoors, and not far from Gorée Village. I want to tell her that this is not like her and she can stop if she wants to. But my lungs are airless, my throat is knotted, my chest fibrillates. She presses, actually presses the heel of her hand into my crotch. I inhale a dizzying draught of air. My throat relaxes. I stop shivering.

As I mount her and we begin to move, I press my lips to hers but do not feel flesh, neither hers nor my own. It feels as though my mouth has fallen asleep. My lips, then the back of my neck, then my fingertips buzz with a deep electrical pulse. Finally, my whole body buzzes this way, except for my penis, which grows harder, stretches deeper within her. I try to lift my mouth from hers in order to whisper something obscene or sweet into her ear, but I cannot raise my head. It is as if another body lies upon mine. I am pressed between succubus and flesh, can move nothing but my hips, though it becomes more difficult with each motion. My penis is impossibly large. I feel it in her stomach, into her rib cage. It widens and spreads, filling her body cavity, till I can no longer move. I hear nothing but the high-pitched squeal. I close my eyes. Brace myself for pain. I try to pull out, but the harder I struggle, the harder I am pressed into Aminata. I feel my heartbeat through my penis, it grows stronger, till I can almost hear it. It beats heavily, as though pushing oceans of blood. The electrical pulse grows stronger. My body fizzes like acid on unfeeling skin. I feel the penis moving again, moving in me. It feels unconnected. I swivel my hips and it slides from my throat to my chest. I buck my hips twice. I feel the penis slide from my chest to my stomach. I try to lift myself again, but cannot move backward at all. I feel the earth pressing my back and the penis slide from my stomach to the very outside of my vagina. This hurts a little, something I had not expected. It plunges back into me and Evan moves slowly. He raises his head, finally, and the buzzing leaves almost every part of me. It feels good and bad. I feel like laughing, but only tears come to my eyes. I look at Evan, and he looks afraid, wild and afraid. This is also something I had not expected. He looks as though he is trying to keep something from slipping from his fingers and falling off the edge of the cliff. Perhaps it is me. A drop of his sweat slips from the end of his nose and falls into my eye. It burns.

"Come with me, Ami," he says. And I do. The world scatters for too short a time, then falls back together.

I lift my cheek from Aminata's, look into her eyes and see that she is crying. "Are you all right?" I say. "What happened?"

"It's not from feeling bad; something is in my eye." She folds her arms around me. "It was good, Evan. Everything was good."

"What happened?"

She releases me, pulls her head to the side, far enough away to look me in the eye. Her gaze is as knowing as Wanda's, and for a moment I feel shabby, juvenile, weak. I cannot keep my eyes in hers. I pull out, rise to my knees and pull my pants up. I should hold her for a while, kiss her, whisper to her, but I cannot. "What did we do?" I say, brushing sand from my palms. I try to look into her eyes, but cannot. "What did —"

"Don't ask me to marry you."

"No, no, for God's sake. Did you . . . Are you . . . I mean —"

"If I get pregnant, I get pregnant, I guess. Maybe we shouldn't have."

I sit lotus-fashion and lower my face into my hands. "Ami," I say, but do not go on. I look up and stare at Koumba's bridge, its metal, the color of dried blood, its cement, the color of aged bone. I am trying to think of one question she might answer: What are you, woman? What is this? Did you feel, did you see, do you know? My thoughts turn till my head thumps. It even occurs to me that she may not even know what I am talking about. Nothing comes to mind. I listen to her braid beads rattle as she sits up and brushes sand from her clothing. I consider question after question, rehearse, in my mind, attitude and attitude, but finally I say, "What did we do?"

"I don't know, Evan, in this thing you're my teacher. Just like with English."

"Do you love me?"

"I think maybe I do. It doesn't mean I'll marry you."

"Why do you keep saying that? Afraid you might say yes?"

"Exactly, and I'm not sure you could afford the bride-price, Evan. N'Gor women aren't cheap."

The bus stops midtown and we walk from Lamine Gueye to Pompidou Street. I do not know where we are going. All I know is that while we were on the ferry, heading back to the city, she told me she wanted to buy something for me. That is all she said, "something." We stop in front of a pharmacy, and I begin to step inside ahead of her, as is the custom here — men before women — but Aminata clutches my hand long enough to stop me, then lets go. "Get on that first," she says, pointing to a chrome-and-enamel scale that sits outside the pharmacy door. I step onto the scale, and Aminata drops a coin into its slot. The needle springs to the right then rocks side to side. It rests on fifty-eight kilos. "How much is that in pounds?" I ask.

"I don't know exactly, but it's around one hundred fifty."

"Jesus Hotel, are you sure?"

"Not exactly. Pretty close. Come on."

We step into the pharmacy, and Aminata and the Lebanese druggist behind the counter exchange arrogant glances. The druggist is very beautiful. Her hair pulled back tight on her scalp. Her oyster-shell earrings brushing against her smooth neck, she looks like a magazine photo, smooth and flawless. I decide I do not like her. She is posing for us. Aminata peruses the shelves and asks the druggist for a packet of quinine tablets. It is the first time I have ever heard Aminata speak French. It sounds perfect to my uneducated ears. It is very nice, for French.

We step back onto the streets and Aminata slips the medicine into her bag. "Will you take them?" she asks me.

"I guess."

"You said you would."

"So why you asking me twice?"

"Because I don't understand why you didn't take it in the first place." She quickens her pace, looks straight ahead. She always walks too fast for me to begin with, but this pace makes my heart beat too fast and my head pounds out of the rhythm I am accustomed to, so I ask her to slow up. "See? You're in terrible shape," she says, "and you're getting worse, man. You better take care of yourself." Her pace is still too fast for me and I get the feeling she is purposely moving at this rate in order to demonstrate to me the extent of my ill health. "Slow up, slow up," I say. "I'm tired, woman. Let's go get some coffee."

"We can stop to get something to drink, if you want to, but I don't think anyone would be selling coffee this time of day."

"I know a place."

And we go there. It is the pastry shop I sometimes go to that is generally patronized by upper-class high school students. I do not ordinarily eat there, because everything they sell is too sweet, glazy, powdery, or creamy. A mere glance at the contents of the display case is enough to make my tongue sour and my teeth itch.

Aminata and I take seats as far away from the large plate-glass windows as we are able. I order black coffee and Aminata orders a short glass of lemonade. She opens her bag and pulls out the box of quinine tablets, drops them onto my placemat. "You can take one now," she says.

"I'll get one later. It'll spoil the taste of my coffee."

She raises an eyebrow. Her face twitches. "You've taken these before?"

"Once. Back in Ziguinchor. Them things taste terrible."

"That's why you don't take them? The taste?"

"No, it's not that, really."

The waiter brings our order, and slips away. A group of French and Lebanese students sits a table away from us, and Aminata looks at me as if to ask me whether we should find another table, but I wave the suggestion away. "How's your drink?" I say.

"OK."

"You know when I was a kid I had yellow fever. You know what that is?"

She shakes her head.

"It's a lot like malaria except there're no chills. There's an awful headache with it, though, and you burn up with this bitch of a fever. It was summer and I was in Louisiana, so of course it was ninety-something degrees when I had it, so that made it even worse. You get it from mosquitoes, I guess."

"Did you take medicine for it?"

"Well there's really no medicine for it as far as I know, but that's kind of what I'm getting to here. We were in Louisiana, you see, visiting my dad's brother. My Uncle A.J. has a small pear orchard, see, and my dad — he owns a produce . . . he sells food . . . anyway, my dad always buys stuff from my uncle whenever he can. It's usually a pretty low-quality crop, but, you know, family's family.

"Anyhow, this was about fifteen years ago so I don't remember it all that well. Besides, I was pretty sick. In a way, it was like being in a place like this. I mean like Senegal, you know?"

"Yeah, some places in the States are pretty nice."

"Well, no I don't mean nice. I hated the weather. It was hot as hell's belly and when I got sick, I kind of wanted to die." Everything I tell her from this point on is mostly a lie, but how can I tell her the real reason I am doing this when I am not really sure myself. I may be doing this for Wanda's respect, I may be doing it because I am in love with Aminata. It may be that, like a rabbit in the glare of headlights from an oncoming car, I am too petrified to move. But this lie I am telling her is not fully untrue. Some of the things I am saying really happened, some are merely truths of my nature, but I mean her no real harm. "Man," I say, "You know I never did acid when I was in college or anything — you know acid, right? — yeah, well I never did it when it was the popular thing to do, because of what happened to me there in Louisiana. I mean I just couldn't imagine a weirder trip. At the time, anyway. Not till now, I'm saying.

"I remember I was sick as hell on the first day, and the very next day I felt OK. Even though my Aunt Rose told my mom I should stay in bed, I whined till they let me go to the living room to watch TV. So I'm there in the living room watching Captain Kangaroo, which I'm sure you wouldn't want me to tell you about. The only reason I remember it is because it was a little kid's show and I was really too old to be watching it. I kept hoping nobody'd come in while I was watching. It was a really silly show. Good for kids, I guess. Anyway, the only ones at the house were my mother and Aunt Rose. I don't suppose they really would have cared about what I was watching. They were in the kitchen, yacking like magpies."

Aminata rests her chin on the heels of both her hands. She stares right into my face as I speak. This does not make me nervous, because she is not looking into my eyes. I think she is watching my mouth. I am speaking rather rapidly, and perhaps she is trying to better catch my words. She speaks English so well that I often forget that she does not have a native ear. I like the way she sits, watching my mouth. She looks radiantly devoted. I realize this sounds paternalistic, but her aspect suggests that I am important to her, or fascinating. Wanda would never look at me this way. Doubtless, Wanda would want me to give her this sort of look. I am almost sorry to be lying to her this way.

Aminata drinks in my words, it seems, as I tell her about Louisiana, Captain Kangaroo, pear orchards, and yellow fever. I tell her that I was lying on the couch, watching a character named Mr. Moose being bombarded by scores of Ping-Pong balls. This was a standard routine on the show. The balls tatted and rattled off the props and the studio floor and suddenly it seemed as though the television's sound grew louder and the sound began to echo upon itself. It sounded like rain. The sound pressed against my ears, so I covered them with my palms. It was to no avail. The sound got louder: first like a shower against a plastic curtain, then steam blasting from a broken radiator pipe, then a stadium-ful of soccer fans applauding a goal. The pressure was so great, I thought I could feel my eardrums bowing in. I wanted to call for my mother, but I was afraid I would not be able to holler above the sound. Suddenly it stopped dead. I heard nothing but my heart knocking in my ears. I kept my palms clamped over my ears and listened to my heart. Then I dropped my hands into my lap and was horrified — I actually use the word *horrified* while telling Aminata about this. I cannot imagine using such a word with any native speaker — "horrified" to find that I could still hear nothing but the sound of my heart thumping in my ears.

Aminata asks me why I did not go to my mother. And I

tell her that I simply could not move. "And I couldn't really tell you why," I say. "I knew I wasn't paralyzed or anything. I was scared, Ami, but that's not the reason I didn't move. It was just so different from anything I'd ever felt. My body felt light, like I could float or something, and there was no sound except for my heartbeat. I didn't feel hot or cold, or anything in particular. Except I felt separate from everything, even myself. I just sat there looking around the room, and I remember just fastening my eyes on this ugly-looking lamp on the end table. Its base was kind of a bumpy ceramic thing, really warty like a toad's back, and it was painted brown on the bottom, white in the middle, and orange on top. I stared at it, and stared at it, then the weird rain sound came back, and all the little warts started . . . I know this is going to sound funny . . . but the little warts turned into people. Little men. Dressed in stretch suits."

Aminata giggles and looks into my eyes. "Really?" she says, and she sips her drink. "Little men?" The high school students next to us are singing a pop tune by the Police; it is bouncy and off-key. "Doh stand so — Doh stand so — Doh stand so close to me." They sing it with a heavy French accent, and I stop and look at them. "Do you want to move?" she asks me.

"That's OK," I say. "It reminds me of home." I lean forward and continue telling her about the hallucination. I tell her that the little men stood up one by one, at attention, as if waiting for orders. Little brown men, little white men, little orange men in spandex suits, they swelled up like popcorn put to heat, their feet rooted in the lamp base. They began to sing to me. Their voices, surprisingly, were not tiny. Instead, deep, rounded bass sounds rumbled from their chests. "You are!" they sang. "You are! You aaaare! You are! You are! You aaaare!" This is all the song consisted of, the 'you' in a low note, the 'are' in a high note, over and over. And then they stretched every third 'are' for a long time. I knew I was on the verge of discovering something powerful, definitive, something for my ears only. "And then my mother walked into the room," I tell Aminata, as she gazes at my mouth, "and asked me if I was OK. And in that very second I was, I guess you could say, 'cause everything was back to normal. A TV commercial was jangling like a son of a bitch, the little guys were gone, and there was my mom with a cup of noodle soup for me — which I didn't want, by the way." I stop suddenly, leaving a long, awkward pause between us. Aminata frowns, leans back in her chair, and folds her arms. She inhales to speak, but I interrupt her.

"So. I guess you could say I just wanna know what I 'are,' Ami. I'm not saying this was my reason from the start for not taking the quinine, 'cause I really never made the connection between the yellow fever and the malaria before. But maybe I made the connection intuitively. I don't know, babe. I'm not sure why, but I think that's why I don't take the medicine. Look, I know it sounds goofy, but it seemed like those third, 'you are's' were getting longer and longer like they were teasing me, building up suspense. Do you . . . know what I mean?" I finish my coffee. It is cold, and I accidentally drink the dregs. Coffee grounds settle themselves between my teeth and on my tongue. "Let's go," I say. The students are now singing another pop tune, which goes, "D-doo-doo-doo. D-daa-daa-daa, is all I want to say to you." But in my aching head I hear two thousand tiny, barrel-chested men singing, "You aaaaaaaaaaaaare . . ."

The bus stops. We get on. We do not speak for the duration of the ride. I think about nothing but our lovemaking, but the memory recedes, becomes no more real than a clip from a film, a story recalled from one's childhood, a week-old nightmare. I can no longer remember the sensations; I can only imagine them. When the bus pulls up to Ouakam Village, Aminata rises from her seat. "Where're you going?" I say. I do not want her to leave. I want to take a walk with her and ask her about what happened to us this afternoon.

"I'm going to see my cousin Koumba. You go back to the village."

"But —"

"We shouldn't go back together. My father will be home by now." She taps her index finger on her forehead. "Let's not be stupid, American man."

"But we —"

"I'll keep the quinine till you're ready to take it. Let me know when you want it." She steps away and off the bus. As the bus pulls away, she turns, smiles and waves. Then she shouts something to me. I cannot understand her, so I point to my ear, and wave her up to the bus. She stands fast, but cups a hand around her mouth, and very faintly, over the grumble of the engine, I hear her say, "I said, 'You are,' man! That's all. That's all." I wave back to her, but do not smile. "Oh, God," I think, "She really believed me." The bus tumbles on, and I settle back into my seat, running and rerunning the morning through my mind's eye, and my mind's ear. I gaze out the window, but do not see the countryside. Instead I see Aminata and myself at lunch, and on Gorée. I see the Africans on the beach. I see the French couple wading with their little boy. And I see, over and over again, my own face as I reach climax, tiny droplets of perspiration on my nose, my top lip, and my forehead, the flare of my nostrils, the magenta blush on my face, my rolling eyes, the patch of sand on my cheekbone.

And then, incongruently, I hear her say, right there in the midst of my lustful reverie, that I will have to kill someone. I hear her words so distinctly that I prick up my ears to the sound. It is so absurd I smile, and then I ask myself, Who is this woman who tells me she does not believe in the bunkum of old women and little boys, but then moments later tells me I must kill some necromancer who seems to have it in for me? And this leads me to ask, Who is this woman who will tell me she despises American men, and then unflinchingly lays me down on the edge of a cliff under the blank sky and takes me so deep inside herself, myself, that no cliff will ever again seem so tall? And she does this without a trace of self-reproach. She does so without the shrug and smirk of a whore. She does so with naked innocence, clear virtue. Who is she indeed? She seems to be whatever she wants whenever she wants, without the slightest hint of hypocrisy. Without any hint of any kind.

The bus stops. I get off. I walk to the Gueye place. The clouds have begun to burn off and the sky seems more lavender than blue. I stand in the esplanade and look at the sky. I watch the clouds roll back onto themselves, peel away, and disappear. I stare so long my eyes begin to hurt. I rub them and continue on toward the house. On the far side of the esplanade I see Phillipe and his father walking toward me. Both of them wave at me, and as we approach one another I notice that both of them are smiling. We shake hands and exchange the usual lengthy greetings. Gueye wears a satiny dark green boubou bordered with gold scalloping. His fez sits snug on his head. Phillipe wears a blue boubou trimmed in white. He wears a lacy skullcap that seems a bit too large. Phillipe shifts from foot to foot as though he is uncomfortable. I have never seen him in such formal clothing, but I do not think his discomfiture has anything to do with his dress. "Ana Aminata?" says Gueye. I shake my head, throw up my hands, and tell him in decent Wolof that I have not seen her since this morning. His eye looks me up and down. I grin at Phillipe and ask him whether I got it right or not. "You're getting it," he says. "Your pronouncing is very good."

"Where are you two heading?"

"Try it in Wolof. Ask my father."

"Fodiem, Monsieur Gueye?"

Gueye laughs and claps his hands, but the eye remains unsmiling. I feel it cut into me, burrow through my veins and marrow. He tells me that they are going to the mosque. "Did you understand him?" Phillipe asks me. I tell him yes. "Do you know where is Aminata?" Phillipe says.

"Didn't you hear what I said before?"

"I won't tell my father. Where is she?"

"We went to Dakar together, but we didn't stay together there. She went shopping. I went to Gorée to see a friend. She said something about going to visit a friend in another village this afternoon."

"Do you know which one?"

"Which friend or which village?"

"Village."

"Nope. And I don't know the name of the friend, either."

"You can tell me, Eva'."

"Phillipe," says Gueye, "Nungidem. Leggi."

"My father say —"

"I know. I've got to get going too." I shake hands with both men and walk on. Perhaps it is my guilt for having made love with his daughter, but I feel Gueye's eye on my back. I feel it bore into my spinal column then split me in two from my nape to my rectum. I feel it pull out organs and toss them aside. There goes my liver. There goes a lung. The eye butchers me as though I am a bull in a slaughterhouse, pieces of me strewn across the esplanade. He roots through me, seeking his little girl. He whacks my heart in two. Is she there? He drills up through my neck and plun-

ders my brain. She is most certainly there. But this should
be allowed, should it not? I can bear it no longer. The im-
agery of my imagination is too lucid, too vigorous. I stop
and wheel about, and sure enough, discover that Phillipe
and his father are standing where I left them. Phillipe's
arms are folded, and he looks away from his father as if he
is waiting for the old man to finish taking a piss. And the
old man is looking at me, staring into my chest, staring
through my chest, staring through my hollowed-out back.
He smiles at me and waves. I return the smile and the
wave, as if I have nothing to hide. I turn toward the village,
thinking, "I am. Is that it? Is that all? Evan, you can do
better."

18 I Visit Whitaker

I get on the bus. I am going to see Whitaker about the job. Today is not a good day for such a thing. The squealing noise is terribly distracting. My headache is barely noticeable, but the "hole" in the top of my head feels as though it is being bored into by a drill. I continually touch the spot, expecting to find blood on my fingertips. My vision is blurry. My speech is slurred. And though perhaps it need not be said, I am in a foul mood. I have gone without sleep for thirty-six hours because of the pacing outside my window and the last bus trip. No, things may not go well with Whitaker today. The only reason I should even be slightly optimistic about my chances is that Allen has promised to speak to Whitaker on my behalf. Still, I cannot be sure. Neither man has any reason to trust me or like me. But I remember Allen's hug. Surely he must have spoken with conviction to Whitaker.

As I step off the bus, I am immediately approached by a street peddler. He holds out his hand in order for me to shake it, but I merely slap my pockets, throw my hands up, and walk past him. He follows me, tugs at my sleeve, pulls himself close to me, gets deep in my ear. "Pssst, bruddah," he says. "Where you from?"

"Look, I'm in a hurry, man."

"You got cigarette?"

I hurriedly fumble through my pockets, find my cigarettes and give him one. "Where you from, américain bruddah?" He feels for matches. I stop to light his cigarette. "Colorado," I say.

"Ah! You joke! My sistah live in Coloralo. She is étudiant at the school in there."

"Nice. Good for you." I try to walk on, but he grabs me by the sleeve.

"Yes, I get a letter from her just today. You want to read it? I bring it for you tomorrow."

"I don't have time."

He slinks his arm around my shoulder. "Hey, bruddah, you wife must needs what I have here, no?" He holds out a gold-plated chain, eighteen or twenty inches long. "I give this you for five thousand franc only. Is of pure gold, my bruddah." His eyes are ebony ringed in ivory yellow, his long nose bejeweled with sweat beads.

"I'm sorry," I say, "I don't have any money."

"OK, two thousand franc only."

"Really, I don't have any money."

"OK, five hundred franc, just for you."

I begin walking from him.

"Fourteen carat of gold," he says.

"Look —"

"Two-fifty franc."

"No." I walk faster.

"Can you borrow me money for the bus, bruddah?"

"No."

He clucks his tongue, and under his breath, says, "Kat'l dem fulay, americano," which Phillipe tells me means 'go and fuck your mother.'

I stop and turn, pushing myself away from him. I reach out with one hand and grab him by the neck. I am generally

not a good fighter, but I have large hands and a powerful
grip. I squeeze the man's throat, cursing him in a strained
hiss. "You bas-tard, you bas-tard, you god-damn bastard."
People stop and look. They gather round us, hollering ex-
citedly. I dig my fingernails into the man's neck, and he
swings and strikes me on the mouth. I taste blood, but I will
not let go. He strikes me twice more, stinging my eye, bruis-
ing my temple. I squeeze harder. I see panic in the African's eyes. He swings two or three times more as his knees
buckle. I hear someone holler in English, "Norris! Goddamn
it! No!" Then I hear the same voice in French say something
like, "Don't — let me!" Someone grabs my shoulders and
pulls me away. I fall backward onto the sidewalk, looking
up at Whitaker, and two cops.

I sit in Whitaker's office, holding a wet rag to my eye, and
swallowing blood. Every place the peddler struck feels hot,
my heart is pounding, my mouth is dry, except for the blood.
I hear Whitaker speaking in French to someone. I stand and
cross the room and stand at the window, listening. I part
the slats of the venetian blind. Whitaker stands in the open-
air corridor, talking to the two policemen. Both cops stand
with hands on hips, their cap bills pulled down over their
eyes. The both of them are smiling, grinning obsequiously
at Whitaker, nodding their heads every now and then. Whitaker confidently smiles, his left hand thrust in his pocket,
the index finger of his right hand pointing at his head. Then
he touches his chest with both hands and shakes his head.
The two Africans lean back in laughter. Then one of them
leans forward, clapping his hands. I draw my fingers from
the blind and return to my seat.

Whitaker steps in and closes the door. He sits at his desk,
slides a pack of cigarettes and a box of matches from his

pocket. He does not ask me whether I want a cigarette. He simply rolls one across the desk to me, lights his cigarette, and tosses the matchbox. "You OK?" he asks me. His tone is light.

"I'm good." I light up and drop the matches on his desk.

"Coulda fooled me," Whitaker says. He plays with the matchbox, taps ashes from the tip of his cigarette, scratches his nose with the thumb of his cigarette hand. We are silent for perhaps a half-minute. "Evan —"

"Calvin, the guy called me a very uncool name. And he had his hands on me first. He kept grabbing me. That's assault."

"Not here. You're not in the States, brother, you're in Senegal. Se-ne-gal. These folks are a little differently oriented to 'personal space.' Thought you mighta noticed that."

"Well, I figured —"

He interrupts me with a histrionic sigh. Smoke issues from his nose in a long stream. "What's wrong with you, man?" he says. He leans forward. "You know, I was gonna hire you. I was gonna have you up to my place on Gorée and introduce you to some of the homefolk in the area. Allen just about had me convinced you were a basically very together brother with a couple of problems. And that's after you sat up here and lied to me like I'm some kinda fool.

"Man, I knew you didn't work for no Father Perrin. Brother, I know Senegal. Just about every-damn-body who's not Senegalese and who's worth a damn comes through Dakar, and about three quarters of 'em end up right here. In my office." He jabs his middle finger onto the desk top, sprinkling ashes on his desk. "And the other quarter," he says, "I end up knowing about 'cause there isn't a whole lot else to do in Africa but talk about everybody. . . . Don't know if you noticed it or not, but this place is the original grapevine, my man. There doesn't happen to be one Amer-

ican resident here I don't get the scoop on sooner or later.
I've lived here twelve years, Norris. I've seen guys like you
come and go, and before they go, I know their name, rank,
serial number, home address, and bad habits.

"You lied to me, man, just like this asshole who came
out here a couple of years ago. I almost hired this boy and
he didn't have degree the first. Came to find he was a goddamn tourist who'd dropped his return flight and ended up
sleeping on beaches and begging for food. This clown —"

"Africa Ford."

"Africa *Mamadou* Ford. I'm not surprised you know him.
He works every side of every street in Dakar. You know
what he's doing now? The boy's peddling T-shirts to Africans, 'cause there ain't shit else he can do to feed himself
out here. Pretty much living hand-to-mouth. I'd've hired
him if he hadn't lied to me. All he had to do was tell me the
straight story." He draws hard on his cigarette, shakes his
head. "Like I said, I was gonna hire you. But you made a
fool outta yourself down there, and if I hire you, I'll look
like a bigger fool than you. You had no reason what-so-ever
to attack that man."

"Maybe not."

"Absolutely not."

"Calvin, man, I need to eat. I need to make a living."

"You shoulda thought about that before you tried to kill
the boy. You been here long enough to know how to handle
street peddlers. Just face it, living in that village has fucked
up your mind. You're forgetting how to act. You're damn
lucky I was down there. Those cops were ready to lock your
ass up. You ever been in a Senegalese jail?"

"Not yet."

"Well, I'm telling you today. You don't wanna be. Talk
to your buddy Ford. Dumb as he is, he'll straighten you
out." He takes another drag on his cigarette, then stubs it

out. He leans even farther back in his chair, lifts his big feet up onto the desk.

"Why'd he go to jail?" I ask.

"Something funny went down there in N'Gor and he went to the cops. He told 'em someone out there was trying to kill him."

"Kill him?"

"That's his story. Dumb son of a bitch. Cops asked him for his papers, and it turned out he didn't have anything but a tourist visa that had been expired for a long time. They put his ass in jail, and Gil Queen up there in Cultural Affairs let the boy's ass cool out in that roach motel for about three weeks before he even thought about getting him out. He begged Gil not to let the government deport him. So, we got him an extension on his visa, but I'm sure he's let that run out too. Which reminds me — you better thank your guardian angel, or whatever, I told 'em you're still legal. But you better know you're not legal for long. You got about a month till your visa expires. If they'd found that out, you'da been escorted to a plane tomorrow morning. If you wanna stay you better find a job. If you don't, you better just pack your shit and get outta Dodge."

"I haven't officially resigned yet."

Whitaker slides the cigarette pack across the desk and nods at them. I take another, lean across the desk so he can light it. Our eyes meet. "Not yet," he says, "but you will be soon as you sign the papers Allen sent me."

I slowly sit down. My headache hammers. "He sent the papers?"

"Um-hm. Sure did. He tells me if you don't resign, he'll can you anyway."

"What am I supposed to do, Calvin? I don't wanna go back to the States. I need money. How am I supposed to live?"

"That's not my problem, homes."

"You guys just can't —"

"Look, man, you're gonna have to go. I gotta meet some-one at the embassy."

"Well, what am I supposed to do? You guys just can't do me this way. I got a life out here. I got a girlfriend."

"Like I said, you shoulda thought about that about a half-hour ago. Listen, I gotta go."

I stand up and make for the door.

"Norris." I turn to see Whitaker opening up one of his desk drawers. He pulls out a well-stuffed manila envelope. He holds it out to me. "Almost forgot this. It's your resig-nation stuff and a few personal letters. He says he wants the resignation back in two weeks. Got two copies in here. You know how the mail is. Don't send 'em both in the same envelope."

"Thanks."

"Ain' no thing."

"And thanks for helping me down there. Guess I lost con-trol. Thanks."

"Don't mention it, man. You just need to get back to the States and regroup. Come on back out in a few months and we'll talk about a job."

I turn and leave the office. I take the elevator down to the street, walk for a long, long time, till the sun is high in the sky, and my head thunders like a Senegalese storm. Then I get on the bus. I go back to N'Gor.

19 I Read Letters

Dear Gentle Giant, begins the first letter, I can't tell you how much Tucker and I miss you. Do you know what Tuck said the other day? We were driving home from the day-care center at Rose Medical, and we heard "King of the World" on the radio. We were singing at the top of our lungs. It was just like you were there. We started talking about you, of course, and then Tuck said, "Mama, you know what? Evan's in Mama's Land." Can you believe that? See, every time he asks me where you are, I tell him you're in the Motherland, and then I explain to him what I mean by Motherland. Can you believe how fast he picks things up? And it should help prove to you my point that he thinks of you more than he does his father. . . . Hey Ev! the second letter begins, You fuckin' dude. You don't mean for that shrimpy little card you sent with the little shack on it and the five scribbled words on it to pass for a letter do you? Be serious, dude-ski. No biggie, I guess. At least we know your still kickin'. You wouldn't believe the shit goin down back here, Ev. Check this out: Mike's been boning Bebe, man! No way, you say? Well it was yers truly caught 'em in my own cama de agua, Jack. They were hammerin' away like chipmunks on mescaline. You know damn well I had to tell Tom. Me and him go all the way back to the 'Jam.' We never saved each other's lifes or anything like that but he was one of the few dudes I got close to not to mention he's a real straight ahead dude. He kicked the shit out of Mike and put his foot up Bebe's ass a little too. But me and Star broke it up. . . . According to our records, says the third letter, as of 05/14/79 you are no longer enrolled in school and your grace period has begun. . . . The fourth letter begins, Dear Son, Daddy finally got his new Plymouth New Yorker. It reminds me of the cars your daddy and I grew up with. You should see it. It's got everything, more fancy doo-dads than you could shake a stick at. We'll let you drive it when you get back. Even tho' Scott is out of school we are still proud of him as he got the manager position at King Soopers. He won't tell us how much money he makes, but I know it's alot because Sherry Long from our church works for Safeway and I know she makes 10 or 11 dollars an hour and she's not even a manager. . . .

Dear Son, says the fifth letter, I know you get busy with all your teaching and everything, but you could drop us a line couldn't you? It's not like you to not write for such a long time. We are used to seeing your letters just about every week. It was nice to hear your voice a couple of weeks ago. Why don't you give us a call if you're too busy to write. . . . The sixth letter says, Sorry this letter is so long, G.G., but I just felt I had to say all this to you. I don't know if you realize how hard it is for a woman of my age to ask you what I've asked you, but it was hard. I want you to know that. I know there's every chance a marriage between you and me could fail, but in my seven years of practice, I've never seen a marriage that didn't have its difficulties. And my asking you to marry me shows my faith in you as a father as well as a husband and friend. It also means I love you. Will you? . . .

As stated in recent letters, says letter number seven, it

is necessary that you resolve the delinquent status of your account. . . . Letter number eight says, Tuck and I will be at this address till the end of the month if you're planning to write soon. But since you don't answer my letters, these days, I'm not really sure why I even bother to give you our new address. I guess I should have known. I should have followed my intuition. Do you still want to see me? Do you still want me to come out there? My vacation's only three months away. . . . The ninth letter says it has been raining like crazy, Love, Little Sis. . . . The tenth letter tells me that Bebe is "knocked up," Tom is in Mexico, and I am a jerk because I promised to write and never did. Letter eleven tells me I am over ninety days delinquent on my school loans and that I will be assassinated by the local CIA representative in my area. It is from my brother, Scott, who rarely writes real letters. But he does send me things every once in a while, things he figures will be good for a laugh: clippings of *Doonesbury,* coupons for feminine-hygiene products, all my junk mail, all his junk mail, tersely written mock letters, telling me the government has put a lien on my angst. ("You are hereby ordered to Mellow Out, Lighten Up, Kick Back, Cool Out, and Live Long and Prosper. Failure to do so may result in a fine of $12.32 or ten years of exile to California, or both.") Sometimes he will write treatises dispelling the long-lived myth that pigs sweat — "Pigs of the World Unite! Do not knuckle under to manmade lies! Our fatbacks are against the wall! If you give a ham about our species, then hotdog, join us in our fight!" I love getting these letters from my brother. He never tells me what I should do, never tells me to hang in there and fight the good fight, never asks anything of me, never tells me how I could better myself.

There is one more letter from Wanda, but just as I begin to open it there is a knock at my door. It is Phillipe. He leans into my room, holding onto the door handle with his right hand, the doorjamb with his left. "Eva'," he says, "Jahkmah bene cigarette." He is wearing neatly pressed blue jeans and a black T-shirt with "Bitch" printed across the front in cursive lettering. I have noticed he rarely wears traditional Senegalese clothing anymore.

"I'm out," I say.

"Do you want me go buy some for you, man?" He pulls himself into the room, sits in a chair. "Winstons?" he says.

"Winstons'll do." Then I wave my hand in the air. "No, never mind, I'll go get 'em myself. You wait here. *Attend ici.*"

"You don't have to speak to me in French."

"I know I don't, but I need to practice French as much as you and Ami need to practice English. I've lived in Senegal almost six months and I still speak French the same way I did when I first got here."

"Everybody understand you when you speak."

"Every one understands your little sister Oumi too, but that's not saying much."

"Oumi speaks the most French in the village for a four-year-old. But you speak better than she does."

"Oh, gosh oh golly, Phillipe, I can't tell you how good that makes me feel." I stand up from bed, slapping my pockets. "I don't have any change on me and I don't think the guy at the store'll have enough change for my bill."

"No problem. I have money."

He asks me if I want to come with him. I tell him I do. We step out into the yellow haze of the afternoon. It is just after midday meal, and there are very few people outside. Most of them are in their homes, taking siestas, or lounging in common rooms, digesting rice and mumbling in dozy tones with lunchtime guests. We pass by house after house, hearing babies cry, men laugh, reggae music thump, women chatter, goats bleat. But the sounds are subdued, as if the sunlight presses them against the walls and the ground. We walk through a small courtyard where three young men are playing the most simple, stirring music on a homemade bass kalimba and two pop bottles. A half-dozen toddlers, runny-nosed and pale with dust, are bouncing on rusty bedsprings in the middle of the yard. The squealing springs give perfect counterpoint to the kalimba player's melody and rhythm. Perhaps the children know this. Perhaps the adage that each culture has its own rhythm is not mere metaphor. I stop to listen to the music for a moment. I close my eyes, thinking this will help me memorize the tune. "Nicena," says Phillipe. I nod, open my eyes and over his shoulder I see a boy pointing at me. He is cockeyed and smiles at me with an unsettlingly goofy buck-toothed grin. His neck is thin, his head is large, hydrocephalic, perhaps. It lolls back and forth, side to side. He drools, his eyes focus then roll, focus, then roll back at me. His finger, however, remains steadily pointing. "Phillipe," I say, "Why's this kid pointing at me? What's wrong with him?"

"Don' know what's wrong with him, but he can see something wrong with you."

"How long will I have to live here before I ever get a straight answer from you guys about anything? Goddamn!" I resume walking to the store. I cover three or four paces before Phillipe pulls up beside me. "What you mean?" he says.

"Never mind."

"What is 'straight answer'?"

"It's hard to explain."

"You think I don' tell true words, no?"

"No, I don't think you tell-true-words-no. I don't think anybody tells-true-words around here. What do you think of that?" He is silent as we step into the store. It is tiny and

157

packed from floor to ceiling with cans, bottles, packages, and boxes of all sorts. Most of these articles are dust covered, their labels faded. The red-eyed Mauritanian who runs the place smiles at me. His expression becomes impassive, however, when he turns to Phillipe, who tells the man what we have come for. Phillipe remains silent as we leave the store. He opens the cigarette pack, takes three cigarettes for himself, then hands me the rest. "You want to go to N'Gor Island?" he says. "I don't feel like swimming today," I say.

"Not for swimming. I want you to talk to someone. He take care of Mr. Wall house there every summer."

"Wall?"

"Wall is a big man at the American Embassy. Lamont Samb take care of his house in the summer. I think you should talk to him. His English is very good. He used to teach at a lycée in Great Britain, but he sell insurance now."

"Sounds like a real interesting guy. How come you want me to meet him?"

"What is 'howcome'?"

"Why. Why do you want me to meet him?"

"He's a nice guy, Eva'. He don' want you to die. He want to help you protect you'self. I can't help you with this problem you have. And my father, he don' know if he will or won't, because he doesn't like you to be with Ami. Lamont, you see, doesn' feel personal for you. So maybe he can help you."

20 I Write a Letter

We board the motorboat to N'Gor Island. There are few people on board. I sit at the stem, where I will be able to feel the spray on my face. "You won' have a nice ride up there," says Phillipe. "The boat is too empty." I tell him I am fine, but he doesn't hear me, because the boatman has started the engine. Phillipe tries to wave me back to the stern. I lean back and turn my eyes away from him. Phillipe slides himself to the front and sits next to me. He tosses his cigarette butt into the water. "What's not right?" he says, and I correct him. "OK, what's wrong?" he says.

"I don't think you'd understand."

"Because I'm a young boy?"

"Later. We'll talk later."

We do not speak again till we get to the island. As soon as we get off the boat, Phillipe lights a cigarette and nudges me on the shoulder. "You want to go swimming later?"

"Not really," I say, lighting my own cigarette. Then I add, "Listen, man, I don't think you're that young. In the States we consider nineteen pretty grown-up. The thing that pisses me off about this place, like I said, is you can't get a straight answer about anything from anyone. I don't know if it's worth it, talking to you or anyone else about some things that are happening to me. I suppose Ami's told

you about some of the things that've been going on with
me."

"No." He shakes his head and points to a trail that leads
to the west side of the island. "My father told me everything."

"How does your father know any — See? That's what I
mean. I never know what's what around here. Fine. OK.
Tell me, Philly boy, how does your dad know what's up with
me?"

"Um, well you brought a jinn here and he can see it."

"You believe in that shit too?"

"Sure. It seem to me that someone doesn' like you at all,
boy. Someone is trying to kill you and should be very careful. My father didn' want you in our house when Mamadou
brought you. He saw your jinn. That boy saw your jinn too.
He is crazy, but he see these things on persons. He see
things that no one, like you or me, can see. What did you
do to this person?"

"What person?"

"The one who send the jinn to you."

"I haven't done anything to anyone, Phillipe. I don't have
any enemies here. None. Not one."

We walk along the strand on the western side of the island. The ocean pounds against the black, volcanic boulders
clustered there. Crabs scuttle out of our path and slip down
into pockets of water between the boulders. I reach into my
pocket, extract a roach, light up, and pass it to Phillipe. He
nods and takes it, inhales, looks at his watch, and tells me
that Lamont is not home yet, that we should wait till two
o'clock or so then walk back up to the Wall place. We sit
and watch the ocean do its work on the rocks, watch the
rocks surrender themselves to the ocean. As I watch the
water slide backward, rush forward, blast into foam against
the rocks, it occurs to me that if I were smart, I would quit

pissing around with these Africans, this malaria, that occult nonsense. I should go back to America, find decent work, marry Wanda, and try to be normal for once in my life. I am accomplishing nothing here. I am changing nothing.

This is not where I want to be. This is not the kind of person I want to be. Since I have been here people have called me "spacey." I am not. People have called me weird. I am not, really. People have said, or implied, that I am not black enough. This disturbs me. I do not know whether this is true. Perhaps I am rootless, but does this mean I am not black?

All that I really know is that I am the great-great-grandson of slaves named Purdy Norris and Norma Jean Evans. I know that I am the great-grandson of Benjamin and Birdie Norris, who picked cotton and sold fruit in Mendon, Louisiana, not twenty miles from where my great-great-grands had been born, horsewhipped, and laid to rest. I am the grandson of Louis and Mayona Norris, who ran a fruit stand in Tyler, Texas, and raised Richard Norris, who turned the fruit stand into a produce company, married Josephine Walker from Waco, Texas, and then had me.

My father's business grew into a small full-service, hotel-restaurant distributorship, and our family grew into nice cars, sharp clothes, big houses, private schools, domestic help, and televisions in the bathrooms. We moved to Colorado in 1962 and my brother, my sister, and I developed new accents, went to school with white kids, listened to and liked Elvis, the Beatles, the Beach Boys, and the Animals as much as we liked Aretha, James Brown, the Four Tops, and Marvin Gaye. But we knew black music better than we knew black people. The black people we did know were not like us. They were nervous about their blackness. They were, I think, ashamed of it. And shame is the pivot that

161

leads sinners to Jesus, criminals to reformation, and black folks to madness.

I knew a black girl in grade school, who, dissatisfied with skin lighteners, hair relaxers, and perfect diction, took a Brillo pad to her arms and legs in search of the rich, creamy center of her being. Derrick Massey, my best friend in the ninth grade, admitted to me once that the reason he never wanted me to spend the night at his place was that he feared I would tease him about the fact he slept with a clothespin clipped to his nose. My brother, my sister, and I were not this way. We would have said, if we had thought about it, our black lives were made richer by the white and brown lives that touched them. But we did not think about it. We did not think about it even when children called us names. My brother and I were not afraid to fight. My sister would tell anybody to fuck off. We did not think about it even when we heard that Malcolm X had been shot down, when we saw, on one of our many televisions, black people in Alabama being hosed, bitten, clubbed, spat on. We shed no more tears for the Kings than for the Kennedys. But really I should perhaps not say "we." I can only say that my brother and sister and I did not talk about our blackness. I, myself, did not even think about it. Much. I do not mean to say I thought blackness was fun. I have myself been spat on. I was placed, untested, in the low-achievement track in my first year in high school. My adviser in college suggested I try vocational school before I even finished the first quarter of my freshman year. I did not think for a moment that these things happened because I am tall and left-handed.

It has only been in more recent years that I have questioned my own blackness, questioned whether my thoughtlessness or indifference to things that tore others apart did not really indicate my emotional barrenness. If anyone is to blame for these questions — if *blame* is the right word — it is Wanda. Her family history is similar to mine: Southern background, upper-middle-class, more televisions than anyone would know what to do with. But she grew up in Chicago. She never attended a predominantly white school until she was in graduate school. She does not hate whites, but she thinks of whites as "Them," those who are separate, have nothing good, interesting, or productive to say to "Us."

I sit and gaze at the ocean, trying hard to peer through the smeary purple belt that holds together the ocean and the western sky. I wish to see all the way home. My eyes begin to burn so I close them. I keep them closed. Dark colors swell and boil. In my mind, I try to write a letter to Wanda. I do not know where to begin.

"No, darlin'," she said to me that night at dinner, "I'm not crazy about you being away from me and Tucker for two years, but why Colombia? Why not Africa, where you can do something for Us?"

"You're the one who's always calling Hispanos our brown brothers. Ain't they part of 'us'?"

"Don't be coy, Evan. You know what I'm trying to say."

"I'm not being coy, babe. I'm waxing rhetorical, maybe, but I'm not being coy. What I'm trying to say is, well, I figure if I help one person anywhere, I'm helping people everywhere. South America. Africa. It's all the same to me. The second reason is that Tom tells me I'll have a good time —"

"There you go — dragging out those tired-ass white boys to back up everything you've got to say. I'm surprised you didn't cite those guys as a source in your Master's thesis. Don't talk to me about what those people say. I don't care. If you're gonna leave me, fine —"

"I'm not leaving you."

163

She poked her finger at me. "Bullshit!" she said. She held her hand there, trembling, for several long moments. I focused on her pearl-colored fingernail as if I had never seen it before. It was so perfect, so polished. I laid my fork down, looked at my own fingernails. They were uneven, a little dirty. They looked like a mechanic's nails. I lay my hands in my lap. "Not really, Wanda," I said. "I'm leaving the country is all, not you."

She slowly brought her hand down, rested it on the table. Then she reached up and wiped a tear from the corner of her eye. I imagined those perfect nails slitting her cheek. She took a sip of wine, pressed her lips together, swallowed. "I'm saying, fine," she said. "Leave. If things are going to work out between us it isn't going to be now, anyway. That's obvious. The simple fact is you've got to grow up a little bit. . . . But if you ever loved me, then listen to what *I've* got to say. Forget about those stupid, pothead, freak friends of yours and listen to me. You can say just about anything you want in defense of those people, but you can't say they love you. And you can say all the rotten things you want to about me —"

"I never —"

"— but you can't say I don't love you. Now you listen to me, Evan. I can't make you take my advice, but I think the least you could do — for once — is listen to me. . . ."

Now I know what I would say in my letter: Dear Wanna, I would say. I did listen to what you had to say. I only pretended not to listen, because you said so many things I already knew I should be doing with my life. I knew it, but it made me angry to hear you say those things. We got screwed up trying to be doctor/patient, doctor/lover, patient/ lover. You told me it would happen and you were right. You said it wasn't fair to me. It wasn't, but then, it wasn't fair to you either. Anyhow, I did listen to you. I'm listening now. I'm sitting on these big volcanic boulders on an island off this village called N'Gor, and I'm still listening. So now I'm 5, 6, 7000 miles away from you, thinking about all the things you said to me that night we had your "first-generation secret spaghetti." I listened to you, and I came here, and now I've got to tell you how I feel about it all.

I have never, ever in my life, felt so miserable. There it is. It's as simple as that. My mind has never burned with such insecurities and questions. I have never felt so angry at myself, never felt so betrayed by you, and by my own blackness. It flickers like the color on a fifteen-year-old TV. I have never felt so homeless, alone, alien to all people, alien to myself. Am I black enough now, Wanda? You told me that all the clouds around my mind would burn off under this invisibly white sun. You told me that the whole idea of Africa being called "The Dark Continent" was either an intentional "white lie" meant to keep the black diaspora from ever coming home to reclaim the power of familyhood, or meant that the Europeans who had sailed down here and plucked this place naked had been blinded by the light of its purity. You were quite the griot that night, Wanda. You were a little drunk but very poetic. You sang the praises of Mama'sland a whole lot better than ever I sang yours. You told me that when you were in Kenya, four years ago, the world bloomed like a black rose and you had never felt so "wired for living." It sounded like some phrase you would coin for a book title. And you were right about one thing, the whole thing about the purity of African light: Things are looking so bright here, love, that I can't see at all. So tell me how you *feeel*. Am I black enough for you?

Love,
Your Gentle Giant

P.S. By the way, a lot of weird things happen here. Things I can't explain. I know. I know, you think I'm too gullible. You think I should drop the whole "neo-hippy mind mess," buy some jeans that don't have frayed cuffs, and try, as you say, to "get from point 'A' to point 'B' on my own two feet" rather than with my "mysto wings." You always have an explanation for things, but I'll bet you Tuck's entire marble collection (clearies included) that you can't explain the stuff going on here. So let's make a deal. If I can make it through 2 years of this stuff without believing any of it, I'll do all the things you ask me to, whether you want to marry me or not. Deal? Write soon.

21 I Have Tea with Lamont

The water begins to boil. Lamont lifts the teapot from the stove and pours the water over the tea in the strainer. Then he pours the tea from cup to cup like a mad scientist in an old horror picture. The cups look like shot glasses in his big hands. He looks at me and says, "Some Americans find our tea a bit too sweet." He speaks with a British accent, round vowels, crisp consonants. There is no hint of French and only a trace of Wolof in his speech. "I've had it before," I say. "I like it."

"Good." He has large, slow-moving eyes that hold you wherever you happen to be. They gaze out placidly, clear to the point of fluorescence, from his triangular face. He is tall, perhaps my height, perhaps more. His muscles lie long and smooth against large bones. He must be a swimmer, and I cannot help but imagine him cutting, spearlike, through water, and never coming up for air. His voice flutes from the base of his throat. It is a drowsy sound, a sound that doubtless sells a great deal of insurance. "Listen," he says, handing me a cup. "Phillipe here has a tendency to exaggerate a little. He's probably convinced you by now that I'm some kind of powerful shaman."

"Well, no, but he did say you could help me. You wouldn't happen to be a shrink, would you?"

He smiles. "If you think you're going mad you might find what I have to say a little more interesting than if you think you're sane and the world is going mad. The world is neither, crazy nor sane. Only people can be one or the other — or both. But some crazy people are dangerous, and if what I hear about you is true, you're in trouble whether you yourself are crazy or not. Do you understand me?" He takes a sip of tea and says something in Wolof to Phillipe. Then he stands, reaches into the pocket of his chayas and hands Phillipe a five-hundred-franc note. He turns to me as Phillipe leaves. "He's going back to the village to get something for dinner tonight. I told him to get chicken. Is that OK?"

"Sure. Fine."

He sits down in front of me, pours more tea. "You understand what I'm saying to you, don't you, about craziness?"

"Yeah. . . . The only thing I don't understand is what you or anybody else can do about it."

"About the world or you?"

"Me."

"I don't know. All I can tell you is that someone may have done something to you, or that you may be doing something to yourself. If someone is doing something to you, I may or may not be able to help you. If you're doing something to yourself, well, I can't do anything about that.

"Ever since I was a little boy I have seen and heard of a lot of weird goings-on in this village. But that's not to say I know the source of these strange happenings. There're some things that I could explain in one way or the other. I could call some of them either true occult phenomena or I could call them psychological or suggestive phenomena. I once knew a girl — she was a virgin, according to her mother — who became pregnant without ever sleeping with a man. She got as big as a woman who's six or eight months pregnant. But she died a few months later and there was no baby inside her. Some say a jinn had sex with her, and that the jinn stole the baby on the night she died. It's ridiculous, really. I believe she had an hysterical reaction to something, probably guilt about some village boy who caught her in the tall weeds one morning. There are cases like these, you know. I have a cousin in Rufisque whose hair turned gray in a period of about six months. He's only twenty-seven now, and this happened five years ago. Most people said that someone was eating his soul. They expected him to be dead in a year or two, but he's not dead. He's not even close to dying. He plays football for the national team. He's bigger and taller than you or I, and hasn't even had the flu in the last few years. He just has white hair.

"As for you, I don't know. These strange journeys you take on this bus you tell me about never happen when you're around anyone. You haven't even tried to take any quinine. You don't eat well, and Phillipe tells me that you go without sleep for long periods of time."

"What about the jinn? I've heard it outside my window. Mr. Gueye has seen it. Today some retarded kid in the village pointed at me and —"

"Phillipe told me about it while he was introducing us. Never mind the retarded boy. He points at anything that suits his fancy. And what's happening to you may be happening to others in the village — suggestion, I mean. You see, the people in this village are as subject to suggestion as you are. You are a stranger, and you act strange. This makes people around here nervous. They're good Muslims and enjoy being kind to strangers, but strangers make them nervous just the same. Strangers who act the way you do make them very nervous. I'm not sure if Mr. Gueye has seen anything or not, but there's no reason for me not to suspect that the jinn he sees following you comes from his anxiety over your presence in his house. Aminata is a very beautiful girl, and I don't think he appreciates the fact that you could wreck his plans for her marriage." He pours more tea for me, saying, "You don't have to drink this if you don't want. It's got lots of caffeine and it could keep you awake for hours tonight." I nod, but sip the tea anyway. Lamont sits back down, hugging his knees to his chest. "She broke her engagement," I say.

Lamont clears his throat, looks at his knees. "Yes, she broke it with me." He sips his tea, looks at me. "Don't worry, boy, it was mutual. I don't want to marry Ami, she doesn't want to marry me. But Ami's mad for you and Mr. Gueye doesn't like that."

"Get outta here."

"She's in love with you, Evan. This, I know. Aminata and I have been friends for twenty-something years. She was my girlfriend when we were at the lycée. She told me herself how she feels about you. She's usually very honest about these things."

"Why did you two break up?"

"We disagree about everything, mainly. It's rather private. But forget about this for a while. Let me finish what I was saying.

"You make these people nervous. As much as they're accustomed to seeing American and other kinds of tourists, they're not accustomed to living with strangers for long periods of time. You do speak a little Wolof and a little French, but not enough to converse with many people in the village. Not really converse, anyway. They don't really know who you are, and some spend hours speculating about your personality and gossiping about some of the peculiar things you are said to do. They talk about you and Aminata too. Mind you, most of these people don't hear these things firsthand, or even secondhand. Some people have never even seen you. I've only seen you once before, and it wasn't even in the village."

"In Dakar?"

"We'll talk about that later. You can stay the night, if you'd like, by the way." He looks at me, smiles, arches a brow.

"Thanks. I like this place."

"Yeah, it's nice."

I offer him a cigarette, but he shakes his head, says, "I don't smoke much. Bad for you." I light up, lean back on my elbow. "So you think I'm just overtired? Sick? Like that?"

"Maybe. But I had a problem like yours a few years ago. That's why Phillipe asked me to talk to you.

"You see, when I came back to Senegal after being away for a couple of years teaching French in Wales, I noticed that some of my friends, family, and acquaintances treated me in a very strange way. They shied away from me, some of them said to me, 'You're so different, boy, are you turning into a white man?' After a while, though, people started warming up to me. But there was one person, a person who, people say, still didn't like me. They say he was jealous of the fact I had been to Britain, that I made good money as an English teacher at the lycée in Dakar, that I had a beautiful fiancée. . . . They tell me he didn't even like the fact that I'm the tallest man in the village —"

"Like I told Phillipe, I don't have any enemies out here."

I am completely supine now. I rest my head in my arms, stare up at the ceiling. Lamont is silent. I lift my head and see that he is lying on his side, his head propped up in the palm of his right hand. We stare at each other eye to eye for too long a time. His gaze is pure, clean, absorbing, fearless. I shiver and look away. "I didn't say enemy," he says.

171

"I said that he didn't like me." He pauses. And then again he says, "I said he didn't like me. That's different. I only consider a man an enemy when I am aware he exists." The *s* of *exists* hisses. It disappears into the hiss of the ocean. He pauses. I hear sea gulls. I hear a breeze. "I don't know why this man didn't like me," Lamont says. "I didn't even know who he was for the longest time. All that I know is that one day I saw myself in a little hand mirror Ami owned, and I didn't recognize my face. It was shrunken and tired looking. It made a better soup bone than it did a face.

"It wasn't till then that I'd noticed how I had become. I had lost maybe twenty kilos but never ever noticed. I ate more but couldn't put on weight. I went to a doctor who told me he thought it was a blood infection but he wasn't really sure. He couldn't find any infection at all, in fact. He just didn't know what to tell me. A second doctor told me it was a kidney problem, but he wasn't sure either. Another doctor told me I was imagining things. He gave me Miltowns and told me to swim every day. Finally I went to see a marabou and he told me someone was eating my soul and gave me gris-gris to protect myself with.

"But I kept getting sicker and skinnier. My gums started to hurt. I had headaches all the time, and I heard funny noises. Sometimes the headache got so bad I would black out for a short while, and when I woke up I'd find myself making love with this . . . this almost artificial-looking white woman. She was — she seemed to be made of rubber. She was alive, but she was cold, like a fish. It was real. I felt and heard and smelled everything. When she climaxed she would beat my sides with her fists and scream. But it was the sound of a cat, and not a woman. The sound terrified me and always made me lose myself in her.

"I didn't mind this at first, as you can understand. The woman felt almost like rubber, but she was beautiful. And she made love better than any woman I'd ever had. She screamed like an animal, but she was good in bed. She made me think of some of the women I had had when I was in Britain. It even made me think that Senegalese women weren't as nice as Welsh women. Very soon I started thinking about going back there. And after a few more times with this woman, I had what I think you could call a passion to go back there. Back to Wales. But I didn't just want to go back for a fast fuck. No, no, I wanted to live in Wales or England or Ireland. I started to wonder why I had come back to Senegal at all and I went to speak to my father about my determination to go back to Britain."

He talks for what seems like an hour. But I listen to every word. I stare at the ceiling and his words carry me into the very center of his past. I can see it all. I see him go to his father, tell him of his desire to return. Then after two hours of his father's close questioning he reveals the dreams, the headaches, the sore gums, everything. I see his father send him to a village called M'Bour, where he meets with one of the most powerful marabous in all of Senegal. The marabou tells him a malevolent spirit has been set upon him. It is powerful and temperamental. "It will take a great deal of work to get rid of it," I hear the marabou tell him. He is there for three days. I see him fasting, praying, purifying himself, wearing gris-gris. But the dreams continue, the headaches persist.

"Then, Evan, when I was back at N'Gor, my father came to my room one night. He pulled out from his boubou a machete this long" — he holds his hands two and a half feet apart. "He handed it to me. 'I've just come back from M'Bour,' he said to me. 'I talked to the marabou. He tells me that the only thing you can do to stop this thing that curses you is to kill the man who sent it to you.' And I told my father I was afraid. I told him that, in the first place, I didn't want to kill anyone, especially with a machete. In the second place, how could someone ninety kilometers away have any idea of who does what to whom in N'Gor. 'And the third thing,' I said to my father, 'I don't believe in this nonsense. I'm sick, and it's because I'm stuck here in Senegal!' I told him I was going to go back to Britain. I told him I was going to stay there. I told him I was going to find a decent doctor to heal me, and that I would never come back to Senegal. My father just smiled at me and said, 'Nyari qui, nyari m'balka,' which means 'two oxen, two streams.' And we mean by this that when a boy becomes a man he must go his own way. He placed the machete on my bed and left the room."

The room grows black and there is no sign of Phillipe. I am still listening to Lamont's story, but an anxious feeling coils up in my gut. My palms and underarms begin to sweat. Perhaps it is the course the story is taking that makes me feel this way, to some degree, but I am most anxious about Phillipe's absence. I think of what Ford told me about the Africans who mine diamonds in the mouths of decapitated and quartered tourists. But the image lasts only a brief time.

I see Lamont's father leave the room. I see Lamont struggle against tears, hatred for his father, the desire to go to Britain. I see him clutch his head in pain. I see him disappear then congeal in another reality. I see him pound away at the artificial woman, plowing her deep, with his fists balled and his teeth clinched. I see her cry like a cat, hunch her back, bow her back, flatten her stomach, curl then flex her toes, bend, then twist herself serpentlike, hammer her fists into his sides. I see him dress himself, stumble from a room he does not know, then suddenly find himself in the space and time he does know.

I see him slip into his dark room. I see his hand clasp

the handle of his father's machete. I sit up, wrap my arms around my knees. I begin to rock back and forth. I see him leave his room, his brain throbbing, odd sounds ululating in his head. He walks to a house he has seen but whose occupants he does not know well. He moves with certainty, though he does not understand how or why. He steps through the front door. He opens the door to the room of a man he has seen before but does not really know. What's his name? he wonders. He hasn't lived here long. He's certainly not family. I see him lift the machete over the sleeping man. I feel the veins beat against my temples. I stop rocking. I see him arch his back, raise up on his toes. I see him cleave the man from this world. My eyes fill up with blood. I cannot breathe. I cannot breathe.

"I'm still not sure who he was," Lamont says to me, "or whether he was the right man, or even if men can do these occult things to each other. No one ever mentioned the murder to me. No police ever came. But everyone knew about it, I'm sure. I really don't know any of these details, boy. I don't know about jinni. I can't tell you about any of this stuff at all. But as you can see, Evan, I'm fine now."

22 I Whisper a Prayer

Phillipe returns with the chicken and fresh vegetables. Lamont cooks a delicious meal, and for the first time in weeks I eat till I am full. As Phillipe prepares the tea, Lamont says his prayers and I wash the dishes, I muse over what question to ask Lamont first. Should I ask him about Aminata first, or should I ask him about when and where he first saw me? I cannot decide, for while I am delighted about what he has said about Aminata, I am unsettled by the way he looked at me when he told me he had seen me before. It was a wry expression, somewhat superior. I wonder whether he saw me in town or on Gorée with Aminata, or whether he saw me throttle the peddler in Dakar. Whatever it was, wherever I was, he did not seem particularly interested in discussing it.

But I am making too much of this. I always do. Besides, I should be thinking about the story he just told me. Having heard it, I am more suspicious of these people than ever. His story parallels mine much too closely. This is all too neat. I do not like the feel of this place at all. Tomorrow I will buy a ticket to some place new. I still have enough money for a ticket to Liberia perhaps, or Ghana. If I do not have enough money, there is always The Gambia. I would be dealing with the same people, I suppose, but at least they speak English and Wolof instead of French and Wolof. I would not be so dependent on others. I would be starting anew. Perhaps I will find work, earn enough money to go home.

"Eva', you want tea?"

I turn to Phillipe, who stands at the stove, smiling at me as if he were a manservant. "Is almost ready," he says. Before I answer, Lamont steps in from the common room. "Let's have our tea outside," he says. "It's perfect out there."

"Maybe we swim tonight," says Phillipe, pouring the tea from cup to cup.

"Good idea, boy!" says Lamont.

"Wait a second. You guys wanna go swimming at night?"

"Sure."

"Why not, Eva'?"

"No thanks. I'm not that good of a swimmer. Anyway, I didn't bring any shorts."

"You won't drown, Evan. I'm a good swimmer. So's Phillipe. And I've got trunks if you need them."

"That's OK. I'll just watch you guys."

"Fine. Won't be very interesting, though, boy."

"Ami told me you were in the navy. You canno' swim?"

"Jesus carp, Phillipe, does Aminata tell you everything we talk about?"

"I don't know, man."

"Well, I never learned how to swim till I turned eighteen — in the navy. They taught me enough to keep my head above water and die gracefully about a half hour later. I do all right, but I'm not secure enough to —"

"I thought they taught sailors to swim in all conditions in the navy?" says Lamont.

"I just plain wouldn't do it. They could've discharged me, I guess, but they didn't. Look, I'll go down to the beach with you guys, but I don't think I'll swim."

177

"Phillipe, do you understand a man who's brave enough to refuse medicine for malaria, but won't swim in shallow water with two expert swimmers?"

"I can't explain this. Maybe he's crazy."

"Maybe I am."

"Calm down, boy. Calm down. Ne pas que la vérité qui blesse. Phillipe, is the tea ready?"

We go out to the picnic table on the patio. None of us speaks for a long while. Then Lamont again attempts to talk me into going swimming. He tells me we will be in shallow water, that we will swim parallel to the shore, that the chance of seeing a shark is very rare this time of the year. "Nice," I say. "What're his chances of seeing me?" We laugh and again fall silent. The island is much quieter than the village. A faint breeze rustles through the tall trees and bougainvillea bushes that surround the house. Crickets bleat. Waves knock against the shore. There are no other sounds. No village sounds: goats bawling, radios thumping, the sounds of five thousand people doing a thousand different things. I do not even hear the high-pitched squeal. "Fanan' nicena," says Phillipe. I agree with him; it is a beautiful night. A swim may not be all that bad an idea. "Lamont," I say, "you got any extra shorts?"

I do not swim but float on my back, paddling my feet. The longer I watch the stars, the more stars there appear to be. They stipple the sky like a spreading rash. I stop paddling. It is so quiet, I hear nothing but my own breathing. The sky is impenetrably deep. Stars materialize. Meteors burn across the sky and I make half a dozen wishes. First I wish that Wanda were more like Aminata. Then I wish that some

force in the universe would fuse their bodies and souls together. Then I wish that I had never met either woman. I
wish that I had gone to Colombia and showered under milk
white waterfalls, chewed coca leaves, and gone on day-long
walks through leafy jungles.

I close my eyes. I try to envision another life in some
other place. I float for a long, long time but panic a bit,
thinking that I may be floating too far out. I open my eyes,
lift my head, and see that I have not floated far. Lamont
and Phillipe, in fact, are farther out than I. I close my eyes
and continue floating. My body feels light. My breathing is
steady and deep. I float for what seems like thirty minutes,
and I seem to be moving, by increments, faster and faster.
The bottom of my feet tingle. I am relaxed, not at all
alarmed at the increasing speed. My hands tingle now, as
do my lips and fingertips — I am sure of it. I *am* moving
faster. It is as if I am moving down a river. Am I heading
toward endless waterfalls in another country? I must open
my eyes, for I am no longer floating but sailing, careening,
hurtling. I open my eyes, expecting to find myself not speed-
ing toward a South American waterfall but on the bus,
zooming down some gloomy street. However, I am not on
the bus but still in the water, gazing into the night sky. I
hear an odd susurration, like wind and rushing water. My
head does not hurt. I feel no ice pick at the top of my skull.
I feel no anxiety, no fear, nothing but unalloyed delight.
Lamont swims by. "It's getting cold," he says. "You ready
to go, Evan?"

We walk back to the house. Lamont leads, I follow, Phillipe takes up the rear. "How was it?" Lamont asks me.

"Nicena."

"I knew you'd like it."

"Unreal," I say.

When we get back to the house, Lamont stops at the front

gate and says something in Wolof to Phillipe. "Waw-kay,"
says Phillipe, and he walks in through the gate. "Let's take
a walk," Lamont says. We do walk, but not for long. When
we get to the west side of the beach, Lamont sits on a large
rock. "Sit down," he says. I sit, offer him a cigarette, and
this time he takes one. I strike the match, and he squints
at the light and nods when his cigarette is hot enough. I
light one for myself. "How long do you plan to stay in Senegal, Evan?" He slides off the rock and sits on the grass
surrounding it.

"Depends. I'd like to stay for at least a year."

"Why?"

"I'm just not ready to go home."

"Why stay here though? Why does it have to be Senegal?"

"It doesn't. I've been thinking of going to an English-
speaking country. The Gambia. Liberia. If I have enough
money."

"I wouldn't go anywhere if I didn't have at least a thousand dollars."

"I could get to The Gambia for a few bucks."

"I suppose so. How did you like the swim?"

"Like I said, it was nice."

"That's right. I did ask you before." He takes a drag,
flicks the ashes, stubs out the cigarette, and puts the butt
in his pocket. "I imagine you felt very good in the water,
didn't you?"

"Yeah, real good."

"Better than you've felt in a while, eh?"

"I guess. What's your point?"

"Are you angry?"

"No."

"Sure you are. You want to know what I'm getting at."

"That's what I said."

"Temper, Evan."

"Shit, why don't you —"

"Do you have any idea why you felt so good when you were in the water? You felt good because whatever it is that's harassing you — a jinn, a ghost, I don't know — can't follow you into the water. Now listen. I know you don't believe me. I don't care about that. I don't care about you, really. I care about Aminata. The girl's crazy for you, and since she is a friend of mine, I'm trying to help you for her sake. You felt good because you were in the water. This thing cannot follow you into the water. Also, it cannot follow you if you cross the water. I mean if you cross the ocean. You know, go back to the U.S. or to Europe. It can't cross the water, I think, because it's a spirit made from fire. Water would kill it, I guess. You can end all your worries if you leave Senegal. That's the whole point of this spirit that's following you. My jinn was trying to get me to leave Senegal. Yours wants the same thing. But Aminata doesn't want you to leave. She wants you to stay here in Senegal, learn the language and the culture. She wants you, man. I don't know why, but she wants you."

"Why couldn't I just go back to the States for a while to break the spell, or whatever you wanna call it, and then come back?"

Lamont yawns and stretches. He looks up at the stars, yawns again, and says, "You won't come back. Even if you want to, you won't."

"I won't be able to?"

"You won't have the courage. I know that. You won't. Besides this, there is nothing to stop this person who's sent the spirit to you from sending another."

"This is crazy. How do you know it's not the malaria?

How do you know you didn't have malaria or something? How do you know the two of us aren't schizophrenic? You said yourself you weren't sure about the guy you killed. You don't know and I don't know. What you're implying is that I've got to kill somebody if I wanna stay in this country. Forget it. You can have your damn Senegal."

"Stay. Go. It's up to you. Kill someone. It's up to you. This isn't my affair. Go back to the U.S. with Aminata next week if you want to. But just remember: she won't stay in your country forever." He stands and stretches, yawns again. "My God, it's late, late, late. I'm going to turn in. Come on."

"I'll be there in a while."

"Come on."

"I'll be OK."

"Up to you, boy." He yawns again and walks away. I turn and watch him go. I turn back, stare at the ocean. I think about how different it really was, being in the water tonight. I think about home. I think about Wanda, her three-week-old letter I have yet to read. I suspect it is a Dear John letter. If it is, I will stay here in Senegal. I will see a doctor, take my quinine without fail. Try in earnest to learn Wolof and French. If, however, Wanda's letter asks me to return home, I will return. I will be whatever she wants me to be.

I stand, walk back to the house, creep inside. I slip into the bedroom, light the candle on the dresser, and undress. My skin feels tight and dry from the ocean salt. I consider slipping out to take a shower, but the house has only an outdoor shower, and it is too cool outside. I sit on my bed, try to think of a prayer, but I am tired. I cannot think of anything to say. I do not know how to pray. I turn and peel back the blanket and sheet, and as I rise to snuff out the candle, I see what appears to be a stick protruding from under my pillow. I lift the pillow and find a lizard. It is dead, of course. Its back is blue. Its belly, I note as I lift it from the mattress, is the usual pale yellow. I toss the lizard out the window, fall to my knees, looking up at the stars, and whisper the only prayer I can think of. "Fuck you all," I say.

23 I Make Plans with Aminata

I walk into my room. The first thing I notice is that the letter is missing. I do not panic. I am not even startled. The letter is gone and I have no doubt that Aminata has taken it. I stand in the middle of this hot, tiny room, feeling little more than disappointment. Then I grab the handle to my door, but I do not open it. I merely stand here. My body feels heavy, my brain like cooling wax. I should be feeling angry, resentful, indignant. Perhaps I should even feel frightened. What is happening to me? What are they doing to me? These are the questions I should be asking, and perhaps in a while I will, but now I feel nothing. I feel nothing. I climb the stairs to her room, torpid and numb. I wish that somehow my legs would buckle, that I would tumble down the stairs, crack my skull, and die. I am really not up to this. I am very tired of people walking into my room without my consent, leaving animals, taking letters, siphoning off my soul. I am tired of the thing that treads outside my door, weary of headaches, high-pitched squeals, bizarre sex, horror stories, hurricane dreams, buses. Lamont says I could leave all this. And I would leave all this if I had some place to go, if I had no curiosity of where this is leading me and what it means, if in some dark way I were not enjoying all this. It sounds strange, I know, to say I am tired of it all, and in the same breath say that I am enjoying it. But I enjoy it in much the same way that a runner enjoys the process of running, not for itself, but for its end — the muscularity, the slow-beating heart, the great appetite for sex and food.

I take each step to Aminata's room as though with every one my weight were tripling, but I feel only stronger for it. With each step I overcome something, bury something, put something to rest, forever. I stand outside her door for a minute or two. I press my forehead against the door then knock. Aminata opens the door. She smiles. It is a beautiful smile, but I am cold to it. "May I come in?" She steps back, her face twitching once, twice. I step forward and point to the bed as if the room were mine. She sits, and I sit next to her, very close. She smells of incense and charcoal. I breathe deep, inhaling her fragrance. It is very nice, more like home to me than anything I have known in the last several months. I thread my fingers together and hunch over. "Why did you take the letter?" I ask her.

"Why didn't you tell me you've got a girlfriend?" She abruptly stands and begins pacing the room. She does not look agitated. She moves with ease, leonine. "You should have told me about her."

"Why? So you could tell your brother so he could put it in the goddamn Village Gazette? Fuck that. And don't change the subject. Give me the letter."

She stops pacing, and stands before me, knuckles on hips. Then she thrusts one finger forward, shakes it at me. "I told you about my fiancé. Why didn't you tell me about this girl, eh? Why is it that men are this way? Why didn't you tell me?"

Suddenly my blood rises to my skin, and with it my anger. I bury my face in my hands and sigh. I know I am being as histrionic as she, but I am so to distract myself from violence. I am close to striking her. "I didn't tell you, because I just forgot."

"Liar!"

I jerk my head up, look at her. She looks me cold in the eye. I suddenly realize that she is not acting. She is not ashamed of having taken the letter. In fact, she behaves as though she had every right to have done so. She folds her arms and starts to tremble. She appears to struggle against the tremor, but it only gets worse. It rattles her hard and she looks momentarily confused — lowers her eyes, blinks rapidly. Her jaw muscles ripple. Her nostrils flare and she inhales deeply. She lifts her gaze. There are no tears. "Don't lie to me," she says. We stare at each other eye to eye. "Don't lie to me," she says again. "Do you hear me? Denga, toubobie?"

"It just never crossed my mind."

"Lie!"

"I swear."

"I gave myself to you. Everything."

"I think I'm in love with you."

"Leave."

"Aminata —"

She reaches into her blouse and takes out the letter, crushing it in her fist. I extend my hand. She lurches forward, and with the fist that clutches the letter, strikes me hard on the side of my nose. I see a flash of light. I hear Aminata gasp. Pain spears from my nose to my forehead and the old pain, the usual pain beats rhythmically in my head, as if she had shaken an unwound clock, making it momentarily tick. My eyes tear up. Blood dots my shirt. "Evan," she whispers. I do not try to stop the blood. I do not touch my nose. I gaze at the crumpled letter at my feet. The image is blurry for the tears. "Evan," she whispers.

"I forgot to tell you about her, Ami. That's the truth. So

much is going on. . . . I just don't know. . . . My mind . . .
everything is . . ."

She moves closer to me, wraps her arms around my head,
being careful not to push against my nose. I suppress a brief
impulse to shove her away, put my arms around her midriff,
pulling her close to me. I feel her tears on my forehead. I
reach up and touch her cheek, then lean away from her.
"You hit hard," I say. "I'm the one should be crying, not
you." I pull her onto my lap, and we hold each other without
saying a single word. Aminata begins to sob. I hold her and
say nothing. I am distracted by the letter at my feet. If I
knew what Wanda says, I would know what to say to Aminata. Aminata stops crying, finally, and rises from my lap,
sits down beside me.

"You're very sick, Evan —"

"I —"

"— do you know that?"

"What's wrong with me?"

"Everything. Just everything, really." She pauses,
smooths her skirt over her knees. She looks at her dresser,
perhaps at the photo of her mother, perhaps her father, perhaps at the bicenntenial whiskey decanter. I cannot tell. "I
think you should go home," she says.

"I don't get you, Ami. Do you want me to stay or not?
Make sense."

"I'm sorry. I will. I know you were on N'Gor Island with
Lamont. I know pretty much what he told you. I told Phillipe to take you there. Tomorrow night Lamont and you and
I will stay on the island. We'll tell you what you have to do
to get well."

"What do you mean? Do what? Listen —"

"We'll tell you tomorrow."

"Why tomorrow? What's Lamont got to do with this?"

"Tomorrow."

187

Aminata stands and walks to the window. She gazes as if looking for someone. She folds her arms. "I'm sorry I took your letter," she says.

"What did she say?"

"She says she loves you and will come to Senegal to live with you. She says she'll come in a month."

I say nothing. I touch my nose once more. It is swollen, but not so tender as I had thought it would be. I am certain it is only a bruise. Aminata walks to me, takes the hem of her skirt and gently presses it against my nose. Gentle as she tries to be, it is painful. After a moment I ease her hand away. "I don't see why you're so upset about the fact I've got someone back home, Ami. Doggish as Senegalese guys are I think you'd be pretty used to this sort of thing. And besides —"

"What do you mean 'doggish'?"

"When a guy screws around on his woman. But anyway, what I was gonna say is we aren't . . . I mean you keep telling me I can't afford this bride-price you keep talking about. I don't understand you."

"And I don't understand you. You said you were crazy about me."

"I am."

"Then you should have said something. You should have told me she was coming. You know I'm leaving in a few days."

"I don't want her out here. Really, I don't. A while ago I did — maybe. I don't know. The truth is, I don't know if I want to be here myself. This place ain't exactly paradise. Things are a mess. You know what Lamont told me?"

"I asked him to tell you these things."

"Figures." I put my arm around her and she rests her weight on me. I am about to ask her why she could not tell me "these things" herself when I hear footsteps on the stairs. It sounds like one of the children. "Should I leave?" I say. "No. It's Oumi. I sent her to the market for soap." Aminata rises quickly and moves to the door. She closes it. Oumi taps lightly. Aminata acknowledges the knock, but does not open the door. The sisters converse for a moment, then I hear Oumi leave. "My father won't be here till noon," Aminata says, sitting down on the floor at my feet. She picks up the letter between two fingers and lays it next to my thigh. "He's at the Grand Mosque in Dakar."

I make no reply. She pulls on one of her beaded braids. "So it's OK for you to be up here, I mean," she says. "I told my sister to watch for him." I touch a finger to her ear, draw a line to her cheek. "Lamont tells me," I say, "that I should stay here, learn how to fit in with the culture and all that. Something tells me this is your idea too. Well, I can't do that, but I will go back to the States with you, if you want. When you graduate I want you to stay with me there."

"When I graduate I'll return here or go to France, but I can't stay there. I don't see how you can stand it."

"Will you marry me?"

"Marry you?"

"Lamont said —"

"Oh, please. We'll talk about this tomorrow, Evan. Please don't talk about this now."

We are silent for a long while. I clear my throat to speak, but no words come. All I can think of is Wanda, and how hard it has always been for me to even imagine being married to her, she who would never steal into my room and read my mail, who would never prevaricate and mystify, who would laugh at the very idea of bride-price, who would never ask or expect me to discipline her child, let alone kill some stranger. How could I so easily ask Aminata to marry me when it is so clear that she could take me or leave me? My mother would have a simple answer for that. She would say, "That's just how you men are." Yes, my mother is right. At least I am that way.

"Aminata," I say, "You're playing with me. You could, if you wanted to, tell me right now what's going on. You told me the other day that you care about me. If you do, you'll tell me." But as I speak these words I know she will not. I no more expect her to tell me what I want to know than I would expect Wanda to drive down to City Park and buy me a bag of dope. The torpid feeling lies over me again, and I feel as though I am sinking into something thick and murky. I want to sleep, to lie down and die, to be buried under ten thousand years of desert sand.

Aminata rests her arms on my knees, her chin on her arms. "Maybe this isn't a good idea, American man. Maybe you should keep your woman, and I'll —"

"Never mind Wanda. Never mind that. Just tell me."

"I can't. You'll have to wait. Just wait till tomorrow and we'll explain everything. You see, there is someone you know, a friend of yours, who did something bad to my family. We think he's doing something bad to you now, the jinn, but I can't tell you today. It'll have to be tomorrow, at the island. Then we can talk about everything, even marriage."

I notice she has a nickel-sized bloodstain on her blouse. Then my eyes travel to her cleavage. There is a little perspiration there. I imagine, and imagine, and imagine. How we are half-undressed, tangled in her bedclothes like netted fish. How I will not care being sucked inside her consciousness as before. How I will not care if, like some insect queen, she devours me whole when we are spent. How I will digest every inch, every flavor, every aroma, every sound, every motion. How I will graze upon each fine hair that spirals tight into dark creases. How I will get us out of this pointless talk, this stupid mess. How I will, like some love-hot soul singer, low from the bottom of my gut, *I'm not afraid,*

Ami. Don't you be. Don't you be afraid to dive down deep down inside me, and have me, deep deep down in you. Don't you be. Don't be.

But I am no good at this sort of thing. I could never say something like this. I touch my nose again. I squint and my eyes tear up a little. I blink. She looks as though she is content being herself. I know I must carry on with this. "What friend?" I say. "If there's one thing I don't have here . . . I mean, besides you and Phillipe, I don't have any friends here. Anyway, whatever you're getting at doesn't really matter. Lamont tells me that if I cross the ocean, I'll get better. That's what I plan to do." But this is a lie. I will stay here.

She throws her hands outward, shakes her head. "Then forget about me, Evan. If you go, we . . ."

I feel the impulse to spring to my feet, but do not. Her arms feel good where they are. And I have the briefest impulse to raise my voice. I do not. "Well, I got news for you. I'm not killing anyone. The whole idea's absurd."

"Maybe."

"Definitely."

"Then why did you kill the crippled man in Dakar? Why are you so afraid of killing another?"

Had she struck me again I would not have winced so. Blood drubs through my temples. My heart beats so hard I can see the middle buttons of my shirt quiver. "Lamont saw you do it," she says. I cannot breathe. I sit back down. I place a hand over my chest and slowly lean forward, down, down. With my other hand, I clutch Aminata's shoulder. "He says you beat him to death," she says. I feel hot. Perspiration covers my brow. I hear a sound like radio static, and the high-pitched squeal pierces every thought in my head. "We were supposed to wait till tomorrow to tell you we knew, but you were making me angry," she says. I roll my head half-right, pull her toward me, and whisper into her ear. "I think I'm coming down with something." Neither of us move. We remain frozen like this for a duration whose length I cannot even begin to guess. A firm tingling takes hold of my fingertips and travels across my skin like a cool flame. The room fades and appears, fades and appears, to the rhythm of my heartbeat. I stand and head for the door. "I'm coming down with something," I say, not turning to look at her.

24 I Do a Little Office Work

I am on the bus. Not my hair, not my clothes. I have breasts. I am a woman. I am tired because I have been working all day for the rust-skinned American. I wash his clothes, his rooms. I cook his midday meal and his dinner. *How can it be that I can be a woman and myself and not myself at the same time?* He is a pig. He never smiles at me and when he pays me he always holds the bills between two fingers and slips the money into my blouse pocket or between my breasts, and says, "Don't spend it all in one place." Why does he always say this? How is it that one could spend all one's money in one place? I must buy clothes for two growing sons, food for my family, charcoal for cooking, soap for cleaning. How can I spend all my money in one place? This is not Europe or America, where one can buy everything — clothes, shoes, meat, rice, candles, soap — in one place.

The bus stops and many people get on. I wish that I could find a seat. Everyone, both sitting and standing, looks tired, but I do not care. I am more tired than they because it is I who feel this. My back hurts so much, one would think some beast is squeezing its talons into my muscle. *Who am I?* Who is this man for whom I have been ruining my back? I know I have spent the day ironing, folding, dusting, lifting, scrubbing, sweeping, and hiding from the gray gaze of that man. Why can I not sit down? This is so unfair. I know I am young but — There is this man standing too close to me. He is tall and has a peculiar smell. If these two men and this oddly grinning boy with the sores on his head were not standing in front of me, I could move away from him. He is pressing his body against me. I am not sure, but I think his penis is erect. If I did not know better, I would think it was my boss. This is precisely the kind of thing he would do. I wish to turn around, but that would mean . . . I cannot turn around for obvious reasons. This feels terrible. This strange electric feeling travels from my bottom to the top of my head, and this makes my head sting in the most peculiar way. At the very, very top. It is like a knife. God protect me. This is terrible. He is sick, this man. He is filthy. I should hit him or scream, but I am afraid. I cannot even move.

This is insane. I cannot take this any longer. This man pretends it is the bus that makes him rub and bump against me this way. I must do something. I will turn around and grab his balls in the same way the imaginary beast squeezes my back. I will squeeze and tug till he falls to his knees. I will not let him go till he apologizes, till he begs Allah for forgiveness. I do not care what anyone thinks. I may only be a village woman, but I will do it.

Suddenly, he moves away. I turn half-left and watch him stumble and push his way to the rear of the bus. He looks American. He looks familiar. Perhaps he works for my boss.

The bus stops. Many people get on and he is pushed away from me. The bus goes and stops four more times. The sick one steps off. I watch him every step of the way. His eyes are big, wild-looking. His skin glistens. I stare at him through the window. He turns left, right, then left again. He reaches up with one of his big hands and clasps the top of his head. As the bus pulls away, he turns right and stumbles down the sidewalk, loping like an old bull. He must be drunk. But as for me, I do not know. I am not drunk, of course, but I feel so strange. *What is my name?* I do not feel like myself today. And strangest of all, for some reason I do not understand — certainly it is not attraction — I wish I had gone with the man who has used me this way.

The bus stops and a man's legs carry me to my room. A man's hands take hold of the handle and insert the key in the lock. He opens the door. Where are my children? No matter: a lifetime of cooking, scrubbing, ironing, nursing, and the like blanch from me like color from sun-drying laundry. I sit on the edge of my bed. Evan's bed. Evan Carl Norris. *That* is my name. Of course. Of course.

I want to be sick. I want to sleep. But I do not have the time. I must go to the American Cultural Center, to that seldom-used office on the third floor. I will call Wanda and tell her not to come. I must tell her now, before I go to jail or go so crazy I will not be able to think at all, or kill myself. Wanda should forget me, find someone who does not turn into women or murder the handicapped.

I take the bus to Dakar. The ride is no more or less real than the last one. I get off and make my way to the A.C.C. Once there I take the stairs, rather than the elevator, hoping not to be discovered. It is late in the lunch "hour" and no one is in sight. No doors are locked. I slip into the office, find a phone, and begin punching in Wanda's home number. It is around seven A.M. there. It rings four or five times, and I hang up. It occurs to me that she has recently moved. I do not have the number with me. It is in one of the letters she sent me earlier. Hoping she has given me the number in the most current letter, I slip it from my pocket and scan it. I see no number, just a great lot of exclamation points, question marks, and underlinings. I do not really read it. Instead I turn to the typewriter and compose a letter. I will send it by facsimile machine to her office. She will get it in no time. I am afraid the letter is a little disjointed. "Don't come!" I say. "I'm in sort of a fix. Legal problems, moral problems, ethical problems, money problems. I've got to train a rabbit to kill a lion. That's the bride-price. Never mind. Love you with all my heart. See you ASAP — G.G." I rip the letter from the typewriter, cross the room, and start removing the plastic covers from all the equipment until I find the facsimile machine. They have changed a great deal since my time in the navy. I study the machine for a good five minutes before even touching it. And just as I reach for the "on" switch I hear Whitaker very calmly say, "Norris, Norris, Norris. Why don't you just go back to the States?"

"It's important," I say.

"Undoubtedly."

"Look, I'm leaving in a few days. I got to make — make arrangements —"

"This isn't a travel agency."

"No, look, I'm . . . It's not about . . . that."

Whitaker sighs hard and sits. He offers me a seat. Our squeaking chairs make the only sound in the room for about a minute. Whitaker stares at me, and I stare at the facsimile machine. Whitaker drums his fingers on the desk. "Norris, my man," he says, "Norris, Norris. What in the fuck do you think this is?"

"Hold up a second."

"Go ahead."

"I've been thinking about what you said to me the last time I saw you. You remember how you told me I need —

maybe — to see a shrink?" Whitaker grins, and then starts laughing. "Yeah," he says. "Yeah, I do."

"Well I'm trying to make arrangements to ... I was seeing someone — getting help, see — in the States, and I was just trying to get a message to her as quick as I could. I'm gonna start seeing her as soon as I get back."

"I see."

"I would have paid for it."

"Let me see the message."

I hand it to him, and he reads it, screwing up his mouth, lifting his eyebrows. "I'll take care of it," he says.

"I could go to Citibank or —"

He lifts his hand, brandishing the note between two fingers. "I got it, I got it," he says. "You couldn't have used it anyway. You have to know the code in order to use it." The finality with which he slips the note into his pocket tells me I need not stay longer. I stand. I feel very tired despite the undercurrent of anxiety that circuits my viscera. "You'll do it today?" I ask him.

"Sure," he says, shaking his head. "You sure haven't given me any reason to wait."

25 I Receive a Gift

Aminata sits at the picnic table, smoothing her skirt over her fine legs. She is barefoot. She has both feet on the ground and flexes her toes up, lets them down, over and over again. Then she idly pulls at her corn rows, then resumes smoothing her skirt. It is a beautiful skirt, huge pink and yellow flowers on a black background. Her camisole is pale yellow, and the pencils of light that fall through the leaves above us sketch flowerlike patterns on it. Her face is completely relaxed, smooth, beatific. The way she looks after lovemaking — and I wonder . . . since she and Lamont invited me here, and she came here an hour and a half before I did. I wonder if they have. Lamont is not here at the moment. He has gone to the village to buy candles and tea. We are to have dinner, talk, spend the night. Aminata's father is with his family in The Gambia, so she is free to do what she pleases. If she is nervous about what her sisters might say, or about gossip, she shows no sign of it. I suppose they are going to tell me how I am to get out of this mess. But I do not really care. Whatever happens will not change the fact that she was mine for a short while.

From the lawn chair in which I sit, I watch Aminata coil one of her braids round her index finger. She gazes vacantly into the air. She unravels the coil slowly, winds it back up.

She does not seem nervous at all. She does not even seem aware of my presence. I should think that she would be nervous, having prepared this semi-"occasion" for the three of us. We are to eat pasta and some exotic seafood called kerr. We are to eat at table, by candlelight. There is wine in the cabinet, fresh cucumbers and tomatoes on the cutting board. We will be Western tonight, as Western as can be. For my benefit, perhaps to allay my anxiety, they have only spoken English to one another since my arrival. But I feel no anxiety. None at all. I only feel tired. I think of floating in the ocean. That is what I will do tonight. I will float on the water, close my eyes and float out to sea. I will never open my eyes again. I will let the fish and the birds pick me clean.

Aminata knits her brow and looks up at me. "What time is it?" she says.

"Three-thirty."

"Lamont won't be back till four-thirty. We have time for a swim, if you'd like."

"No thanks. Maybe later. Maybe tonight."

"It's nice today. I like this time of year."

"Spare me. What's on your mind?"

She pushes her braids out of her face and shuts her eyes, whispers something to herself, clucks her tongue. "I'm sorry I hit you. How's your nose?"

"Hurts, but the swelling's gone down some."

She looks away from me, nodding. She folds her arms, leans against the table. She remains silent for half a minute or so. "Why don't you trust me?" she finally says.

"Let's not start this, Ami."

"I hit you because you don't trust me. If you had said something about your girlfriend —"

"This is making absolutely no sense. You don't tell me everything. I don't tell you everything. N'est-ce pas? You

199

hit me because you were jealous. Period. I got a feeling that what you're saying now hasn't got much to do with where you're going. I'm sorry, but I just find that irritating. Why don't you just get to your point."

She sits up, her arms still folded. "I don't want to be rude, like you, and be blunt about everything. That's the main thing I don't like about your country. That's why I don't want to live there. Everybody just throws words out as if they were nets to catch fish. They don't think about what they say — they just spit out words, like machines.

"What I'm trying to tell you is that you have to trust me. You have to believe me. You have to understand that I want this life to go well for you. The things I have to tell you could —" She springs to her feet, folds her arms tight over her breasts. "I hate English," she says, pacing. "Too cold. I wish that I could speak to you in Wolof. I think if we spoke Wolof to each other you would believe the things I tell you. Your language is made to expose things and arose suspicion —"

"Arouse."

"I don't care! Don't you ever listen to me? Is all you can do is listen to your stupid English? Listen to *me* when I speak, not my words." She points to her chest, then to her mouth as she speaks. Her face is a deeper color. The beads in her braids rattle against one another. "You say you love me, man," she says. "You say you love me, but you don't listen to me. You don't trust me, and the only part of me you understand is my English. If you would learn to take my language seriously, I would know that you take me seriously —"

"I do —"

"Wyyo!"

"I do."

"Byma."

"I do. I swear."

"Why didn't you tell me about the murder then?"

"I didn't think it really happened."

"And you believe all the other strange things you did were true?"

"It's not the same thing. It was worse than the rest. It wasn't because I didn't trust you. I was confused."

"I knew you would say that."

"Get off my ass, all right? What am I supposed to say? You want the truth? Here's the truth: I don't know nothin'."

"Anything," she says, taking a step toward me. I shrink back a bit, almost involuntarily. She puts her hand in her pocket, and takes out a tubular leather belt. It is made of goatskin, and attached to it is a leather packet, about the size of a matchbox. At one end of the belt is a leather button; at the other end is a loop. Aminata clasps the belt by the end with the button, as if it were a snake. "This is for you," she says. "It's to protect you."

"What is it?"

"Here. Take it."

I take the belt from her, turn it over and over in my hands. "What's it for?"

"To protect you."

"Protect me from what?"

"Lamont will tell you later. It's called tere. Sometimes it's called gris-gris, but the real name — in Wolof, any-way — is tere. It means book. And it's called book because inside it are some verses from the Quoran. There are herbs in it too. Powerful herbs that will protect you. Put it on."

I put the belt on, making self-conscious comments: It will not hold my pants up; it does not match my sandals; the leather packet would make a nice billfold if it were not stuffed with all the herbs and hadits. Aminata smiles but says nothing. She sits down on the end of the lawn chair, places her hand on my knee. I take her hand and we thread our fingers together. "What's on your mind?" I say.

"My father, he doesn't want me to marry you."

"I know that."

"I've never disobeyed him. Never in my life. It is a father's choice who his daughter marries. Some people say this is an old-fashioned way of thinking, but others say 'Kou yague deme yague gisse,' which means 'the one who travels farthest sees the most.' My father has traveled farther than I have, Evan. I'm afraid to disobey him."

"You don't want to marry me?"

"I didn't say that. I said I am afraid to disobey my father. Papa knows many ways to make a person change his mind. When we talked about the things a marabou can do to you I didn't give you the right impression."

"Go on." She squeezes my hand.

"A marabou is not a witch doctor, he's a scholar of the Quoran. He doesn't practice witchcraft. Everything he does comes from God. Some do practice these old things. But my father doesn't practice these things really. He practices only things that are in the Quoran. The Quoran is more powerful than anything because it comes from God. My father is a very religious man. He is pure in everything he does. In all my life he has never hurt me. He always speaks with a gentle voice and has given me only good things in my life. He would never harm me. But he could do something to you. The only reason he hasn't is because he knows you've never tried to take me — Don't interrupt me. I know what we did.

"But you're an atheist. He doesn't like this. How do you think you would feel if you were the most clean and spiritual man in your village and your daughter married a man who had no religion at all? Maybe you don't understand how it would feel, but I will tell you. It would bring a man shame. It's as simple as that. I would say it would be a good idea if you were to become Muslim, but I don't think you will."

"I wouldn't be a good one."

"I know. And Papa knows too. So this is why you should be careful. My father knows ways to make a person blind to love. Don't interrupt. I don't know how these things work. All that I know is that he knows ways to block your eyes so that you won't see me as beautiful. Don't interrupt me. You will look at me today and love me. You will look at me tomorrow and you will hate me. That's what happens. People here can do these things. Something like this happened to Ford when he was here. He fell in love with me, but I didn't like him at all. I couldn't stand him. This is when my mother was alive, and it was she who told my father about the way Ford used to bother me.

"At first Papa had Lamont talk to Ford. He told him in a very European way — direct, you know? — that he shouldn't bother me, but Ford thought that Lamont was in love with me. He challenged Lamont to fight, but Lamont didn't want to fight. Then my mother went to an old woman she knows who makes powerful love tere. She put Ford in love with a woman named Fatima, who is a prostitute who works at the Meridien. He followed her for a few weeks, but Ford is smart; he went to a marabou in M'Bour, a bad marabou, the kind who only care about money, and practice more of the old things, witchcraft, you see, than they practice the things from the Quoran. Ford paid this marabou to break him from the hold Fatima had on him.

"Well, he did. My father knew this even before I did. And he wouldn't let Ford back into our house. But Ford didn't leave the village. He was making money, by this time, selling American things to people in Dakar. He moved in with the N'Doye family. He paid them thirty-five thousand francs per month. No one said anything to N'Doye, because this was so much money, and it wasn't his problem. But Ford bothered me every day. He would follow me to Dakar, Ouakam, Gorée, Rufisque, everywhere, everywhere, everywhere. He would beg to marry me, and speak in a loud voice in public to tell the whole world I was his fiancée. When he didn't have money, he would steal things from the markets and give me them, but I wouldn't take anything. He would do all kinds of things like this.

"One night, when my father was at his other house with his other family in The Gambia, Ford came into my room to get in bed with me, and sleep with me, but I screamed, and my mother and brother came running into my room. All of us began to hit Ford, and Phillipe went to get his machete, and he was saying, 'I will kill that half-breed dog. I will cut him in two.' Don't interrupt me, Evan. Phillipe went to get his machete, and when my mother saw it in Phillipe's hand, she yelled at Phillipe to stop. He did stop. And everything was quiet. Everything was quiet except for the light bulb in the ceiling of my room. It's only a light bulb, but it sounded, on that night, like dry wood burning. Then the bulb went black, and I screamed. We heard someone fall on the floor.

"I thought Phillipe had killed Ford, and I ran to my door to go in the hall to turn on the light there. But when I got to the hall, Phillipe was already there. And he turned on the light. We ran back into the room, and saw my mother on the floor. And Ford was gone."

Aminata and I turn toward the gate as we hear it squeak open. Lamont strides toward us, carrying a plastic sack in one hand, and in the other, a baguette. "Whotcha, boy?" he says, "Nangadeff, Ami." His smile looks artificial. "What are you two discussing?"

"I just told him about Ford, when he tried to get in bed with me."

"Aminata," says Lamont, "What did I tell —"

"But I haven't told him about the jinn."

Lamont throws his head back, squints. He whispers to himself in Wolof, then in English, says, "Stupid girl, I told you not to tell him anything until I got back from the village!"

"Tell me what?"

Aminata threads her fingers together at her waist. She lowers her head. "But I didn't —"

Lamont clucks his tongue and swings the bread, sword-like, in the air. "So you know then?" he says, turning to me.

"Know what?"

"Lamont!"

"Shut up, Aminata! Yes, Evan. Ford. We want you to kill him."

"Ford?"

"Yes," says Lamont.

"He caused my mother to die, Evan," Aminata says in a rush of words. "He gave her a heart attack. Don't you see? If you do this my father will let you marry me. It's your bride-price. It's the only way. You don't have to do it if you don't want to. It's up to you, mostly. It's up to you."

My head spins from all this talk. None of us speaks for the longest time. The air is as still as the three of us. I stand with a silly grin on my face. I look from Aminata to Lamont, and I can tell by the way they stand, the way they refuse to look at each other, that they are furious with one another. Yet I cannot help feeling that there is some truth to what Aminata has told me. Her desperation, her urgency lead me to the sense that I will very soon get to the bottom of this. But there is something I do not understand, and I turn to Lamont for my question. I gaze at him for a moment. He looks uncomfortable, shifting from foot to foot, and he grins back at me with the same inappropriate grin I am wearing. He hands the sack and the baguette to Aminata, who turns and steps silently away. "If you hadn't come," I say. "She would have told me about how Ford had sent the jinn, or whatever, to me, right?"

"Yes," he says. His throat sounds dry, gravelly.

I am angry, but more than this I am embarrassed for the both of them, and this tempers my anger. My eyes are downcast, my hands in my pockets. "I don't understand everything that Ami's been trying to tell me," I say, almost in a whisper, "but I think I get the idea. She wants revenge, and so does her father, and I guess I'm supposed to be the triggerman. OK. OK, fine. But what I don't get is —"

"Why, and how has Ford set this jinn on you, right?"

"Exactly. I mean, yesterday, from talking to Ami, I've learned she's got the impression that Ford and I are friends, that we've known each other awhile. Well, I only met the guy a few days ago. I hardly know him. I spent a few hours with him in the Blue Marlin. We had a couple drinks, went out and smoked some pot. I'm afraid you guys are . . . well . . ."

Lamont sighs, folds his arms, shakes his head. "In your country you would say 'fuckin' up,' right?"

"I'm afraid so."

"I knew it. I just knew you would say something like this. I told her to keep her mouth closed until tonight. I told her things had changed, but she's a vain and stubborn girl. She seemed to think that you would do anything for her, but her father and I know differently. She wanted to go soft with you, make you do this whole thing for love, but I told her you wouldn't. Am I right?"

"Looks like it."

"Well, my friend," he says, his tone firming, "we still want you to do what we say. Only things will be different. Just a little. In fact, things will be easier for you."

We stare at each other for a long time. I do not know what to say. Can he really insist on going on with this stupidity? "Look, Lamont —"

He raises a hand. "You want to know what's going on with you, don't you? And how to make things better, right?"

I say nothing for a few seconds, then look him so hard and deep in the eyes it is a wonder he does not melt away. "Yeah, I do, but my guess is you people don't have a fucking clue."

"Then you guess wrong. Let's eat, boy. Let's sit down and chew the fat."

26 I Eat, Talk, and Go Swimming

The kerr is wonderful. It tastes like a combination of shrimp and clams. It is in a rose-colored sauce, which is ladled over the pasta. In the semi-dark it looks almost like marinara sauce, my favorite dish. I have seconds on almost everything, and drink perhaps two thirds of the wine. Aminata and Lamont eat only a little bit, and Aminata periodically cautions me not to eat too much of the kerr, telling me that those who have never eaten it before, or who rarely eat it, often complain of severe gas pains the morning after. I ignore her. And whenever the two of them try to discuss anything about Ford, jinni, Mrs. Gueye's death or what have you, I nod and say things like, You don't say? or, Well I'll be, or, Good for you, or Do tell — my, my, my, my, my. After what I would guess to be thirty minutes of this sort of thing, Aminata claps her hand against the table top, causing utensils to rattle, the candle to topple over. "Evan," she says, "this is not a game."

"You don't say? My, my, my —"

"Stop it," she hisses. She narrows her glare. She rights the candle. Her face shifts from shadow to shadow in the bending, weaving light. I grin at her.

"Stop what, babes?"

"Evan," Lamont says, looking and sounding as controlled

as Aminata looks and sounds agitated, "we understand how you must feel. All you have heard is kill this person and kill that person, beware this spirit, look out for that ghost, since you came here. I know it must be driving you mad, boy. But please understand that this is not the true Africa. Not really. This isn't the way we spend our lives from day to day. We are both as afraid of this whole thing as you."

"How did you find out about the guy I killed?"

"I'll get to that in a moment. But first let me say this: Whatever you decide to do is up to you." He pauses, takes a sip of wine, clears his throat. "To a degree. But I might as well tell you that Ami, Phillipe, Mr. Gueye, and I are the only ones who know about the murder, I think. We have you over a barrel a bit. We want you to kill Ford. Kill him, and Mr. Gueye will allow you to marry Aminata — if you want — or you can go back to your country in peace. Do you understand?" He scratches his nose, sips his wine, looks at me with his large slow-moving eyes.

I say nothing.

"You don't understand. Look, Ami, he's confused. He thinks —"

"I speak English, Lamont," she says.

Aminata is not eating. She sits hunched over, hands in her lap.

"I know you do," says Lamont. "Look, Evan, what Ami and I are trying to tell you is that what's happening to you is very unusual. This is not the kind of thing that happens every day here. Listen . . . We thought they were, but Ami has found that . . . Listen. The thing you don't understand is that you have a very serious problem. We didn't realize this till a few days ago. At first we thought you had a jinn. Ford has one. Do you know that? His jinn is very dangerous. It is evil."

"Don't change the subject."

"Evil to you is an abstract. You read about crimes in your newspapers. You hear about robbings and murders, wars and things. And of course these things are evils. Of course they are, but you really don't understand what evil truly is. You don't understand that it's a living thing. This is not to say that there is less evil in your country than there is in ours, but there is less awareness of it in your world because you are all so distracted by superficialities."

"Get to the point."

His voice raises a pitch. "Evil tastes bad. It smells bad. It feels bad. Evil is alive. It moves and breathes as you and I do. But when a Westerner encounters it, he tries to spray it away with air fresheners, flush it away down toilets, pay it off with money, turn on the TV and tune it out. You ignore evil as it eats away at you like cancer."

"Lamont," says Aminata. "Tell him."

"Have some wine, Aminata, don't behave like an American," Lamont says.

He turns to me.

"Listen, boy, what Ami wants me to do first is apologize for joking with you. About —"

"About what?"

"About the things I said to you when you were here the last time. I was only joking, you know."

"You never got sick —"

"And I never killed anyone."

"You were kidding."

"Well . . . sure. Not like . . . It wasn't for laughs, Evan. I — You mean you believed me?"

"What if I did? Maybe I did. Why couldn't you just —"

"I was just trying to teach you with a story. I was trying to tell about jinn. That's what Ami wanted me to do. Listen, I don't know exactly how these things work. Jinn, I mean. I just figured that if I took the things that Ami told me about you, and put them in a story about me, that you would . . . would . . ." — he begins to wave his hand in small circles — ". . . understand better what this whole thing was about. Of course I was joking. I thought you knew!"

I lean forward and rest my elbow on the table, my forehead on my fingertips. I say nothing, but I begin to wonder whether Aminata has been "joking." I begin to wonder just how stupid I have been. I feel the impulse to laugh, to lash out, to cry, to run, but God help me I can do nothing but wait to find out what is wrong with me. And if and when they tell me, how will I know whether to believe them? My head begins to hurt. My hands shake. I push my plate away and listen. That is all I can do. "But, listen, my friend," says Lamont. "Listen to what I have to tell you. As long as Ford is alive he's a danger to everyone in N'Gor. He's possessed by a powerful jinn. He may not even know that the marabou he deals with is using him."

"I don't have any quarrel with Ford."

He smiles at me. "No quarrel? What did I tell you, Ami?"

"So why didn't you tell the cops?"

"Mr. Gueye wants him dead, not deported or even in prison."

"Why didn't he kill Ford? Why not you?"

"Ford," says Aminata, "is protected by very strong tere. As long as he doesn't come into the village no one can harm him." With her right hand she twirls her fork around in her plate. She holds it awkwardly, clearly unaccustomed to its feel. She rests her chin in the palm of her left hand. "But," she says, "what Lamont is trying to tell you is that we were wrong about the jinn . . . yours, I mean. There is one that follows you. Phillipe told me he heard it outside your window not long ago —"

"Yes," says Lamont. "Yes, it's there, but it can't touch you because Ami's father —"

211

"Remember what I told you about the lizards? They keep the jinn away from you. Papa's been doing this for you because he wants you to do this thing for him." Aminata will not look at me, but I do not take my eyes off her. I sit and wonder what her motive might be, why she is going through such great lengths to get me to commit murder, *another* murder. Oh well.

I clear my throat, and still staring at Aminata I say, "No. See, Ami, you told me your father dropped those lizards all over the damned place to protect you all —"

"Both," she says.

"No! No, goddamn it. You're not helping me. You said you'd help me. You said you'd help me stop this goddamn, goddamn sickness and all you do is fucking lie and give lectures. First you say I kill Ford as a bride-price, and for Ami's honor and all that. Then you imply you've got me over a barrel because you saw me kill someone. Then you imply the old man's been protecting me so I'll be grateful and kill Ford as repayment. Then you tell me that this fucking genie — Do you know what's wrong with me? Do you or don't you? If not then just leave me the goddamn hell alone and let me go mad on my own. I don't need you people to push me along."

Lamont pokes his fork into his salad, shoves a piece of lettuce into his mouth, wags his head and waves a hand in my face. "I suppose your next question is, if I or Phillipe, or Mr. Gueye can't kill Ford, how can you?"

"Jesus God, man, my first question is —"

"The answer is that you wouldn't be able to if it weren't for that belt you've got on. It'll protect you for reasons I can't completely explain, because I don't understand these things very well, but it has to do with the fact that you and Ford were born on the same side of the ocean. You're like brothers or something. I'll ask Ami's father if you want me to. But Monsieur Gueye wasn't protecting you so you'd be grateful. He was protecting you because he knew he could use you. And if you want to know the truth, he really doesn't want you to marry Ami. He thinks Americans are crazy and dangerous children. The fact is he'd like to see you imprisoned for what you did, but Ami wants to marry you, I think. Do you, girl?"

Aminata whispers something in Wolof.

I lean toward her "What did she say? Ami, what did you —"

"She says she does, but she won't do this unless you pay the price, right, Ami?"

Ami lowers her head, saying nothing.

"She's shy, Evan. Embarrassed, you know?"

"How did you find out about . . . what I did?"

"Just be patient."

"I've been patient, motherfucker —"

"Evan," says Aminata. She touches me on the arm, and I relax.

"I want him to tell me."

"I'll tell you. Give me a cigarette, will you, Evan?"

I take my cigarettes from my pocket and slap them on the table. "Tell me," I say. I stare into Lamont's eyes. We stare at each other for a quarter of a minute. I have the urge to take up my fork and pound it into his eyes. My stomach undulates. My heart rocks my chest. Pain rises in my head like steam, filling it, packing it tight, till it throbs. My right eye twitches and tears up. Then the other eye tears up and I blink. "Thanks," says Lamont. He lights a cigarette and flips the match over his shoulder. "It's simple, really," he says. "I was at a friend's apartment — leaving his apartment, I should say. I don't suppose it matters. But I had been recording some tapes, Weather Report, Ornette Coleman, and Santana, I think. But you don't want to hear these details. Well, this friend of mine, Vieux is his name, lives pretty close to Fosse. You know, Fosse? The ghetto? That's where I saw you. That's where you did it."

"I wouldn't know. I don't remember. Just get on with it."

He looks at Ami, then quickly away. "That's right. American-style. Like Hemingway, right? Well, good. Fine. I saw you when I was walking up the street, looking for a cab. I was in a hurry, and didn't want to wait for a bus. I was about two or three blocks behind you. You were much bigger then. Huge. Ninety kilos, it looked to me. And you looked drunk. You were staggering to-and-fro, side to side. I thought it was funny, at first. I imagined you were late getting home from work, and that your wife would be angry when you got home.

"Anyway, you were walking, but then you stopped and just started to totter, side to side. Then you fell to your knees. Then you fell on your face. I was going to help you, but before I got to you, the man with no legs was there. He stood beside you, and I guess he was trying to take your money. I don't know, it was pretty dark. I stepped up closer, but not too close. I mean, it was none of my business. You looked rich and he looked poor. But then you yelled in a loud voice and you hit him. I couldn't believe it. Here this man — with no legs — was trying to help himself a little and you hit him. I mean, all you had to do was get up and walk away, no? You hit him on the side of his head — three or four times. And then I heard you yell at him in English, and push him to the ground. You wouldn't stop hitting him. I couldn't believe —"

"Why didn't you stop me?"

"I was scared, man. You were big."

"Why didn't you call the police, call someone for help?"

"I was in shock. I couldn't believe what I was seeing. It was like a dream."

214

"So you didn't do anything."

"No."

"And you haven't told anyone but Ami and her father."

"I don't think so. I only —"

I spring from my seat, clutch Lamont by the hair, and jerk him toward me. I am one breath and one beat from blasting him with my fist, but Aminata grabs my arm, and calls my name twice, "Leave him," she says. "Let him be. Please. Please, Evan."

I stop and turn to her "Why? You fucking him? Huh? You goddamn fucking him!" I do not mean to say this, but I am drunk. I let Lamont go. Aminata freezes. Her eyes are large, then they tighten to slits. She opens her mouth as if to speak. She closes it, opens it again. Then her face relaxes completely. She sighs, turns to Lamont, and says, in Wolof, she is going to bed. Then she says something I do not understand. She walks inside.

"Ami —" I say, but I know it is useless to speak. "She's hurt," I say, stupidly.

"Sure she is," Lamont rubs his scalp, stares at the door through which Aminata has walked. "Why did you say that? Why would you say that? She —"

"Stupid."

"Yes."

I slump into my seat. "Goddamn it. I should go talk to her."

"That would be stupid too. Have some more wine."

"No thanks."

"Do you want to take a walk?"

The tide is low. The night buzzes with silence. It is very warm and streams of perspiration snake down my neck. Lamont and I walk to the east side of the beach, a short walk, but I am tired, and my head still hurts. I tell Lamont I do not feel like walking after all. I take out my wallet, finger around for a joint. I find one, light it, and offer it to Lamont. He shakes his head, sits down, saying, "Bad for you. You really shouldn't smoke so much."

"What difference does it make?"

"You need your wits."

"For what?"

"You never know. We have a saying here that goes, 'You never know what your ass is for till it's time to sit down.' Ford is pretty smart. You'll have to be very careful with him. You may need more of your brain than you think."

"Understand this. I'm not going to kill Ford."

"You don't have the choice."

"Maybe. But do you think the cops are going to believe a guy who's waited almost three months to tell them what he'd witnessed?"

He pokes a finger into the sand and moves it around in a circle, making a small hole. Then he lays his cigarette in the hole and covers it with sand. "I'm a good liar, don't you think? I have this way about me. The police will believe me. I'm not worried."

I snuff out the joint in the sand and drop it into my shirt pocket. "You are, Lamont. You're a real good liar. If it weren't for the fact you know about the murder, I'd swear you were lying about that too." I take off my shirt, kick off my sandals, stand up and pull off my jeans. "You people can kiss my ass. If I go to jail, I go to jail. If they want to hang me, they can hang me. I don't care anymore." I stride toward the ocean.

"You don't want to go to jail here, boy. It's filthy. Full of rats. They feed you sour rice. Nothing else. I know you don't mean that. You don't want to go to jail. You really don't." He stops trailing me.

"Hey, Evan," he hollers, when I am no more than twenty yards from the water. I keep walking. "Hey, Evan. Do you want to know what Ami said to me before she went in?"

"Fuck you," I say without turning around, without slowing my pace. I hear Lamont run up behind me. He does not pull up parallel, but stays a step or so behind.

"She says she must be crazy for loving a soul-eater, a demm, but that she loves you just the same."

I stop. I do not turn to look at him. "Always something out of the hat, Lamont. You folks are really pathetic. Look here, asshole, why don't you and your little —"

"You're one, boy. A disease, it is. You've got it. Can't change it, Evan. No cure as far as I know. It's a disease. That's what Monsieur Gueye thinks, anyway. I don't know how you got it. I don't know how anyone gets it; and until now, you're the first American I know of who's ever had it. But listen. We've done all this pretty badly, you see. We've lied to you a lot, and I'm sorry if you don't believe me now. But what I tell you is true."

"Why did you —"

He holds up his hand. "You know, Phillipe kept insisting that you were a demm, but we all argued that it's not possible for you to be one. We never thought you could catch it like grippe or something. We really thought it was just the jinn. Yes, you do have a jinn, but Monsieur Gueye has pretty much been keeping it away from the house. He's very afraid of them, you know. One once caused him to lose his eye, and, well, you know what Ford's jinn led Ford to do to Madame Gueye.... Really, we don't know much about them, Ami and I, I mean to say. We're losing our culture, I suppose.

"But listen, this is good news, really. Things will be much, much easier for you. You actually do happen to be a demm. Ami found out when you and she went to Gorée. The funny thing is that she just mentioned it in passing. And the silly girl never realized how important that was, how simple this makes everything." He chuckles to himself. "Ami won't tell me how she knows, but she says she knows for sure. She seemed very upset about it, quite sick in fact because . . . Listen. It's not really that bad. Phillipe is one. He can —"

"Phillipe?"

"Yes, yes, didn't you ever wonder how he can do all those crazy things, speak your words as you say them? All that sort of thing?"

I shake my head slowly. "Does he have the headaches, does he —"

"No, nothing like that. You see, he was born this way. Your illness has been caused by, well, malnutrition, you could say. Soul-eating is Phillipe's nature. And listen, boy, he can teach you to control it. He can do this if you'll just agree to do what we ask. Evan, listen to me, boy. Ford is breakfast. Ford is lunch. Ford is dinner. Eat and he dies, boy. Eat and you live. It's simple. You've got to learn how, or it'll kill you. If you don't eat the soul, well, you'll starve to death. But look how simple it is, Evan. It takes months to eat someone's soul. Ford won't even suspect what's happening to him. It'll be easy. No evidence. No fingerprints. No —"

"Bride-price."

He is silent for a long time. Suddenly, I feel hungry. I tell myself it is the pot, or else suggestion. My stomach groans and I am momentarily dizzy. "Oh. Yes," says Lamont, "I don't suppose that is necessary either." He pauses, absently rubs his scalp, folds his arms. "You see?" he says, smiling. "You see how badly we've done this thing? No bride-price. That's right."

"Figures."

"She does care for you."

I say nothing.

"She probably does love you."

"I see."

"Except . . . well, she really doesn't have much choice, my friend. She pretty much has to marry me. I know she doesn't love me. And I don't particularly have any strong feelings for her one way or the other, but . . . Well, it's politics, you see. My family and hers have made the arrangement, and I'm afraid —"

"Fine."

I resume my walk. I keep walking because I know. He need not tell me more. I know. I knew. Suspected. Felt it inside, outside. Felt it walking, sitting, standing, lying. Lying. Truth. In truth. Knowing. Not lying, walking, keep walking. Now wading. Deeper. Swimming, pushing water, fine wet beads, liquid pearls, foam. Swimming nowhere. Now here. My middle passage. Onward. Forward. Ford-ward. Ford would. Eat and taste. Eat and live. Dinner is he. Lunch is he. Breakfast is he. Demm. Souleater. My, my, my, my, my. You don't say.

27 I Hear Odd Sounds

I tire, stop, tread, float. I rock on the water. The water vibrates with a plangent sound as I lower my ears into it. The water bounces me and I relax. The water feels as though it weaves through me like a long row of cursive *W*'s. Behind my closed eyes, I see an image of Ford's cool-jerk face, those globelike eyes, that roundsmooth face. My body momentarily stiffens. I tremble, relax again. I soften, melt. I am oil on water. I spread out under the quarter-moon sky, reflect the stars back onto themselves. I spread thin across the ocean. My left knee brushes N'Gor Beach, my right, N'Gor Island. My scalp, my face, spread round the island, encircle the island. I cover the water like a dark skin. I bleed my way from Africa to America. In time I will no longer be able to hold each particle together. The slow boil of the ocean will break me down, atom by atom. Some atoms will be consumed by microscopic creatures, some will harden, sink, and bury themselves beneath the ocean sands; some will float upward and upward, burst in the heat of the day. My consciousness will rise up like vapor, will steam and roll, half-invisible, far into the sky, get caught up in the clouds, choke them till they can hold no more of me. The clouds will cast me down in a silent dry rain. I will hang in the air, between sky and soil, sky and sea, floating in disjointed voiceless madness for all eternity. The wind will rise and push these fragments around the circuits of the world. Everywhere, people will breathe my hunger, grow dizzy with the pangs of emptiness, consume one another. There is never enough to go all the way around. Look out for the hungry ones.

I paddle to shore, get my money belt, my wallet, my sandals, and the tere. I slip my wallet into my money belt. I cinch the money belt around my waist, thread the tere through the sandals, and fasten the tere around my waist. I return to the water and swim, taking very long, relaxed strokes. I am not a bad swimmer. I lied to Lamont and Phillipe. I did not trust them. I had the conviction that they meant to do me harm that night. Silly me.

It is a long swim. It is some ten minutes by motorboat, and I am uncertain whether I am up to it. And it becomes apparent to me now that I am less than one quarter of the way to the village. Silly me. My shoulders burn so badly it feels as though my bones will melt and fuse together. Every breath I take scrapes my lungs. I am breathing hot sand. My thighs and calves and stomach muscles cramp, and I stop, tread, float, try to relax. But treading makes the pain worse. I cannot call out for help, for who would help me? I imagine my legs and arms folding spiderlike toward my chest; my muscles would tighten, lock into immovable hardness. I will sink, my muscles gripped so tightly I will never decompose.

I swim on, dog-paddling, crawling, scuttling, till, one thousand years later, my fingers touch pebbles. I stand and walk to the shore. Already I can feel the pain in my head, far away now like distant hoof beats. The moment my feet find the strand my head is torn in two as if it were ripe fruit. I hear myself scream, and everyone on the bus turns to look at me. "Excuse me," I say, and then, after a relatively long pause, "but I thought this was my stop." The bus stops, but I do not get off. I stand fast and watch each passenger disembark. There are seventy people or so, and as each exits he or she wishes me a good night. I do not acknowledge them, even though each good night seems sincere. It appears that the boy with the peppercorn hair is nowhere around. As the last passenger exits, the driver stands, turns and waves to the cageman. The cageman grins, pushes his glasses up on his nose, rises, and leaves. Then the driver himself leaves, switching off the overhead lights as he does so. I stand and listen to the sounds of the bus as it cools and settles. It squeaks, groans; fluids trickle, drip, hiss. Someone taps me on the shoulder. I turn and hear the boy's voice, but I can scarcely see him. "Back, I see," he says.

I stare at him a long time. His image slowly bleeds from the darkness, yet his features remain muted. I see them best out the corner of my eye. When I look directly at him his features blur.

"What's going on?" I say.

"Now, you ask?"

"I just want to know what's going on. I just want to know if I'm crazy."

He pauses for a long time. He is very good at these pauses. "Listen," he says, "Why are you here? You're wasting your time. Go home."

"Just tell me. Tell me and —"

He raises his hands. "Never mind, 'merican. It's not worth it. You shouldn't be here."

"Am I crazy? Is that what this is?"

He shrugs. "Sure. I think so, but so what?"

"And I really killed a man?"

"Now, you ask?"

"So sue me. And I want to know if I'm really a soul-eater too."

"Let me ask *you* something."

"Tell me. Please. Tell me and I'll go. Just answer me one question, not both. Then I'll go. I swear. I promise."

He scratches his nose, lowers his head. I see the dull glisten of his wounds. "Ndeysahn," he says. "Ndeysahn, ndeysahn, ndeysahn." He leans very close to me. His eyes look as dull as the memory-light that floats behind just-closed eyes. "Where are you?"

"Excuse me?"

"I ask where you are."

"Where am I?"

"Yes."

I pause for a long time. Long enough to hear a jazz rhythm in the hiss and drip of the bus engine. It is Connie Kay brushing the high hat on "Django," a cool, cool sound. Finally, as if answering a trick question, I pop my fingers and I say, "I'm on the bus . . . I'm on the bus."

The boy pats my shoulder, whispers, "Well, get off."

Without words, without hesitation, I turn from him, step off into empty air, and fall straight down on my face. When I come to, I am again on the beach. It is still night. I am still naked. My mouth is full of sand. My nose aches. My body is stiff, and as I push myself my head booms painfully. I lower my head to the sand and begin to cry. Nothing makes sense, I whisper. I am crazy, I whisper. That is all. That is all. I am stupid and crazy. I push myself up into a sphinxlike position and find myself staring into the muzzle of a large black hound. It sits, staring at me, panting. I cannot see its eyes, but feel them. I smell its breath. "Get away from me," I croak. To my surprise, it does. It is so dark that it disappears when it has taken only a few steps, but I hear it pad against the sand for what seems like ten minutes. It cannot be that long.

I rise and steal through the village. I go to the Gueye place, brush away sand, spit sand, and dress. My body itches everywhere, and I consider taking a shower, but instead I sit and smoke a joint. Then I have a cigarette, and before long I begin to notice how tired I am. I kick off my shoes and lie back on my bed. My eyes grow heavy. My chest slowly rises and falls. I feel the dark sweet lassitude of an endorphin-marijuana-nicotine high slip through my veins and bones. I am near sleep. But then I hear the most peculiar sound, and open my eyes. It is guttural, growling, moaning, grunting. At first I think it is Old Gueye coughing in his sleep, but then I note that it is coming from down here, on the ground floor. Gueye, like the rest of his family, sleeps upstairs. I sit up and listen. It is silent again. I tell myself that I have merely had one of those auditory hallucinations that occur between waking and sleeping. But I hear it again before I can once more lie down. Guttural, growling, moaning, grunting, it is animal, but no animal I have ever heard. My skin tingles with fear. The high-pitched squeal kicks in; the pain at the top of my head burns so sharply I feel it on my tongue. I stand, slip on my jeans, take my flashlight, thinking to use it as a weapon rather than a beacon. I walk into the common room and am immediately bowled over by a hideous stench. The common room is cold, so cold I can see my breath. "Goddamn," I say, "What've we got here?" I am trying to be brave, I suppose, but I am so afraid I can scarcely move.

I go back to my room and close the door. I sit in a chair, thinking, so this is insanity. It's not so bad, really. Then I hear the growl again, only this time it lasts longer. The sound is not loud, but it shakes the entire house. I do not suppose that 'shake' is the right word, for it is not as though

I were in the midst of an earthquake. It is nothing of the sort. It is more like the low-note tremble of a bass. And though it may be a hallucination, it is a complete one, for I notice that the vibration causes the sand on the floor to shift and dance, settle in starlike patterns on the floor. Then the whole pattern begins to rotate, to spin into itself, making a perfect whorl. Images of dust devils, hurricanes, whirlwinds, draining sinks roll through my mind, and I know he is here. Old Gueye is here, disinviting me from his home. His presence lies heavy on my back. I want to vomit. A bead of my sweat slips from the side of my nose and falls into the middle of the whorl. My window cracks. My room fills with the awful smell. I look around, back and forth, to and fro, and I cannot help being as fascinated as I am terrified. But I am also angry because I am curious and know there is probably no one here who could or would explain any of this to me. Except perhaps Phillipe. I will go to his room. Maybe he will be able to explain things.

I climb the stairs to Phillipe's room, and am glad to see a slice of light at the bottom of his door. Phillipe, like myself, is a night person. He stays awake late, often reading the English newspapers and magazines I give him. But even if he were not awake I would still come to see him. I stand before his door and listen. There is no sound. I knock. There is no answer, so I knock again. "Phillipe?" I say. "C'est moi. Something weird's going on, man. Open —" The light in his room goes out. It just goes out. I know this sounds strange, but that little blade of light vanishing so suddenly, with such finality, stuns me more than anything else that has happened tonight. The world empties of all good, all purpose. I have been so stupid. I am afraid. I am hungry. I am insane. I descend the stairs, go back to my room, slip on my shoes, my shirt, take hold of my pack, and leave the house.

28 I Go Nightclubbing

It is a beautiful, clear night. Someone is following me. It is a beautiful, clear night. Perfect for walking. The quarter moon lays a blue-white glow on the tall grass that surrounds the village. I am sure someone is following me. The blacktop sparkles here and there, and I follow it as if it would lead me to mountains of diamond dust. I have no idea where I am going, but it is beautiful and clear. It is so quiet, I hear the buzzing of telephone wires, and this reminds me that I must call Wanda to tell her I love her. I do love her. I think I do, anyway. I strain to see her in my mind's eye, but her image — large eyes, glistening coiled hair, triangle face — her muscularity, her white teeth, swirl into one another in a dust-devil haze. I cannot see her. I cannot feel her. The image is buffeted away, and as my mind's vision clears I sense, but do not see, the presence of Aminata. Her impression. Her heat. But I cannot see her either. There is nothing but this night and my benumbed fear that weaves it together. I stop to listen for footsteps. I hear them. It is a four-legged trot. Such a beautiful night. The ocean smells like sex. I see someone up ahead, just off the road. He looks familiar. I stop and wave, walk closer. "Hi," I say, grinning. "How are you? How the hell are you?" I step closer. It is a small tree. It is a small tree. My heart jolts, my temples drum, my face flushes, the ice pick presses deep into the crown of my skull. *Keep walking. You don't want to be that crazy, do you?* No, I do not. I do not want to be that crazy. I will not talk to trees. Who it was I thought I had recognized I do not know. I must keep moving. I must not think about it.

Such a beautiful, walkable night. I have walked maybe three miles, and the only thoughts I allow myself to think are the Lord's Prayer, the Sh'ma, Nam myo ho renge kyo, Om Mani Padme Hum, Allah Akbar, Hail Mary, full of grace . . . Anything to keep it all away. It is a beautiful, clear night. Up ahead I see Ouakam Village. As I approach the village, a cab drops off a couple at the bus stop. I run, wave my arms, holler. I know the cabbie sees me because he flashes the lights and waits. I wish he would meet me halfway. I am tired. I climb into the cab, and for some reason say, "It's me." The cabbie snaps his head around and says, "Comment?"

"Dakar," I say. It occurs to me I have no money with me, but I say nothing to the driver. I have seen Dakaran cabbies bullwhip nonpaying fares. If this one tries to whip me I will run. It surprises me, the fares who do not. They stand there, perhaps astonished by pain, and take as many stipes as the cabbies wish to lay on them. At the most they will raise their hands and back away, yet they never run. But I will kick him in the balls and run into the night. I rehearse this in my mind, over and over, until we pull into Dakar. We roll by the little boulangerie where I met the legless man. I think of Ford. I think of tearing into him with claws and teeth. I think of devouring him in bloody chunks, sucking his bones clean, howling at the slivered moon. It is odd, but as we drive I still have the sensation I am being followed. I look around but see no one. "Place de l'Indépendance," I say. He takes me to the Cultural Center, and I exit the cab.

The driver also exits, stands before me and tells me how much I owe him. I apologize, tell him I have no money, but assure him I work at the Cultural Center. "Look. Understand me," I tell him in terribly bad French, "I can pay you. I just don't have any money right now." I begin patting my pockets. "Avez-vous une plume? Du papel? Je tu donne . . . ma . . . ma . . . adresse." The cabbie stands back, shakes his head, waves his hands and says, "Is OK. Pas problème, pas problème." He slides into the cab and scoots away. He must have found me pretty pathetic. Or perhaps it is the tere belt.

I walk around the city as if on an evening constitution, aimless, almost serene. Since I do not know where I am going I am in no hurry. I walk round and round the square. The only people I see are the guards who stand outside the better buildings, or sleep on their cardboard mats in front of them. I gaze longingly at the sleeping ones. I want more than anything to sleep, and I keep my eyes peeled for a convenient spot. Out the corner of my eye I see a large black hound. Perhaps I should say The black hound, just as I say The boy with the peppercorn hair, for I am certain it is the same beast I have seen at various times and places since coming to Dakar. "Come here, boy," I whisper. And I step toward him. "Come here, dog." I come within fifteen or twenty feet of him and he lopes away, then stops. He stands there as if waiting for me. "Come on, boy." I again approach him, come within several dozen feet, and he again moves away. I follow him this way up Pompidou, I think it is, close to a jazz club, the name of which I can never remember. I call it The Coltrane Club because each time I am near the place — I have never entered it — I hear "My Favorite Things," "Afro Blue," "Nancy," or some other Coltrane number. Tonight "Central Park West" curls out into the air and the dog sits before the yellow light that shines above

the club door as if he is listening, as if he is waiting for me.
"You hungry, boy? Come here, boy. Come here."

"Your dog, Mr. Norris?"

I turn. It is Whitaker. He is with a beautiful Senegalese
woman dressed in tight French jeans, red high heels, and a
gold lamé tank top. For a moment I think she is Aminata.
I stare at her as I answer Whitaker. The woman looks back
at me blankly at first, then, as my gaze remains on her, her
face tightens and she looks at Whitaker.

"Hello, Calvin."

"You're still here, I see."

I look at Whitaker, finally. He is dressed in white. He
looks sharp and tall. His gray glasses look me up and down.
I shove my hands into my pockets and raise my shoulders.
"You don't look too good, my man," he says.

"Bad night," I say. "Do you have time to talk? I know
I'm not dressed or anything, so I can't go in or anything,
but if —"

"Casual place. Come on in."

Perhaps it is the way I am standing — I do not know —
but he puts his arm around the woman, whispers something
to her, kisses her cheek. The woman walks into the club.
The dog, of course, is nowhere in sight. "Bad night, huh?"
says Whitaker.

"Something weird happened at the village. I had to get
out. I walked first, then I found a cab at Ouakam."

"Something weird, huh? What happened?"

"You ever see *The Exorcist?*"

He smiles, shakes his head, pushes his glasses up his
nose with his middle finger. "That bad?"

"Worse. I left without any money. I was wondering if you
could loan me some francs. I could stay in a hotel tonight
and maybe —"

"How much?"

"Couple thousand. Twenty-five, maybe."

"Damn, you gonna shack at the Terenga?"

"I need something to eat, too. I —"

"Never mind. Just playing, brother." He takes out his wallet, removes the bills, and holds them between his index and middle fingers. I reach out my hand, but he steps closer, stuffs the bills into my shirt pocket, and says, "Don't spend it all in one place." For some reason his words sicken me. My skin prickles, and I shiver. I feel for a brief moment as though I am a full foot shorter, and I look up at Whitaker through eyes that are not my own. He is less handsome, his mouth crueler, and I am afraid of him. I stand before him trembling, staring at him. An uncomfortably long period of time goes by, then Whitaker says, "Thank you, Calvin."

"I — No."

"Say again?"

I take the money from my pocket and give it back to him. At the same moment my own vision, my own sense of stature and balance, are restored. "I need help, Calvin," I say. "I don't need money, I need help. I killed a guy," I tell him. "I killed someone."

Whitaker sighs hard, drops his head, folds his arms across his chest. "Mo-ther-fuck," he says. He stuffs the money into his pocket, and spinning around says, "Don't go anywhere. Don't fucking move," and trots into the club. He comes back in a couple of minutes. "I told you to get out, man. Didn't I tell you to get out? Goddamn, I told —"

"I just —"

"— you to get —"

"— couldn't —"

"Shut up! Just shut the — What're you talking about? Who'd you kill?"

I say nothing. I shrug. Whitaker collars me, nearly pushing me to my knees. I feel his energy twitching through me.

230

I could eat him if I wanted to. "You better answer me, man," says Whitaker, "or I'll knock your weak ass out and take you to the cops, right now. Right goddamn now. You dig what I'm —"

"A cripple! I killed a cripple! He had no legs, man . . . no legs . . . wanted to . . . wanted . . . tried to help me . . . can — can you believe that? He was trying to help me, see, but I'm sick, man. I'm sick. Help me. I don't care if you call the cops. I don't care if I die. I got . . . I got . . . Do you know what I am?" He lets me loose and paces in front of me. "Stop crying, goddamn you," he says. "I said stop crying, boy. And you're not making any sense." He stops pacing, calms his voice. "Slow it down, Norris, just slow it down. Come on. I need a drink."

As we step in, I watch the jazz combo lay down their instruments, wipe their brows, smile and nod at the sparse applause. A fat Senegalese man in a green sport coat and blue trousers rises from his seat near the bandstand, clapping, nodding, grinning. He shakes each band member's hand as they file past him. He slaps the drummer on the back and offers him a seat at his table. They both sit. The big man picks up two swizzle sticks and begins drumming glasses, ashtrays, and so forth. Both men lean away from the table, laughing. The club smells of liquor, weed, cigarettes, fried food. It is not nearly as crowded as I had thought it would be. There are perhaps only twenty patrons here, most of them tucked away in booths, their voices sounding like boiling liquid. Whitaker and I slide into the booth with his girlfriend. He tells me her name, but I do not catch it. She slips a cigarette from her purse and offers me one. I feel her eyes on me as she holds her lighter for me, but I do not look at her. There are two drinks already at our table. Whitaker asks me whether I would like anything to drink. I tell him I do not. "She doesn't speak English," he says, "but keep your voice down. Can't tell who does around here. You said you were hungry?" Not anymore, I tell him. I tell him I feel tired and sick. He sips his drink, looks at his girlfriend, and pats her on the hand. Then he turns to me. "Norris, Norris, Norris," he says. "Guess you been busy lately, huh? Now . . ." He lights a cigarette. "Now I want you to tell me everything. I want you to take it slow and easy, you understand?"

I do not tell him everything. I tell him merely what I think he needs to know. I tell him about the headaches, about my passing out and being roused by the man with no legs. I tell him that I did not know I had actually committed the murder until tonight, till my conversation with Lamont. I tell him that I do not care if he wants to turn me in, but that I want to be committed to a mental institution. He listens, pulls on his cigarette, nods, drinks, but asks no questions, shows little emotion. "Are the cops still looking for me?" I ask him. The combo takes to the bandstand. I note that now the big man is setting himself behind the trap set. Whitaker shrugs as the band begins "Naima." "Are they still looking for you?" he asks.

"Are they looking for the murderer, I mean."

"Keep your voice down. When did you say this thing happened?"

"About a month before I met you?"

"August?"

"About then."

"I see."

The sax groans, then wails loudly, so Whitaker leans closer, slips off his glasses. The whites of his eyes are clean, sober, and the irises are a startling hazel. He locks them into my eyes for a moment, then looks away.

"Looking for the murderer. Well, now, I don't know for sure, you understand. But, like, you know Dakar is a pretty good-sized city, Evan. Million and a half or two million. It changes, season to season, you know?"

"Yeah. Sure . . . OK."

"Pretty mellow place, too. These niggers are as laid back as a Mexican's hairdo. You must know that. Not a violent place at all."

"I guess that's so, but I'm not —"

"Do you have any idea what the average murder rate is here in this city?"

"No. No idea."

"Well neither do I, really, cause my math's no good. But there were four murders last year, two the year before that, about two the year before that. You know how many murders there've been so far this year? Do you have any idea?" He lifts his hand before I can answer. "Now I know Dakar, you see? This is my hometown, practically. Like I told you, I know everybody who's worth knowing in this city. Ev-ree-body. And that includes the top man on the police force. So, I'm up on the inside and the outside, OK?"

"Sure."

"I read newspapers, watch TV, party with everybody but President Diouf, OK?"

"All right."

"You know how many murders have been reported in Dakar this year?"

"No."

He raises his hand, bends thumb and index finger till they form a circle. "That many," he says. "Zero."

"There was a witness, Calvin. Look, do you think I'd be telling you —"

"Did you hear what I said? Zero. Nothing. Zip, OK? So what if you did" — he leans toward me and whispers into my ear — "kill someone? As long as no one's reported the damn thing, you're cool." He waves backhanded at me. "But

I don't care," he says, leaning away. "I don't care what you do, see? And if you wanna know the truth, Norris, if you did off this guy, if I had one suspicion that you did do something like that, I'd turn your ass in yesterday. Bank on it, home, cause I know that niggers like you can fuck up things for niggers like me. You come here and act like fools and —" He leans back farther, slaps his hand on the table, shakes his head. "Don't get me started. But look here, Norris, if you don't believe me, go ahead and take your crazy ass to the cops. They might lock you up for a couple days till they check things out. They'll tell you what I'm telling you now. Then they'll deport you, of course. And when you get back you can check into a nut ward, just like you want."

"You don't understand. I —"

"Now you got just a couple days to pack your trash and zip on back to the crib, Norris, and if I was you, I'd do it. Yesterday." He finishes his drink, asks his companion if she would like another. She says yes, and he waves to the barman. "You sure you don't want something, my friend?"

"I'm OK."

He snorts. " 'OK,' " he says. "Look here, I got a place here in the city. I know I'm being just as crazy as you for saying this, but you can spend the night there. Then you can go back to the village in the morning and pick up your things. Then you can make reservations to go back to the States. Then you can split."

"I don't want to get in your way."

He waves away my comment just as he had before. "Big enough place. You won't be cockblocking if that's what you're worried about." He leans back in his seat as the barman makes his way to our booth. He makes the order, wraps his arm around his girlfriend's shoulder, nods his head to the rhythm of "Soul Eyes." After a moment, he leans forward and says, "One thing you can say about Senegal, my friend —" The barman returns, exchanging drinks for money. "One thing you can say," says Whitaker, "is Senegal's just about as deep as you can go. The place is deep, Evan, deep." He leans back and squeezes the woman's shoulder. He leans his head close to hers, whispering. His attention is fully hers. It is as if I were nowhere around.

29 I Cut Out

My dream is all colors, splashes of them — purples, yellows, blues, oranges, greens, reds. It is almost the same effect as closing one's eyes, pressing and rolling one's knuckles over the lids, only a thousand times more vivid. They mix, tumble, swirl. I am disconcerted. I wish to wake up. I cannot. Color upon color, hue upon sickening hue. Colors boiling, spilling, vomiting, spinning, freezing then breaking into shards. They fall away, leaving blackness so deep my sleeping head twirls. Then colors burst bright from nowhere, like the birth of a new universe. I struggle to wake up, but I cannot move. My body heats up, head rocks and buzzes, my lips and fingertips, neck and back are numb, and the ice pick, a vortex of diamond-hard colors, bores from the top of my head and down through my body. I feel my teeth clenched. I cannot breathe, and I struggle toward consciousness. Soon, every muscle is as tight as piano wire. I tell myself that if I can move one finger, one toe, crack one eyelid, make one sound, that I will awaken, but I cannot reach the level of consciousness that will permit awareness to become volition. I am as close to it as skin is to muscle, but I cannot move. Then color folds upon color, roils, thickens, curls inward like a fist. Suddenly it stops, leaving the image of my face. It is not my face.

I jerk into a sitting position. My sweat-covered body shivers. I lean towards Kene and place my hand on her hip. *Kene? Interesting.* "J'ai petit mal," I say. She merely grunts, pulls the cover over her shoulder. My stomach twists, and I leap from bed, feeling for my glasses. *My glasses. My glasses. Interesting.* I cross the living room and stop outside his door. I listen. No sound. He must be sleeping. Crazy bastard. I will get the police here first thing in the morning.

I make my way to the bathroom. I flip on the light and lean over the basin. *Basin? It is a sink. I call it a sink.* I look at myself in the mirror and am surprised to see that I really am Whitaker. Rather, I "possess" him. I must be "eating" Whitaker. I become dizzy, looking at the new face with its startling, startled eyes, the muttonchops, the penny-colored skin, the mole on our right cheek. I must admit that we are handsome. I look at my long thick fingers, my relatively hairless legs, my sex-stretched penis. I chuckle, but this causes my stomach to heave, and I fold myself over the toilet and heave out everything I ate last night. I lose Whitaker as well. The food floats in the bowl, chewed, but wholly undigested. It smells the same as it did when I ate it. I sit down on the floor, draw my knees up to my chest. I sit until the sky turns deep blue. After a while my lips and fingertips become numb. I feel cold. A strong pressure pullulates in my head and I prepare for the great pain. I wait. The pressure builds, but there is no pain. Instead, there is but a dull thump deep inside my brain. And that is all. That is it.

I rise and look at myself again in the mirror. No longer Whitaker, no longer hungry. I feel fine. I head back to the bedroom in which Whitaker has billeted me. I decide that I am thirsty, step into the kitchen, and switch on the light. I fill a glass and drink, fill it again and drink. I lean against the counter, fold my arms, and survey the apartment. From

237

the light in the kitchen that shines into the living room I
see a telephone. I stumble into the living room, sit down,
and dial Wanda's number. I will call her, tell her I love her,
tell her I will never go back, tell her to forget me. I am sure
she will have no problem forgetting me.

Her phone rings for almost a full minute, but there is no
answer. This is curious because Wanda's phone has an answering machine. Why has she turned it off? My head fills
with images of Wanda and some well-coiffured, smooth-
skinned man in her bed. They pound away at each other,
exuberant but silent, as Wanda would like it. One would
hear no breathing, no grunting, no sound of any kind. The
bedsprings — even their bedsprings would not so much as
whisper, yet their teeth would clench, their eyes tear, their
bodies grow hot and wet. I see all this in vivid detail, from
glistening skin to entangled tongues to the galvanic shud-
dering of orgasm, but I do not feel the usual surge of jeal-
ousy. Only a torpid annoyance, the regret that I have not
written her, and the memory of one of our last conversa-
tions. I told her one night, after a long, silent meal, that
she could see whomever she wanted to after I left. This was
stupid of me. I regretted my words the moment I had said
them. I had been wiping down her counters as she was load-
ing her dishwasher. After my tongue let slip the final word
of my remark, my hand ceased its circular motion on the
countertop, my eyes closed, I tipped my head back and
sighed. I waited. So did she. But she did not wait motionless
as did I. She waited, scraping, rinsing, stacking, arranging
in deliberate motion. In deliberate motion she filled the de-
tergent receptacles, closed the machine, set the dial, dried
her hands. In deliberate motion took up the foil-wrapped
leftovers and put them in the refrigerator. I could wait no
longer. I said, "I didn't —"

"Sure you did, Evan."

"What I was trying to say —"

She rested her knuckles on her hips. "Trying? Trying? Let me tell you what —"

"— was you don't have to —"

"— trying to say. What you were *trying* to say is that you don't —"

"— see? I didn't —"

"— to feel guilty for what you're going to do, and what you might do. But don't you dare try to absolve yourself of . . . of —"

"Now wait a second. Wait a second. That's not true. That's not —"

She raised her hand sharply, then pointed one perfect finger at me. "Don't worry, Evan. I will. I mean this is extremely big of you and everything, but if you don't mind I'll just live my life according to my rules. I mean, don't get me wrong, big papa, cause I know how in control all you —"

"Wanda, please —"

"Nigger, I'll see whomever I want, whenever I want, for whatever reasons I want, and I don't need your permission, your blessings, your pointers, or your goddamn pity. Do you understand me?

"You know, Evan, you never cease to amaze me. Just when I think . . . I don't think you understand. I don't think any of this has ever been clear to you. I've been doing, and will continue to do what I want. I make my choices. Some of them are bad, I know. . . ." She turned and began wiping the counters on her side of the kitchen. "I don't know," she said. "I don't know. God, what's wrong with me?" Then she stopped wiping, lowered her head. Her sobs sounded like stifled laughter, and for a moment I thought perhaps she *was* laughing. Then I was certain she was crying. Then I had no idea what to think. I moved to her, slipped my arms around her shoulders, squeezed her tight. I wanted to tell her I would come back. To her. I wanted to tell her that nothing was wrong with her. But me. I wanted to turn her around and kiss her to the roots of her disbelief in herself and in me. I wanted and wanted and wanted, but it never really occurred to me that she, too, wanted. What she wanted. Why she wanted.

"You love me," she said.

I wanted to say something good. Something she would remember. I am tired, I would say. I am lazy. The world's last shiftless darkie. Love is work. I am the Stepin Fetchit of love. But I said, "I do. I really do."

"I'm a good woman," she said.

You are *the* woman, I thought about saying, but your kisses don't get me stoned. Your sex is no deeper than any other woman's, your philosophy scares me, your blackness blanches me, your intellect probes me deeper than I am. "I know. You are," I said. "You don't have to repeat that."

"I deserve better than this," she said.

"Better than me," I said.

"I'm the best thing that ever happened to you."

"I know."

She turned around. She was laughing. She had tears in her eyes, but she was laughing. I stood there with a stupid half-smile on my face, unsure of what to do or say. "Go home, Evan," she said. "Go on home. Oh, Lord, you kill me. I really do deserve better."

"I know —"

"Oh, shut up." She pulled away from me, patted me on the chest. "You'll make a good husband someday, you big self-loving, morbid jerk," she said. "Go on. Go home."

Strangely enough I almost did go home. I made my way down the hall, to the bedroom, got my hat, coat, and shoes. I stood in the hall, slipped on my shoes, and began putting on my coat. Wanda appeared at the other end of the hall, leaned against the wall, folded her arms. I tried to smile at her, but she looked at me as though I disgusted her. It took me seconds to realize that this indeed was the case. She was being coy about her wanting me to leave. I had never before known her to be coy. She is (should I say was?) up-front about everything, seldom euphemizes, metaphorizes, seldom evades, feigns. I had never before known her to be anything but direct. I had never known her to be wrong, either, about anything that had to do with me. I rarely contradicted Wanda when it came to my self-image, my habits, my future. Even when I did argue with her I always felt I stood on the same rocky ground from which a young child argues with a parent. She argued from a higher moral plane, from a deeper love, from age and experience, insight, intuition, and education. I did not bend to Wanda's will for sex, or peace of mind, nor out of indifference, but from the belief that she was my better. I had grabbed my things without question, by reflex. She is always right. I must go —

"I can stay if you want me to."

"Don't put yourself out, big papa."

I pulled off my coat, dropped it. "Well, what do you want?"

Leaning her back full against the wall, she let herself slide to the floor, and sighed. She closed her eyes. "Well, I'll be goddamned. I'll be goddamned." She shook her head. "Um-m-m-m-m. You really are like this, aren't you?"

I had no idea how to respond to that.

"You really are," she said. "You know, when I first met you, all I saw was potential. Potential for growth, for friendship and love. I said to myself, Wandagirl, will you just look at this big, fine, articulate educated Negro. Will you just look at this big ol' gentle giant. All this brain and talent and looks and he doesn't even know it. The boy don't even know it. Gotta help him finish that degree, tell him how

241

beautiful he is inside, clean him up, sharpen him up. Gotta help him all I can 'cause he just don't know. And you know this has never been a secret: I wanted you for myself."

She drew her knees up to her chest, rested the back of her head against the wall. "You see," she said, "being around Them has done you some serious damage, the way I look at it. They keep you around like a showpiece, like some kind of pet. Look how passive you are. 'Should I stay? Should I go?' God's sake, Evan, be a man. Be a man. Seems like all you want to do is please other people. You bend to every-damn-body, accommodate everyone. You don't know that, Evan. You simply do not know . . . that white people are just not capable of loving black people. I think, somewhere in the back of your mind, you sense this. And it frustrates you that no matter what you do, they don't seem to love you. So you dance and dance and grin and shuffle —"

"I'm not a Tom."

"I didn't say that. And I'm not saying they're incapable of love. I'm saying they're just not capable of loving Us. You want some tea?" I had a sick taste in my mouth and told her I did not want any.

"Suit yourself." She yawned and shivered. This irritated me. "I need a cup, if you don't mind." She stared at me. I could not tell whether she mocked me or was embarrassed that she had unintentionally echoed me. "I don't mind at all," I said.

"If there's one thing a black man needs," she said, yawning again, "it's the love of a good woman. White women just can't love black men. The cultural gap's too wide. Probably wider now than a hundred years ago. And if I let myself be real objective about it, it's kind of sad. The both of them try so hard that it damn near kills them. Or they damn near kill each other, or do kill each other. They keep trying to shovel into one another's hearts and souls, but it's as futile as day trying to dig into night. What looks like a solid mixture turns out to be transitory. Dawn or dusk." Then she rolled her eyes toward me, paused as if to say, See? I can use metaphors.

I sat down where I had been standing. I did not know what to say. I wished for a cigarette. "The whole not equal to the parts," she said. "Evan, honey, we are, and always have been, locked in a struggle, with Them, that is beyond all our ideas and emotions. Just like day pushes out night, white people are bound and determined to push black people off the face of the earth. Because they have to, darling. Because it's their nature to do so. But you don't know that."

She unbent her legs, sat lotus-style. She hugged her arms round herself and shivered. "Come sit by me," she said. And I sat down in front of her, a crude mirror of the position in which she sat. I took her cold hands in mine, squeezed them. "You're saying," I began, "that I act white, but that's not true. Even if it were true, even if I acted white, white folks never let you forget who you really are."

"That's just what I'm saying. They can't help but tell you, as obvious as it is, that you're different. Yet you keep going back there. You keep going back, letting them define you in that negative, destructive way. You've had to empty yourself, let others define you, shape you, in order to please them. And I'm not just talking about those who don't — aren't even capable of loving you." She slowly rose, walked to the kitchen. I followed her. I watched her prepare tea, lay out cookies, fruit, and cheese. She worked silently. Overhead, the lights hummed; outside, traffic groaned past. "Chamomile?" she said. "Whatever you're having," I said.

"There it is!" she said. Her response made me start. "That's just what I'm saying, Evan. Whatever I want. Whatever They want. Whatever anyone wants. Don't you get it? You join the Peace Corps because that's what they want.

You decide on Africa rather than South America 'cause that's what I want. Them. Us. It's all the same to you. You really don't care. Just as long as you —"

"Wait a second —"

"But the difference —"

"Wanda —"

"But the difference is that when you go . . ." — she held me with her eyes — "when you go they won't care all that much either. But I will. I do already. I'll miss you. I love you. But you don't know that, do you?" She rolled her teacup between her palms, shivered. "You just don't know that you don't have to be me to please me."

Nonsense. This is nonsense.

This is her old number, and besides, she would be at work now. It would be something like three P.M. there. I pick up the phone and dial her office number. The connection is poor, but apparently Wanda's receptionist can hear me well. I, however, hear his voice as though he is speaking from an open phone booth in the rain. I ask to speak to Wanda. "She won't be in for a few days," he says. "Is this an emergency, sir?"

His tone is somnolent, indifferent.

I tell him it is no emergency, and that I would like to leave a message.

"Evan?" he says.

I say yes.

"This is Mike. Don't you recognize my voice?"

I tell him the reception is bad, that I am sorry, that I should have known it was him.

"It's OK. I suppose it's been a pretty long time. How's things out there? Run into Tarzan lately?"

I tell him I have not, but that I have been busy. I tell him that, in fact, I am in a hurry right now, that I would love to speak with him someday, but that I must get in touch with Wanda.

"Now that's interesting," he says.

I ask him why.

" 'Cause she's been trying to get in touch with you. Literally, dude. She left for Dakar this morning. She'll be getting there Thursday on flight —"

"Hold up, Mike. You're saying she's coming out here? To see me?"

"It's OK, Evan. We've known about you two here for some time now. She really changed when you left. I think she's considering quitting."

I say nothing.

"Yeah," says Mike, "she was pretty flipped out about the phone call she got from your boss."

"Allen Weitz called her?"

"Nope. No, that wasn't the guy. Hold up a sec. Let me see." There is a pause. "Yeah, yeah, it was a Calvin Whitaker. Friendly guy. Hey, what the hell's going on out there with you?"

I thank Mike, tell him I must be going.

"Don't you want to know when she's —"

"No," I say, and hang up. I return to the room, dress, and leave.

30 I Lose My Temper

"Bullshit," says Ford. He sits in front of me at our table in Chez Marie, a small café a few blocks north of the square. Finding him had been easy. I left Whitaker's place, slept on a bench in Place de l'Indépendance, awoke stiff and more weary than I have been in days. Fog rose up as the sunlight pressed down. And each time I blinked it seemed that more people, more noise, more heat filled the streets. I walked to Lamine Gueye, went left two blocks, and there he stood, T-shirt in hand, green khaftan, shades, skullcap. "Les chemises américaines!" he hollered. "Bon marché et toutes couleurs. Les chemises américaines!" He nodded to me but continued to cry out. I stopped within a couple feet of him. "I thought you said you didn't speak French," I said. "You can call it French if you want to, homes," he said, not missing a beat. "These motherfuckas don't. Where you been?" He held out his free hand and we shook. "Nangadef?" he said.

"Still here. You eaten yet?"

"You buying, I'm flying."

Ford forks, spoons, and fingers his food into his mouth. I cannot eat, but I am hungry, and my mouth waters at the sight of the grilled fish, the rice, the salad, the French bread. "You ain't hungry?" Ford asks me. I tell him I will eat later, and I watch his Adam's apple bob up and down as he drinks his water, then his soda, then his coffee. A little coffee streams from the corner of his mouth, down his neck, and disappears into the V of his khaftan. "Stone bullshit," he says. "Got any squares?"

"Gauloises."

"Damn, blood, why you smoking *them?*"

"Money."

"Right on. Right on."

He smokes. I do not. I watch him. He French-inhales, regards the cigarette. "Caint believe Ami told you that shit," he says. "Why she wanna do me that way? Damn. Lamont I can see. That nigger unhinged, ain't fit to sniff glue, but that don't sound like Ami." He inhales more smoke, shakes his head, exhales, chuckles. "Said I followed her, huh? And tried to rape her, huh? What else all she say?"

"You mean besides about her mother and all that? Not much else."

"Um." He stands, stretches. "Thanks for the chop, Ev. Look here, I'ma head on up to Ouakam f' some herb, you need some?"

"I could use some, but I need to hit the bank first."

"I'll cover you. Get me back later."

The bus is crowded and hot. Lunch hour has just begun and people are eager to be home. They do not speak much. They perspire and stare out the windows as if their gazes could more quickly pull the bus along. I sit between Ford and a teenage boy with a slender feminine face. He is very pretty, aloof and innocent-looking. There is something finished about him, well defined, complete, as though he were an evolutionary notch above the coarse Ford and the ill-formed me. His skin is perfectly black, his posture, perfectly straight, his breathing — even his breathing — seems so as-it-should-be, effortless, smooth. The bus stops. Ford nudges my arm and points out the window to a hedge of bougainvilleas. I nod appreciatively. "Naw, man," says Ford, pointing again, "look at that." I see a web that is some three feet in diameter stretched tautly across the bush. In the middle of the web rests its builder, a green, black, and yellow beast with a leg span approaching twelve inches and a body the size of a wine cork. I do not like spiders so I look away, to the people boarding the bus. "It's one powerful poison in that spider," says Ford. "Use it right and you can make a man blind in three days." I look again at the spider as the bus pulls away. I make no reply. For perhaps one minute, Ford is silent. He reaches into his pocket, pulls out a short string of amber prayer beads. He begins working them, one by one, between his index finger and his thumb. "But ain't nothing in Dakar that's bad as the shit out in the bush. You been out in the bush, homes?"

"I used to work in Ziguinchor."

"Out there, huh?"

"I was there a week or two."

"Whitaker say you was out there in the Pee-Cee."

"I was never in the Peace Corps."

Ford steadily works the beads, looks out the window and grunts. "Yeah," he says, "lotta mysterious things out in the bush. I lived out there f' six months out near M'Bour. Studied Quoran with a powerful marabou. Same cat who healed me off that sister I told you about. Taught me a lotta stuff. . . . Lotta stuff." He puts the beads away. I note that the young man to my left seems to be listening in on our speech.

He looks too young to have much knowledge of English, but one can never be sure. I cock my head closer to Ford's and blend my voice to the hum of the bus. "Tell me something," I say. "How do they make someone crazy? Some kind of drug?"

Ford leans away from me a bit. "Let me ast you something, bruddah. Why you out here?"

"I thought I told you first time we met." I am hoping he will not ask me for details about my "research," because I do not remember much of what I told him. Something about history, I think.

"Yeah, right. How's that research coming?"

"Gave up on it, to tell you the truth. And I'm having visa problems, so I might have to go back to the States pretty soon."

"Sheeit, don't no one here care about your papers. Senegal free. You can stay here as long as you want. But you ought to think again about living with them Gueyes."

"Look —"

"Soul-eaters, like I told you."

"Africa, I don't think so. I just don't think so."

"Stay out there. You'll see."

The bus stops. The boy to my left stands and exits. I slide a few inches away from Ford. "Who was the woman who put the spell on you? Was it Ami?"

"Fuck naw."

"Then who —"

"Ami's stepmother did it. Oooh damn, this is our stop. C'mon, homes."

The dealer is a wide-nosed Nigerian who calls himself Sam. His room is on the second floor of a large house near the

mosque. The room is very dark because of thick burlap curtains covering the windows. The place smells like cologne
and churai incense. A Bunny Wailer tape thumps from a
player in the corner. The red lights on the boom box flash
to the beat. I shake hands with Sam. His grip is stiff and
weak, a mannequin's hand. He does not smile or look me in
the eye. "Sit down, brothers," he says. I cross the room and
sit at the head of his bed while Ford sits at the foot. Sam
closes the door, turns and frowns at me. "Don't sit there,
man," he says.

"Excuse me?"

"You don't supposed to sit at the head of a Ibo's bed, Ev,"
says Ford. He is still wearing his shades. "See, Sam's a Ibo."

"No offense," I say.

Sam points to a beanbag chair in the middle of the
room. "Sit there," he says. "Always remember," says Ford,
"when you go to Nigeria, blood, you don't put y' ass where
a man lay his head. You'll be cool." Then he yawns, folds
his hands behind his head, lies back and says, "Oooh,
man, man, man. Tired . . . Had to be up at four this morning to pick up a load a pot holders my sister sent me.
Them things selling like hotcakes." Sam turns to Ford
and speaks to him in what seems to be good French. "Pas
problème," says Ford. "He's all right, Sammy. Told you
I wouldn't never bring nobody over here but homeboys."
Sam produces a goat-leather bag from beneath his bed, and
from it he removes a large plastic bag of pot. Using an
eighth section of a *Le Soleil* page, he rolls a spliff. He
then moves to a footlocker on which rests a plate of incense. He lights several sticks. The fragrance of sandal-
wood plumes thick in the air; the smell reminds me of
the smell of my apartment back home, and before I have
taken my third hit on the spliff, I am more there than

here. Actually, I am in both places, my room superimposed over Sam's as if beamed from a slide projector. I am with Wanda. She moves ghostlike about my room/ Sam's room, touching furniture, books, lifting dust from everything. She is comparing my room to an opium den she had once visited in Thailand. "I can't breathe," she says. "Can I open this window?" She crosses the floor and spreads the curtains, throws the window open. "You shouldn't live like this, Evan. No question why you get depressed."

"Go ahead; I don't mind."

"Excuse me?"

"If you open the window. I say, I don't mind."

"Well, I figured you wouldn't —"

"It's OK. My home's yours."

"Fresh air and sunshine are good for the spirits, 'G.' How many times have I had to tell you that?"

"I know. You're right. But I'm tense. The sun won't help. You see that fat guy over there?"

"Of course I do. He's sitting right there."

"Well, I'm supposed to kill the fucker."

"Would you mind not —"

"All right, all right . . . I'm supposed to kill the gentleman. Better?"

"Thank you."

"Who you talking to?" says Ford.

"What?"

"Is the music too loud?" says Sam. He stands.

"Leave it," I say. "I was just singing along. The music's fine. Real good."

As Ford offers me the spliff I catch a glimpse of another dream fragment. Ford sinks a blade into my chest. Sam unloads three bullets into my skull with a pistol. I take the spliff, heave, blow, pass it to Sam. He has yet to speak to me, except for his having directed me to the beanbag. Ford stands and reaches into the pocket of his khaftan. I stop breathing. My body locks. Ford hands Sam a wad of bills, tells him that we want two bags. I pocket my bag without checking it and we leave.

The sky is a blue dome rimmed with a pale yellow smaze. It is very hot, but I can smell autumn. Aminata tells me it will get cooler soon. She loves autumn, she says. Curiously enough so does Wanda. It is the only similarity between the two women I am aware of. It somehow seems right that one should be arriving, the other leaving, at this time of year. I wonder if I will find the nerve to face either of them again. Aminata would most likely laugh in my face. Wanda would probably scratch my eyes out. Or would it be Aminata who would tear at my face? Perhaps I have infected her, if this is possible. What would she say? Look what you've done to me, American man. Not only have you taken away my virginity, but you have left me with these horrible headaches, this hunger, this dizziness, numbness, squealing sounds. My friends fear me now. Lamont won't marry me now. My father has taken ill and it is only days before he will die. Look what you have done with your 'doggish' lust. Is this what she would say? But if even half of what Lamont surmises about my condition is true, how could Aminata live among demm without becoming one? I suppose Phillipe could have told me that. And would it be Wanda who would laugh in my face? After all, I have been very stupid about all this. Where is your proof? she would say. Have you seen a doctor? What have you been eating? Why didn't you take your quinine? Look, if you give me just one smidgin of quantifiable proof, Evan, I'll try to help you, but it looks to me that you're just suffering delusions. Now this is something I'm not qualified to treat, so I can't begin to tell you what's going on. I think you should see a psychiatrist. But I'll stand by you, darlin'. I'll be there for you. Just be open with me. Tell me how you feel. That is precisely what she would say. But it occurs to me that the only way I can complete this journey is to face them both, to find out exactly what each will say or do. If I hide from them, I will have learned nothing.

There is no breeze, but I breathe the dust that our sandals kick up. My head begins to hurt. I feel my pulse throb in my neck. My mouth is dry and I tell Ford I am thirsty. He suggests we go to the Blue Marlin, the bar near N'Gor, but I tell him I would rather be in Dakar.

"Geting to you, ain't it?" he says.

I know he means my life in N'Gor, but I do not answer him. We walk silently, till Ford says, "You ain't looking so good, man." I tell him I need an aspirin. "That's why I need to hit Dakar. I'm not paying a buck an aspirin at the hotel." Ford grunts, then tells me he knows a good restaurant near the airport, and that the airport annex sells things as cheaply as any place in Dakar. My head floats two feet above my shoulders. I watch us stride to the bus stop. A little boy sidles up to me, grins, asks me for money. I distractedly give him a five-hundred-franc note. "Shouldn't a done that, hometown. How long you gonna be here before you know how to act?"

I throw up my hands. "You got me, Africa. Maybe the kid's got strong tere."

"Naw, it ain't that; you just ain't learned how to give alms. That kid looked well fed. You cain't just throw y' money away like that. That's why you smoking Gauloises."

"Yeah, I guess. I'm just stoned, I guess."

Ford grunts. "My man say 'stoned.' Whycome you use them toubob words, Ev? Brothers don't say 'stoned.' "

I stop, shove my hands into my pockets, and stare down at the back of Ford's head. He stops and faces me. "Why don't you get off my ass about how I talk, and how I think? I'm black, OK? Negro, colored, Afro-American, coon, jigaboo, soulman. Why is it every time —"

"Look here, man —"

"— open my mouth for two seconds, you gotta throw my words or whatever —"

"Cool on out, now, homes, you —"

"— right back in my — And quit fucking calling me 'homes,' goddamnit. You don't know nothing about my home, or me, or who —"

"Look here, boy —"

"Fuck you! Fuck you!"

Ford pushes up his glasses. He folds his arms and grins. I had not been expecting this, a grin. I wanted him to swing at me, give me a reason. "Hand me a square, soulman," he says. "I don't mean nothing. You just funny, that's all. But you wrong about what I don't know about you. I know a whole bunch about you. You hungry?"

"I don't get you."

I hand him the cigarette and light it for him.

"Hungry. Food. You know, chop?"

"You just ate."

"I'm asking if *you* hungry. You ain't eaten yet. As for me I could eat again. Munchies, you understand."

"I'm not hungry, really. And I've got some things to do. A friend's flying in tonight, probably, from the States, and I'd like to look her up."

"I understand. But you got time. I'm in that airport more'n Air Afrique. Won't no U.S. flights be in till eleven

P.M. or so. And, hey, I figure the least you could do is let me have my say."

"Well, I'm not really hungry, like I say."

"Mm-hm. That headache, huh?"

"Yeah."

"Aspirin for you, grub for me. I'll buy. And I'll tell you about Ami's stepmother, and some other things you don't know." The bus stops. We get on.

31 I See Spot

His second lunch is not sumptuous, but it looks good: Mutton, cold potatoes, hard rolls, and a small salad of onions, beets, and lettuce. Ford eats leisurely, with a certain fluidity. He moves as if conducting a tea ceremony. There is grace even in the way he waves flies away, the way he wipes the perspiration from his brow, the way he presses his lips together after every sip of lemonade. We sit at a corner table. There is a plate-glass window behind me, and one to my right. Under the white light I can study Ford in minute detail. Long yellowish fingernails, pinkish lips, beardless full cheeks and sparsely bearded chin, burn-marked wrist, thin eyebrows, close-cropped hair. He wears what I am almost certain is a tere around his neck. It is a goat-leather pouch attached to a slender leather choker. And oddly it is the pouch that disturbs me more than the fact that Ford has still not taken off his glasses. I watch him and say nothing. He eats and says little. His only words for fifteen minutes or so are "Mutton's a little tough," "Spud's good," and "Why don't you drink something, Ev?" Finally I say, "So it was Ami's stepmother."

"Heart attack is what killed her. Whudn't but thirty-seven. Fine, too —"

"Really? When you —"

He holds up a hand. "I know, I prob'ly said the broad was ugly, or something like that. Naw, Aita was fine, all right. But when you forced to love someone . . . like, you attracted and drove back at the same time. You can see the ugly side no matter how good she look. See?

"And I know what you thinking, Evan — Why would anybody die over a fat motherfucka like me? Eh? That's what's on y' mind, ain't it?

"That's OK, soulman, you ain't got to say a word. Not one word. But it's nothing I could make you understand. You kinda had to be there. Aita and me just got along good. The broad was funny. Didn't have to say a word and she could just make me laugh. Anybody laugh, really, but it was like she and me was hooked up with wires the second we met. Ka-doom-doom! Just like a drumbeat right out the bush. For me it wasn't a sex thing. Not till she dropped them bones on me, you understand. It's just that she could look at me and crack me up, and I could do the same to her.

"Man, when she and me and her old man be in the living room, just sitting around talking — Gueye and me would talk, really, not her — well, Gueye'd be sitting up there with his old sour-prune lips, talking more smack than a four-arm junkie, and Aita'd . . . Well, man, she'd give a look that'd last like a second, and I'd fall out. We just dug each other. I don't know. I mean, and she'd bring me extra grub at night, or gimme ice water on hot days. I'm saying she would send one a her girls down to market to *buy* me some ice if the fridge wasn't working. And me, well, until I started working I couldn't really give her much, but I'd run errands for her and that kinda thing, and, hey, things was just copacetic between me and her. Cain't explain it."

The more Ford tries to explain, the less I understand or care. They simply fell for each other, and because of Ford's reluctance to sleep with her on those nights Old Gueye was

257

off to The Gambia or wherever with one of his other wives, Aita used — I have no other phrase — supernatural persuasion. Ford broke things off by the same means. I can scarcely keep my mind on his words. I keep thinking of my impending meeting with Wanda, and am trying to engineer a way to see Aminata as well. My anxiety builds by degrees, and little dramas flit through my head: I am kissing Wanda on Gorée and suddenly Aminata appears; I pay Ford to take Wanda on a tour, while I go to N'Gor to seek out Aminata; I take a cab to the airport and find the two women conversing. It goes on and on, and I can barely hear Ford. I close my eyes a moment to focus. I lean closer to him. I struggle to listen. "But what I'm getting to," says Ford, pressing his lips together, setting down his glass, "is that she was in love with me, but the fact I cut her off didn't have shit to do with the fact she died. 'S matter fact, Evan, she died two, three weeks after . . ." He leans toward me, spears a hand forward, chops the air with it as he speaks. "Look, lemme get down to it. I believe that one-eyed bastard killed her. Her own gotdamn husband, Ev. And I know for a fact he want me dead too." He drops his hand and leans back. Then he folds his arms across his chest. "She never did wanna be married to him. Not ever."

I am on the verge of asking Ford to remove his glasses. I want to see his eyes. My head no longer hurts, yet I still cannot think clearly. I want to know, but cannot tell. He gives me no reason. All that I can see is Ford/me and Aminata/Aita making love. All I can see is Old Gueye's black-and-amber eye. I think Ford is truly in pain, truly horrified of ever setting foot on N'Gor. From behind those shades Ford is still in love, sick in love, with Aita. I have no reason. I cannot kill him.

"How's your headache?" he says.

"Gone."

"You hungry?"

"I don't know yet."

A bus rolls by and our windows vibrate. Our waiter strides over, grins at us, and, in English, says, "Everything fine?" He stands back, hands on hips like a lion tamer. I take it that he thinks we should be impressed he speaks English. "How much?" says Ford. "Eight-fifty franc," the waiter says.

As we stand waiting for the bus, I tell Ford about the lizards, the bound chicken, the footsteps, but say nothing of the bus or the legless man, or anything else. Ford listens intently, his head cocked toward me. He nods from time to time, but says nothing. When I finish he straightens up, and it surprises me when he says, "So what's y' point?"

"What do you mean, 'what's my point'? You think this kind of thing happens —"

"You want me to tell you what it means, then —"

"Yesss, I want you to tell me what it means. Why do you think I've told you all this stuff?"

Ford turns away and looks down the road. He stands on his toes and stares for a moment, then looks at his watch. "Well, Ev-man, let's not play games. Someone's throwing bones on you for something you done or something you are. So you got to tell me more. 'S matter fact, you could tell me more if you wanted to. Sure you could, but you just want me to tell you if this . . ." — he arcs his hand across the horizon and looks at me — ". . . all this shit, where y' standing and what you hearing and all, everything around you, is real. Boy, what'd I tell you about this place? You damn right it's real! I told you. Man, I told you that."

"I don't *know* what I did. I didn't do anything."

"Sheeit."

"Let me put it this way: I didn't do anything before all this stuff started to happen."

"How do you know?"

"Because I got along with everybody in Zig," I say, thinking of big Ruth Barron, her yellow face, pulled-back shiny hair, her thighs, dimpled elbows, arching eyebrows. "This is the only place I've had trouble, except for the malaria. Shit started happening here before I even knew anybody here."

"Then it musta been in Zig. It musta been something for some reason, man, don't play with me. Now see I done been here for a while an' I seen things and I know things. Dig. Do you know what kinda world this is? F'get about all them stories you've read about in supermarket magazines about beans and fish and frogs and ice blocks falling out the sky. F'get about spontaneous combustion, astral projection, reincarnation, alien babies, elephant birds, Bigfoot, and telekisi-call-it. F'get it. Lemme show you something." He bends down, picks up a walnut-sized igneous stone, the same kind, dark gray, porous, lightweight, that scatter themselves, boulder and pebble, on N'Gor Island and Gorée. He rolls it between two fingers and a thumb. He tosses it to me and I catch it. "Put it in y' mouth," he says. And I do. Ford stands before me, knuckles on hips, grinning from behind his glasses. "Would you care to tell me why there's a rock in your mouth?" he says. I stand before him stupidly. He knows both that I do not need to answer him and that if I were to answer him I would have to remove the stone. I do not know what to do. I stand. "Well take the fucking thing out y' mouth, Ev," he says. I spit it into my hand and drop it onto the shoulder of the road. A small red sports car blows by and I watch it, the driver's hair sucked backward and wriggling like worms.

"You beginning to get the point?" says Ford, with intimate softness. "Evan, my brother, the onliest reason you put that rock in y' mouth is 'cause I told you to. That's real. You seen that. You did it. Ain't no kinda way to explain that. It's just something that I did and you did. Understand me, Grasshopper?

"I can put a peanut in my mouth and my enemies won't be able to see me. I can get money from anybody I want. I can follow a man anywhere in Senegal without even leaving my room. I can take a knife in the gut and don't bleed. I can make a man crazy as a dickless dog, just by touching him with a little something in the right place. Learned all this stuff 'cause I had to. I'm here by myself, understand, and I've made my mistakes. Same ones you making. It's cost me, but I have learned. I learned life ain't no game, but you can play it just like it was. Life clay, homeboy, and the world is a potter's wheel. If I'm lying may Allah strike me down." He pulls off his glasses and levels his big eyes on mine. They are as clear as a baby's. I cannot look away. "I know you believe me," he says, "but tonight I'ma show you something that'll make you understand me."

The bus pulls up, stops. We get on.

We are at Ford's place now, in his common room. I watch him make tea over one of those small dangerous butane stoves that are so ubiquitous here. He pours cup-to-cup, in the usual mad-scientist fashion. He moves with the same fluidity with which he moved at the restaurant. As I watch him I ponder his story, and I try to imagine him courting Aita, the woman in the picture on Aminata's dresser. But this leads me to thinking about Aminata, her chest against my chest, her cool tongue in my mouth; and then Wanda, the heat of her presence growing warmer out there, outside. She may be in some hotel out there right now, or in Whitaker's office, grilling him about my whereabouts, getting back from him nothing but invective that must surely sound insane to her. And I think of Ruth Barron. She sits naked to the waist, next to a campfire, holding an Evan Carl Norris voodoo doll over the flames. If Ford is right, who else could it be? Ruth, what have I done to you? Did Allen Weitz, with his little tweezered beard and pink cheeks tell you how very much I despise you? My stomach twists at the thought of Ruth killing me. My breath ceases at the thought of Wanda finding me. My heart leaps at the thought of Aminata leaving me, heading back to my country, as I inadvertently cannibalize souls in hers. My fingertips ache for her, my throat closes like a rifle chamber.

Ford hands me a shot glass of hot sweet tea, then calls for his housekeeper or woman or wife — I do not know what she is to him and I cannot catch her name. She bends close to Ford, who sits cross-legged on his bed. The girl is too young for Ford, I think. She cannot be older than sixteen, curve and cushion notwithstanding. "Non," says Ford's woman, and if I understand her French, I believe she has said that dogs are filthy and she will not allow one in the house. "Then we'll do it outside, just go get the boy like I ast you — leggi, leggi." He points at me. "Go ahead, Ev, drink y' tea. Ain't no poison in it."

Twenty minutes later Ford's woman returns and says, "Mamadou, sont ici." I rise, following Ford into the enclosed courtyard just outside. All afternoon long I have been amazed at the size of Ford's home. I had always imagined he lived in a shabby two-room apartment, but apparently he is the sole owner of an entire two-family, two-story building. He notices my gaping and rubbernecking, and tells me there are fourteen fully furnished rooms in his place. He is quick to add that he is not wealthy by American standards but is doing better than he had ever done in the States.

"Used to drive a dairy truck in the mornings," he tells me, "and run a little blow and reefer in the evenings. Never could get all the way over. Sometimes I couldn't even make rent. Money was all right, but I went through it like water." He tells me that one night his supplier brought him a few ounces of cocaine and an ounce of angel dust. Ford himself carried several thousand dollars that night, money belonging to two Oakland dealers. Ford pulled a gun on the supplier, stole the man's car, and drove directly to the airport with nothing but his passport, the money, and the clothes he wore. "Took enough blow for just me and left the rest of it in the car." He remembers asking the woman at the ticket counter whether he could get a ticket to somewhere, anywhere in Africa, and she told him there was a flight from New York to Paris to Dakar, a two-day trip. "Then I ast the broad where Dakar was and she told me Senegal, and I said to myself that a place with the name a Dakar, Senegal, got to be a bad motherfuck. Ka-boom, I was gone."

As he speaks my attention sunders and I watch a European boy, twelve, I would say, release a tall, gray terrier from its leash. The dog is poorly trained and it continually springs up, bounces its forepaws against the boy's chest. The boy shouts. He wrestles with the dog. He beats it about its muzzle and ears until the dog finally sits, its tongue lapping its nose. It breathes hard, and is on the verge of whining or barking. "Now check this out," says Ford, and he steps toward the dog with an outstretched hand, slaps a one-hundred-franc note in the boy's hand with the other. The boy leaves, but the dog remains motionless. It stares at Ford's left hand. Ford points at the dog with the same karate-chop position he brandished at me during lunch. He steps toward the dog, holds his hand an inch from its nose. He points his index finger and begins shaking slowly, as if shaking seasoning on a meal. He slowly backs away, still

wagging the finger. He backs carefully into a patio chair.
He sits. He drops his hand to the side and watches the dog
for two or three minutes. He slowly turns his head and looks
at me, but I note in the corner of my eye that the dog turns
its head in synchrony with Ford's. Ford's eyes are on me;
the dog's eyes are on me. I look from one to the other,
squinting my discomfort.

Ford raises his hand, points at me, and wags the finger
in the very same way he had wagged it at the dog. He drops
his arm, sits back in the chair, and closes his eyes. "This
your dog?" I say.

"Don't look at me," he says, "look at him."

The dog stares at me. "He's well trained," I say.

Ford scoots his chair round till his back is to me.
"Trained! Sheeit," he says. "Lookidizise."

"What?"

"Look-at-his-*eyes*."

It hits me immediately. The dog stares at me with Ford's
eyes. There is no doubt about this. The eyes are large, intelligent, detached. They are as close to human as a dog's
eyes can be. They study me, measure me. Ford chuckles. "I
seeeee you!" he says, and adrenaline and blood and fear
surge so hard through me that I feel as though I have been
kicked in the groin. I actually tremble. My mind races with
explanations, but nothing my mind says quells the way I
feel. "Bus," I say. I do not know what makes me say this.

"Say what?"

"Can we stop this?"

"You look scared."

"Well this is sort of weird." It occurs to me that I am
addressing the dog rather than Ford. This makes me all the
more terrified. I squat low and fold my arms around my
knees. Ford has lit a cigarette. I can smell it. "Africa," I
say, "do you know how tired I am of all this shit?" My throat

clutches itself, but I will not let myself cry. "You know," I continue. "You know, when I first got here, and got sick and all . . . Africa, I've seen some pretty weird things too. I mean I hallucinate sometimes, like I told you. And when I first . . . when all this stuff started happening to me, I kind of liked it. It's like drugs. It's scary, and everything, most of the time, but always interesting. Fascinating. I thought it was all making me stronger. Like when I joined the navy. I thought I'd come out stronger. But when I got out I was lazier, did drugs, hated work, hated being organized and on time for things. . . . Listen, could you get rid of this mutt?"

I hear the patio chair creak, and Ford shuffles to me. He places a hand on my shoulder. The dog lies down, yawning. "M' boy Anton'll be by to get him tonight. You OK?"

"Oh, yeah. Yeah. But I think I'll just go back home. I'm not stronger. I don't care what you say. I think I'm insane."

"See, Evan, it's like this: cain't no man really turn into an animal. When people tell you that shit they don't know what they talking about. You don't turn into one, you go inside one. Wild, tame — don't make no nevermind. If you was to leave right now, and I wanted him to follow you, he would, and he'd die before he'd take his eyes off you. Some cats keep two, three dogs around to cruise the compound at night. Sometimes they'll just set one on one fella, follow him around all day, all week, all year if they want to. All I gotta do is close my eyes and think about you and there you'll be — right in my head, like a memory, but it ain't memory." He drops his cigarette butt, steps on it. A wisp of smoke rises and vanishes. "You know," he says, "I been keeping a mutt on you ever since that night I seen you busting up all that sidewalk outside the bakery."

I close my eyes. I open them and stare at the end of his cigarette. I say, "That's a nice way of putting it."

"Excuse me?"

265

"Oh, Jesus, Ford. If you saw me kill that guy, just fucking say so! Get it over with." I am afraid I will cry. I keep breathing deeply so that I will not. "Don't play with me."

"You killed someone? When?"

"If you saw me outside the bakery, you saw me kill the amputee."

"I seen you, all right. You tried to give the dog a piece of bread. Next thing I seen, you was picking up a big-ass piece a sidewalk and chucked it on the ground with everything you had behind it. I got to say, you one cockstrong nigro."

I place my hands over my face. I press my fingertips down over my closed eyes. I can say nothing. Nothing comes to my mind. Ford, too, remains silent. He coughs once, then twice, then clears his throat, but says nothing. Then after a very long time of listening to crickets chirp, engines grunt, car rapide boys hollering the names of their vans' destinations, the laughter of a young couple on their drunken way down some sidewalk, I say, "Lamont saw me."

"Lamont Samb?"

I speak so softly that I am unsure whether he can hear me, but then I do not really care. "There's no way you could have seen me try to give the dog the bread, unless you were there with him. . . . You guys are trying to make me crazy, aren't you? You're in this together. I don't understand what I did to any of you people. I'm sorry for whatever I did, but —"

"Fuck Lamont," he says. And he says he is in nothing with Lamont but a struggle. Lamont, he says, is cunning, cold, clearheaded. He has no great knowledge of supernatural arts, in fact he knows very little, but it is he Ford most fears. Neither Old Gueye nor any other jinn, kouss, or spirit, no master of any esoteric art, can harm Ford if its origin is from N'Gor. "Got protection," he says. "The most

266

powerfullest marabou in the country is backing me. But Lamont, see, he don't work with the clay. He work with wood, metal, bullet, fist. He want Aminata's hand, and offing me is the onliest way he gonna get it. But I been smart. I steady keep a dog on him. Had one on him that night. I know f' sure he didn't leave N'Gor Island. Had me another dog cruising the city. The one that seen you. If you killed something that night it mighta been some insects or shit, but you sure didn't kill no man." He chuckles. "Coulda killt someone, though. I mean, you let that motherfucka fly."

"I don't know, Africa, I don't know. I'd like to believe you. I want to believe you, but I mean . . . I remember killing him. Lamont says he saw me —"

"Did he mention the bakery?"

"No."

"Did he say what you was wearing?"

"No, but he's a human, at least. You're trying to tell me a dog —"

"Jeans and a salmon-colored plaid shirt. Dogs is color-blind, but when I see through a dog it see in color. Did he describe the dude you killed?"

"Yes! Yeah, he did; he knew I killed the man with no legs. He couldn't have known any other —"

"Maybe you told someone."

"Right. Like, I'm sure I went around announcing to the world I killed this guy."

"Maybe you talked about it when you was sick in bed that one week."

"So you can hear what the dog hears too, right?"

"Nope."

"Then —"

" 'Cause I seen your mouth moving. I seen old man Gueye sit and watch you moan and groan and twist up that sheet for five days. I seen him give you tea. I seen Aminata bathe you, feed you, talk to you, check out your passport. I seen Binta sweep your room, dig through your pack. I was there, Ev. Watching, looking, thinking —"

"Why?"

"Huh?"

"I said why? If you're so afraid of Lamont creeping up on you and cutting your throat, why did you spend all this time watching me?"

"I wasn't on you the whole time, man. Don't you worry about me. I could run four, five dogs if I wanted to. I'm the one worrying about you. You in trouble 'cause you hard-headed. Don't believe in shit. Same as me when I got here. I know what it's like, bruddah. I know what you going through. I shoulda told you straight up you was in trouble when I met you, but that bullshit you told me about that research you was doing made it kinda hard." He pauses as if to let this sink in. I feel myself blush. "Hm," he says. "What was I supposed to tell you then? 'Say, m' fella, I know you lying. See I can see through dogs' eyes and . . . '? Naw, I couldn'ta did that, could I? And besides that it woulda been hard even if you hadn't lied. Had to let you see for yourself. Had to watch Phillipe leave them damn lizards all over your room, had to watch —"

"What about the bus?"

"Excuse me?"

"The bus. Did you ever see me just get . . . How do I put this? Did you ever just see me, well, disappear? Or just stand in one place for a long time and just stare into space, or pass out?"

"What you getting at, homes?"

I tell him about the bus, the times I had been on it, what I had seen, and whom. As I tell him I see his face shift from expression to expression, but I do not see anything that could be interpreted as recognition. As I end my story, his face exhibits bewilderment. "So what I'd like to know," I say, "is where was I? Did I just walk around in circles till the hallucination ended, or did this really happen? Did you see anything that might explain this?"

He pushes his lips forward, shrugs. "I don't have no idea, man, but I will say that you the onliest person I ever followed who the dogs is afraid of. They don't like to be nowhere near you." He shakes his head. "But that don't mean nothing," he says. "Someone's put jinn on you, or slipped you a mickey, is what that bus shit's all about. Both them things can be used to drive you crazy. See, it's real and it's not real. If there's one thing I cain't do with them dogs is see inside you. Now someone put a jinn or something on you, and Lamont and Gueye and them is smart enough to use it to turn you around, make you do something you don't wanna do. He squats beside me. "Wanna tell me, Ev?"

"There's nothing to tell."

He takes out his bag and some papers. He fixes a joint and lights it. It has begun to grow dark. A slight breeze spins the smoke round and round and carries it away. "What'd y'all talk about on the island last night?"

"That was your dog last night?"

"Muslim don't own no dogs, man. I borrow 'em, or find strays. And by the way, you cain't hear a jinn walk. That was my mutt making all that racket outside y' window."

"So you should've borrowed one that could swim."

Ford throws his head back and laughs. "Man, you crack me up. Say I shoulda got a dog that could swim. Sheeee . . . Naw, man, it ain't he couldn't swim. But someone coulda spotted the mutt — Lamont, you know? And Lamont woulda killt it." He offers me the joint, but I refuse. "So you gonna tell me?"

"Tell you what?"

"Evaaan, now come on, man. Don't do me like that. Now

I know something heavy deep musta made you swim a whole quarter mile to get off that island. Talk to me, homeboy."

I sit cross-legged. I sigh. "Well, if I'm crazy I don't suppose it makes any damned difference. Lamont tells me I'm a demm. They sent me to eat your soul. He said since I . . . well, you know. Blackmail."

"A what?" He begins laughing again. "A demm? Aw, man, naw. You believed him?"

"Well —"

"Evan, you got to be born a soul-eater, don't you know that? You don't come to Senegal and turn into one a them things." He stands, reaches his hand out to me. "You look tired, man. You can crash here if you want to. Get up feeling good. Have a big breakfast. I owe you one, anyway. Don't worry about y' friend. We'll pick her up and y'all can stay with me." He tells me that he has grits. His sister sent him some in the last shipment of T-shirts. He clears his throat. "Now, you do eat grits, don't you?"

I take his hand and pull myself up. "Don't be ridiculous. I grew up on 'em."

"Soulman eats soul food, *and* souls. Hey, hey, hey. So they sent you here to share food and shake hands, breathe my breath, smoke with me and stuff like that so you can eat my soul?" His grip is very strong. He holds my hand for longer than he should. I nod and pull my hand away. And he says, "So that's why you ain't ate nothing all day?" I nod. "That damn Lamont," he says. "Now why would he tell you that kinda thing? He'da been better off giving you a gun. Cain't no demm take me." He fingers the tere around his neck. "Demm. Damn." He folds his arms. "Something's going on and I'ma figure it out."

I step back from him. He offers me the roach. I shake my head and say, "Look, Africa, goddamn it, if I'm not what

Lamont says I am then what's wrong with me? I mean, I hallucinate, I black out, I get headaches I wouldn't wish on the devil. *Something*'s going on. Sometimes . . . Sometimes, I feel like I'm inside other people."

"Sound like a jinn to me, man. Shot a quinine in y' ass, a little kinki-li-ba tea, a little rest, you be strong enough f' me to take you to the great marabou. He'll make you right. Copacetic, homes, copacetic. Off to see the Wizard. Yes! Then click y' heels together three times and roll on home." He slaps me on the arm, nods toward the door to his room, and we walk inside. "Or stay if you want," he says.

32 I Ask for a Loan

As we enter, Ford's woman steps into the room and lays a few sheets of newspaper down on the floor. She leaves and returns with a large, covered bowl, two spoons, and a plastic pitcher of water. "Hope you don't mind left-overs," says Ford. He offers me a seat on the floor as though he were a waiter in an expensive restaurant. I sit, then he sits. He uncovers the bowl. "Folks don't cook much in the evening," he says. "Me, I don't care. Grub is my life. Hell, if I owned a car out here, I'd have me a bumper sticker on it that say, 'I break' — b-r-e-a-k — 'for snacks.'" I grin, but do not laugh. He hands me a spoon, but sets aside his own and digs in with his hand. "Tastes better this way. Go ahead, man, don't be shy. Spoon, hand, don't matter — just eat." The steam carries the aroma to my nose. There is rice cooked in tomato sauce and fish broth. Sweet carrots, tender yams, baby eggplants soft as breasts, whole peeled turnips, cabbage, onions, okra, and a large dark fillet of fresh tuna. "Tjebugin," I say, almost moaning the word. "Um-hm," says Ford, and he conveys an oily hand to his mouth. "You gonna eat it, or announce it?" I spoon a flake of fish, scoop some rice. "God, that's good," I say, chewing.

I eat my fill, past my fill. And as we eat we talk about all manner of things, but they are mundane things — the coming of the dry season, the best fish markets, local politics, which, I admit to Ford, do not interest me in the least. We talk about football and basketball. We talk about women. Ford tells me the young woman in his home is the sister of a friend of his. Khary is her name. His friend is an unemployed lawyer. There are over three hundred unemployed lawyers in Dakar, he tells me. "So they got all this education," he says, "but cain't use it, just sit at home, feeling frustrated and outta joint. Some of 'em get ministry jobs or hotel jobs, but how could a fella be happy with that?" He is paying this young woman a small salary and putting her through school. "Her brother's kept me outta jail more than once. I'ma tell you something, a lawyer's better 'n good tere in Dakar." He sucks his teeth for a moment, picks them with a finger for a moment. "And I want you to understand something," he says, shaking a finger at me. "I don't sleep with her. She's a kid."

"I didn't —"

"But you was thinking it. I know how niggers is. 'Cept you, I ain't so sure about." He quickly changes the subject to the Senegalese economy: unemployment, peanut crops and farming in general, neocolonialism, President Diouf's indifference to the common people. My eyes get heavy. I am too tired even for the anxiety of meeting Wanda, of explaining to her why I will be going to M'Bour. After a while I do not even respond to Ford's words with so much as Uh-huh's. He talks until the muezzin's call to prayer wafts into the room. "You look tired man. Whyn't you lay down for a while. Got a room upstairs you can use. Khary'll take you up. I gotta do m' prayers."

"What time is it? I still wanna make it to the airport tonight."

He looks at his watch. "You got plenty a time. I'll flag you a cab when I get back. Go ahead on, man." He rises and calls to Khary. Before he leaves he turns half toward me. "Before I take you up to M'Bour, you got to do a few things f' about seven days to purify y'self. Got to bathe in the ocean three times a day. You got to lay down about three times a day and imagine bathing y'self in white, white light.... Hell, naw I'm not kidding.... Listen to me. Don't eat red meat or bird, but fish is OK. Don't smoke nothing. Don't drink no alcohol. Stay away from coffee and tea. Stuff like that. Another thing you wanna do is draw a circle on the floor, or make a circle with salt or sand and put a picture of y'self — y' passport or something — in the middle of it. I'll get you a tere you can put over the picture. This'll protect you and purify you. Understand?"

"I don't know if I can remember all that."

"I'll write it down for you. Don't worry." He turns full away, making to leave.

"Africa, one more thing."

"Speak."

"I told Whitaker about . . . you know. I ran into him last night when I came into town and I confessed."

"Confessed? He ain't no cop, and he sure ain't no priest. I don't see what difference it make. You ain't done nothing."

"Well, I'm still not positive about that, but even if I didn't kill anyone I still got problems. My visa's dead. I think he might try to turn me in."

Ford belches. He stretches. "Alxamdulillah," he says. "Don't worry, Ev, he about as simpleminded as they come. I'll turn his ass into a lizard. Ain't no problem about the visa. Grease a few palms, you cool. I done it. Lots a folks do it. Hey, Mah Selamah, homes. Have a peaceful night."

Khary walks me up the stairs to my room. I am so heavy with food that I can scarcely move. My skin feels tight, my very bones are lead. I ask her to show me the bathroom so that I can splash water on my face. "La lumière est brisé," she says, snapping the switch up and down. "That's OK," I say, "I'm used to being in the dark."

"Eh?"

"C'est bien. No problem."

When I come out she leads me to my room. It is large and spare. There is a double bed whose pale green brocade spread is already turned back. The sheets are clean and tightly tucked around the mattress. Against one wall is a teakwood dresser upon which rests a candle, a copy of the Quoran, a brush, a comb, and a gold-plated hand mirror. The face of the dresser reflects off the clean linoleum floor. A large Naugahyde-and-cane chair sits in a corner by the window. I walk to the window and look out. "Fananl jamm," says Khary. "Good night," I say. I hear the dooor latch behind me. The building next to Ford's is so close I could lean out and touch it. I look down, thinking, momentarily, about the cliff on Gorée, the blind man falling head over heels over head over heels. I think about being inside Aminata, about the lie I told her about the yellow fever. I think about every moment that has brought me to this apartment, looking down on the litter — old boxes, bottles, flattened cans, banana peels, crumpled paper — covering the alley below. I open the window, am blasted by sound and smell, but the air feels good. Though I may not be, I feel innocent. I feel like no murderer. I drop to my knees, as if I were to pray. I will not pray. What possible good could prayer do in a world such as this? Still, I feel good, thankful, lucky. "Zero. Nothing. Zip," said Whitaker. ". . . mighta been some insects or shit, but you sure didn't kill no man," said Ford. I kick off my sandals, peel off my shirt and jeans. I slip into bed, thinking of Ruth Barron, naked to the waist, holding the Evan Carl Norris doll over the flames. I imagine myself dressed in a blazing gold boubou. I have a long white beard and carry a cudgel like Old Gueye's. I stand before the half-naked woman. I shake the cudgel at her in the same way Ford shook his finger at the dog. Ruth drops the doll into the flames and the flames go wild, begin to spin like a tornado. Her body, as if it were made of dust, shreds apart, is sucked into the flames. She doesn't speak or scream, but the words "I'll be back" crackle out of the dying fire. I turn and sit down at a card table. My father is at the table, as are Tom, Star, Bebe, Wanda, and Ruth. On a dust-covered phonograph, Asleep at the Wheel plays "It's Only a Paper Moon." Bebe is suddenly sitting on my lap, singing the song into my ear. I have an erection.

My father deals the cards. Each player gets thirteen. The cards are very strange, rather like Tarot. "What game is this?" I ask. "Paper poker," my father says. It is a very complex game. Cards fly from hand to deck to hand, till I cannot keep track of what I have. "How'm I doing?" I ask my father. My father pokes his cigar into his mouth, shakes his head, and says, "Ain't no son of mine." Bebe sings: "But it wouldn't be make believe if you believed in me." We bet with barbecued ribs and chicken. I have five or six aces. Bebe gives me a long wet kiss. "Now we can have a baby," she says. Wanda throws her bid on the table. They are cooked hands, human hands. "They're your hands," says my father. I look at my hands, saying, "No, mine are right here," but they are large, fat, ending in long yellow nails. Then my arms begin to swell, my chest, my stomach, my legs, all grow and fatten like water filling balloons. I fear I will explode. "Oh, God," I say, and rise up from bed, my stomach still full, roiling. I try to leap up from bed, but my legs are heavy. I rise as if I were carrying myself in my arms. I stumble into the bathroom, drop over the toilet, and vomit out my dinner. It explodes out of me, and I cough till tears come to my eyes. "Oh, God," I say again. I rise and go to my bedroom, fumble through my pants until I find my matches. I walk back to the bathroom, strike a match, and hold it over the toilet bowl. There floats my food, chewed, but undigested.

Yet I still feel heavy, bloat. I plod back to my room, fall to my knees, and fold my hands together. "Oh, God . . ." I say, but my mind is blank. I kneel there, squeezing my hands together in the semi-darkness of this room. No words come. Something snaps against my window and I start. This causes my head to thump, but there is no pain. I listen. "The jinn," I say aloud. I listen: "Pssst. Psssst . . . Eva'." It is Phillipe. I creep to the window on hands and knees. I draw myself up, peer out, but say nothing. "Eva' Norrits, is me, Phillipe. You must come back." I cannot see him, but call out in a conversational tone. "You were there, Phillipe. Asshole. You were in your room. Why didn't you answer your door?"

"Eva', please, come out. Ford will kill you," he hisses.

"Not before I kill you. Get lost."

"Eh? You coming down, Eva'?"

I feel murderous. I slip into my clothes, my stomach still so full that I can barely button my pants. Carrying my sandals, I ease open my door and slip down the stairs. Why I am being quiet all of a sudden I do not know. When I get to the side of the building I stride right up to Phillipe and blast my fist into the side of his head. "Get up," I say, but he refuses. "I was not in my house, Eva', is true. Binta say she hear' you talking in a high voice, but she was afraid."

"Why don't you get lost?"

"I was no at home, man, is true."

"I said get lost."

"I don't under —"

"Leave, go, *pars, sors*, split, walk, exit, move."

"Come with me. Ford will kill you this night, and, Eva',
your 'ooman is there."

"Tell Aminata I said good-bye."

"No! No! Wandah." He accents the second syllable, and
for a moment I am not sure what he is saying. "She is with
Whitaker. He bring her there. Man, you must come."

"Are there police?"

"Police? No. No police, just Wandah, and Whitaker."

"Get up."

"Don't hit me more, OK?"

He stands.

"How did you know I was here?"

He tells me that he has a cousin in Ouakam who saw
Ford and me at Sam's.

"Figures. Tell them to come here. Tell them to bring my
stuff. You can have my cigarettes, my dope, and I think
there's a couple thousand francs on my shelf. You can have
that too." Phillipe makes no reply. He stands here, retuck-
ing his shirt into his pants. "You understand me?" I say. He
is dressed in jeans and a short-sleeved sport shirt. In this
darkness the shirt seems to float in the air. It is spotted
with blood. "You must come. Aminata is getting lost tomorrow and she want to see you."

He does not, of course, understand why I am laughing.
"If she wants to see me before she gets lost she can come
here, too."

"Ford is dangerous."

I turn and head toward the front of the building

"Evahhh! Please!" There is something in his voice that
is so little-boylike, so hurt and surprised that I stop.
"Please."

I turn and look at him. He stands motionless, as though
he is holding his breath. He looks so thin and small. He

looks no more than thirteen. I am almost sorry for hitting him. "You know, I loved y'all, Phillipe. There was a time I loved everyone a y'all."

"You comin' back?" he says, sliding his hands into his trouser pockets and taking one step toward me.

"No, I'm not."

"Don't be afraid to eat soul, Evan. Is good. It make you smart. You can understand every book. You can know what genius know, or old man know. You are not a demm, Evan. You are not that, and I am not that. But we are brainmen. Smart ones, you know? We live to be eighty, ninety, one hundred years in one day. We know good, we know bad . . ." He pauses and lowers his head. He lifts it and takes one more step toward me. "And we know the world. . . . Do you see?"

"Look, Phillipe, I can't go back there. I can't. Listen here. I can't. Understand that. I won't go back there. You guys tried to screw me. I didn't ask for this bullshit, homeboy, and I ain't asking for more. You dig this?"

"But —"

"Naw, now if you so concerned that fatboy up there is gonna kill me go get me some money so I —"

"Eva', why you talk this way? I don' understand you."

"What way?"

"Fast like that."

"I'm . . . sorry." I have been doing my father routine, strutting, huffing, preaching Texas thunder. "I'm sorry, Phillipe, but look here, I thought you said you knew the world. Why —"

"I only understand when I am hungry."

"OK, I see. Only when you're hungry. I like that." I smile at him, and for the briefest slip of time I almost wish it were true, what he has been saying. But I think

of how Ford made me put the rock in my mouth, how Lamont drew me in with his artificial woman, how Chuck,
Star, Alice, Tom, Bebe, and Wanda drew me word pictures
so exotic and lush that I, as of yet, have been unable to
hack my way out of them. I consider telling Phillipe that
he is wrong about me. I am neither "brainman" nor demm,
but I am merely gullible. That is what it comes down to.
I have nothing of my own. "Phillipe," I say. "You don't
trust Ford. I don't trust you. If all those people want to
see me, you go home, get some money — eighteen, twenty
thousand francs — so I can go to the Pompidou Hotel. You
know it?"

He nods.

"I'll be there, you dig?"

Phillipe stands and says nothing for a minute. He lowers
his head. "He kill my mother —"

I collar him, push him through the garbage and pin him
to the wall. I am surprised at how quickly I have come again
to feeling murderous. My breath is foul; my body stinks; I
am fibrillating with anger. I could bounce his skull off this
wall a thousand times. "Don't you dare! That's a lie! Your
own father killed her, you understand me? Do you understand me, boy?"

Phillipe trembles, and I feel bad again. I feel gullible
again, but I force myself to go on. "Just get me some money.
I'll check into the hotel, and Wanda, you, and Aminata can
come. Understand? Ford won't be there. Lamont won't be
there. Whitaker won't be there. Now, I will not stand out
here in this rank-ass alley debating this with you. You come
back, throw the money into my window, and meet me in
the hotel one hour and thirty minutes after you bring the
money. Do you understand me?"

"I will be back," he says. "I will bring you money and
find you in the hotel. . . ."

"One hour and thirty minutes *after* you bring the money here. Denga?"

I let him go and he falls, stands, backs away. I think there are tears in his eyes. He turns and runs.

I move my bloated belly back inside and upstairs. I sit down on the bed. I wait. I feel sick. I feel pregnant.

33 I Get on the Bus

I am nervous. I pace across the room, out the door, down the hall, back to the room. I stop at the bathroom every now and then and regard the cool porcelain, the tile, the water. I would rather feel my head rocket with pain right now than vomit again. But I do not think a headache is due, for my head painlessly thumps away, tumbling like shoes in a dryer. It is a wild rhythm that my footfall cannot match. I sit. I stand. I smoke. I pick up the telephone and punch out the operator's number. I hear his voice. I hang up. Why should I call home? What can I say to my mother? What possibly could I tell her?

I rehearse aloud: Mom, do you know what kind of world this is? ("No, son, what kind of world is this?") Well, Mama, life is clay and the world is a potter's wheel, OK? ("Yes, go on.") This is the kind of world where beans, fish, frogs, and ice blocks can fall from the sky. This is the kind of world where people, sitting up in their living rooms drinking Fresca and watching old sitcoms, can, for no reason you could put your finger on, burst into sun-hot flames. Christ, Mama, I don't know. This is stupid. Wait. Let me tell you what kind of person I am. ("I'm listening, son.") OK. Good. This is the kind of person I am. I believe in everything. I believe that if a guy wants to get from point "A" to point

"B" he's got to rise from wherever the hell he's sitting and walk, you know? Or drive or ride a bike or whatnot? ("Whatnot?") Or whatever. I've picked up a word or two from this guy I know. Anyway, Mom, I believe also that the same guy can get from the one place to the next just by tapping his heels together and thinking it. Is this making any sense to you? ("Not a bit, son. Go on.")

And I do go on, pacing, smoking, rehearsing things I will never say to my mother. My ankles hurt, as do my knees and shoulders. I weigh ten thousand pounds. It is clear to me what is going on. I look at my thick fingers, through half-closed eyes, as though squinting at a half-healed wound. The long nails like yellowed ivory could scratch out eyes. The lifelines, deep slashes, are the work of some mad artist. The backs are almost hairless. Two knuckles are stiff, sore. I hurt them. . . . I do not remember how at this moment, but I will soon. For there is no doubt — I am digesting Ford. I do not feel bones shift or hair curl out or pull in as happens in high-tech horror films, but it is between seeing and not seeing, between remembering and not remembering, between hunger and no hunger, that he unfolds, unravels before me. It is exquisite. Memories open like roses, physicality hardens like cooking egg. Names, snatches of conversation, faces, places, ideas burst forward in flashbulb brilliance. Colors shift, just slightly. The pulse changes, just slightly.

Mama, this is the kind of person I am. Remember the time that the five of us went to New York for New Year's? Do you remember our walking up Fifth Avenue and stopping before that enormous dark building as, one by one, all the lights were snapped on, all the way from the bottom to the top? That is me.

Do you remember that night in Louisiana when you, I, and Uncle A.J. were sitting on Grandmama and Granddaddy's patio? Remember? There was no moon, and the sky was thick with clouds. Do you remember that warm, bayou-scented wind that came out of nowhere? Do you remember Uncle A.J. pointing his pipe to the sky and saying, "Look at them clouds roll away." And as that gray peeled back, how many stars did we see emerge from the black sky? You said, "Just like bubbles rising up in soda water." That was the first time I had ever heard you use that word, soda water. Well, anyway, that's me.

Mama, I remember when I first got here, Aminata — or was it Aita? — told me a story about this old woman who was laid up in bed. She was so sick that she could not feed herself, and that was very very unfortunate for her because her husband, who had been kind and a good provider, was dead, and all her sons and daughters were lazy, and would often forget to change her bedding. She would go without food or water for as long as three consecutive days. Each day she would grow weaker. She would cry out to Allah to take her. "What have I done? How have I sinned, Great Allah, to have borne such callous children? They have money, I know, because I hear it rattle in their bags when they walk by. I know they have food because I hear them pounding millet, slaughtering chickens; I hear the clatter of calabashes and bowls. I hear throats pull in cold-smelling water. I smell the sweet smell of rice nearly every day. I smell the okra and yams and the salty fish. But they bring me nothing! Ndeysahn, ndeysahn, ndeysahn, Allah. I have borne these children till my bones cracked, suckled them till my breasts hung like dead fish, wiped them — front and back — held them close and closer, told them story, daubed their wounds, picked them fruits and seeds and berries. I have pounded their millet, spooned them couscous and yams, mended their clothes or sewn them new ones. I have risen with their cries and sung them to sleep, let myself sleep only when the last of them lay dreaming, covered or swaddled by my own hands. Great God, I beseech Thee! Take me. Send an angel."

But instead of an angel appearing to her, late one night a mouse crawled out of her bedroom wall. A little gray mouse, with black eyes and sharp teeth. She watched it slip from its hole, scramble up her bed, and duck beneath the covers. "Ayy!" she screamed, when she felt the little animal's sharp teeth take a tiny bite out of her toe. "You have bitten me!" she protested in her cackling voice. "Curse you, you issue of Bouki the Hyena and Golo the Monkey!" Her oldest daughter, Debo, came slowly shuffling into her room, saying, "Mama, why do you wake me from my sleep? Are you complaining again?"

"My child," said the old mother, "I do not mean to disturb you, but there is a mouse in my room, and the little rascal has taken a bite from my toe. Could you please find a way to dispose of it?"

"What?" said the daughter. "You wake me for this? Wyyy! You old bag of hay. Fine, Mother, as you wish, but I will get it when I finish my nap."

Well, needless to say, the daughter never returned to get rid of the mouse, though she, or some other indolent daughter would deign to bring old mother a sip of water or a morsel of food. And each time one of them would happen to appear, she would ask that he or she do something about the mouse. But the room grew dustier, and the mouse remained. And each and every night the mouse would creep into the room to nibble away at the poor old woman. It happened with such regularity, became such a routine, that after a while the old woman did not even complain or cry out. Her body was slowly disappearing, and she was thankful. On those rare days when one of her children would remember to pay her a visit, they would say things such as,

"Mother, you really should eat more. You're becoming so small," or "Mother, these covers are too many for you. Why don't you let me take these? The nights are getting awfully cold."

So the woman, night by night, was reduced to a torso with arms, then a torso with no arms, then a head, then but two eyes. And when she was but one eye, she said, "God is Great! for my suffering is nearly done!" Then, on the last night, the mouse scurried upon the bed and raced to the eye. And the woman said, "My little mouse, before you devour me, this night, please be kind enough to tell me why it was that Allah sent you, and not a merciful angel." "But dear woman," said the mouse, "I am a merciful angel. Now close your eye and give thanks to God." The woman closed her eye, and the mouse swallowed it whole.

But this is not the end, for the woman opened her eye and was astonished to find that she could open her other eye, and with her two eyes she discovered that she again had legs and a body and hair and a tongue. But all had changed. Slowly it dawned on her that she was no longer an old woman, for she had hair where she had never had it before. She had a tail and paws and long teeth. She was a lioness! And she was hungry! She stood up on her bed and called out in a loud voice, "Children! I am hungry. Please have mercy on an old woman." The first to appear was Debo, and she very quickly disappeared. So Debo, Aida, Koumba, Mamadou, and all the rest were devoured one by one. The lioness ate a long and happy meal, and when she was done, she closed her eyes and slept. When she awoke, she awoke in Paradise, and she was no longer a lion, no longer even a woman, but a soul at rest.

Well, I'm all these things, Mama. The mouse, the Louisiana night sky, the Fifth Avenue building on New Year's Eve. I believe in everything. Everything you taught me, everything the old man taught me. Everything I have ever heard or seen or felt, understood or misunderstood, I have believed. Aita . . . No, no, I'm sure it was Aminata this time, who once told me that I should respect the things my elders say. I remember it was she because we'd been embroiled in one of our many arguments about her father. We were on our way to Le Café Lyon, this little place near the wharf. We went there for what you might call a date. I was drunk sick dead in love with her, but I couldn't really tell how she felt about me. It was her father that made me feel that way. You know, sometimes when I'd try to imagine kissing her all I could see was her father embracing her. No, don't get me wrong; the man's no daughterraper. It wasn't like that, not that kind of embrace. It was an embrace so tender that I knew I could never match it. It was like you hugging me, or Wanda holding her boy.

And I was thinking about all this hugging and holding right there in the middle of our argument, right there in the middle of my asking her how she could love someone she didn't really understand? "He hardly even looks at you," I said. "He never *asks* you to do anything, he orders you to . . ." and so on, and so on. She folded her arms, Aminata did, she sighed, and stared out the bus window. "Evan," she said, "what's wrong with you? Are you crazy? What kind of person would try to make a daughter hate her father? Listen to your voice, American man. Listen to yourself. Cutting yourself from your olders is stupid. Where is all knowledge then? Where is everything? Here we say that when an old one dies, it is like a library burning down. Do you understand what we mean by this?" Of course I did. I shut up for the rest of the bus ride, Mom; I couldn't say a word. And when I really thought about it I knew she was right. What you and Dad taught me is more deeply embedded than any book, any broadcast, any journey. But, Mama,

287

you taught me that life is fat and sweet and the old man taught me supply and demand. And Aminata, remember, said 'olders.' This includes not only you and Dad, but Wanda, Tom, Star, Bebe, Chuck, Ruth Barron. Who doesn't it include?

Mama, in just a few minutes, two of the thickest volumes in my life will come walking through that door. Aminata is a novel, full of more life and more expressiveness than Dickens. Sometimes I doubt she's ever told me the truth about anything, but I don't think I've ever cared. Not really. Not when I am near her. Now, Wanda — you know, I never liked that name — Wanda is nonfiction, tough as Foucault. ("Who?") Never mind, Mom. Just some guy. My point is she keeps me honest, cuts beneath my bullshit. She's never ever lied to me, and I've never ever understood how rare that is in humanity. Not really. Not till now.

So what do I do now, Mama? Ami's leaving soon. Wanda's just arrived, but they'll both be here in a little while, and I have no idea what I'll say or do. I would like there to be tears and fists and long pink nails slicing my flesh. There should be accusations, stinger-sharp, zipping round this room like mosquitoes. Wanda will be packing heat. "You ripped me, motherfucka. Where's my money at?" she'll say. I'm sorry, Mom. That's someone else. Someone else's voice, not mine, not Wanda's. And, no, Wanda doesn't carry weapons. Neither does Ami, but she may, blind and hot, grab whatever weapon she can get to. Both women will shriek, pummel me into consciousness. (No, Mama, into consciousness — I'm still holding out for the possibility that I am dreaming this, that I lie dead to the world on the floor of a Vietnamese restaurant, or in a hospital bed with clear fluids dripping from bottles to tubes to veins in my arms.) Then they'll lift me, with Phillipe's help, and toss me out the window so I can breathe for once, think for once. Ford's essence and mine will explode upon the streets like a sack of flour. Ford will find himself at his mosque in prayer. I will find myself somehow, somewhere. As long as it's not here.

That's what I'd like. But what is most likely to happen is that I will have to suffer their silence for what will seem like an eternity. There will be no hugs at the door, no words at all. I will offer them seats. They'll refuse them. I'll sit on the very corner of the bed, thread my fingers together as Dad would, tremble a bit. I'll look from Wanda to Aminata, from Aminata to Wanda. I'll clear my throat and say, "I'm sorry. To both of you. I can't explain any of this." Then Wanda will say, "Aminata says you've asked her to marry you. You could have written. You could have called." Then Aminata will add, "He all the time lies, Wanda. Every word . . . And he killed someone." "Yes," Phillipe will say, "is true. I have call the police already." Wanda will close her eyes and sigh. "Jesus, Jesus-God," she'll whisper. But I'll ignore this part. I'll probably just sit there with my ever-bloating self, and regardless of how I feel about each woman, I'll probably lie to Wanda, say, "But I did write you, Wanna. Of course I'm all right. No, nothing's changed." And to Aminata I will tell the truth. "You hurt me. I'll never forgive you. I'll always love you."

I'm losing sight of all this, Mama. Or more precisely these images are alternating with images of bags of white powder, fistfuls of money, dark glasses. *"You ripped me, motherfucka. Where's my money at?"* I fear these images no more and no less than I do the images of what may happen when my two ex-lovers come pounding on my door. It's strange, I know, but I haven't been feeling so hot lately.

There is a knock at my door. They are here. Perhaps she will not recognize me. I let my pacing carry me to the door, and I open it. It is Lamont, and he is alone. He offers his right hand in greeting and we shake. "Where are they?" I say. He does not answer. He does not release my hand. Instead, he grips it as tightly as he can, reaches into his pocket with his left, and removes a handkerchief. I notice on that hand he wears a rubber glove. He wipes the cloth on my face, first the right cheek, then the left. "Motherfuck," I say.

"It doesn't hurt," he says, "but it will paralyze you. I'm sorry, boy. I've got to do it while Ford is in you. You go and he goes with you." He drops the handkerchief to the floor. "Motherfuck!" I say.

He smiles at me. "Got you," he says. He wears a mustard-colored khaftan. His hair glistens with pomade and his shoes are carefully buffed. He regards me with his big slow-moving eyes, and I almost feel admiration for him. "You put up a good enough fight," he says. "You should be proud."

"Was Wanda really there?"

"Who's asking?"

"I'm asking f' him. He still here, you know."

"Well, good. That's kind of you, Ford. So Evan, boy," he says, raising his voice a little as though I were in the next room, "she really was there, but when Phillipe returned for your money, he told her and Whitaker that you weren't at Ford's but ran away to Banjul. She cried, man. I sort of felt bad for her. I feel bad for you, too." He bends over, picks up the handkerchief. He grabs for my wrist. I am not quick enough to move away. He wipes more of the chemical onto my wrist. All my guts and all my veins pound against my bones and skin. "Please, Lamont, don't do this." I am whining, sobbing like an idiot. *I don't play that bullshit, man. Cut that shit out. Crying like you need a motherfucking diaper.* "Lamont. Lamont. Ain't no need for this. Ain't no need for this. Dag, man." Lamont rubs my wrist as would a doctor an arm before giving a shot. My arm and face feel a little warm, but there is no pain. "I don't know how fast this is supposed to work," says Lamont. "Monsieur Gueye says that when he was young they used to use a needle hidden between the fingers, but I couldn't figure out how to do this and Monsieur Gueye couldn't remember. But anyway, that would be too much like a spy movie, don't you think?" He lets me go, looks me straight in the eye. He is no longer smiling, but I cannot read him. "I'm not enjoying this at all, Ford. I know how Ami's mother felt about you."

"Stepmother."

He arcs his brows. "Aita was Ami's mother, boy. I mean, you could tell, couldn't you? All you had to do was look at them. Listen, I don't know if she told you this lie so you would think she was younger, but I knew Madame Gueye before Ami was born." He rubs the cloth on my face again. He need not have done this. The chemical had begun to take effect soon after the handshake. I can scarcely move. "There," he says. "Monsieur Gueye told me that when he was a boy they would use a sliver of roundwood, or something like that, and it would always work perfectly. . . . But anyway, I wanted to finish answering Evan. I was angry with Phillipe at first because I knew you were there; I knew he was lying. But I'm glad you decided not to come to the village, after all. It's much easier this way. Whitaker brought coppers. We would have had all this explaining to do, and it would have wasted time. You won't have your 'teeth' in Ford forever, you know. We would have to have tried this whole thing over. It would have been much harder to do."

"They'da believed you just like last time."

"Excuse me?"

"Ford. It's Ford talking."

"Oh. Well, they didn't believe us that time, Ford. You went to jail for bad papers, not murder."

"Well . . . Fuck you anyway."

He smiles, then chuckles a little. He is very handsome. I suppose I can see why Aminata is willing to marry him, but she will never love him. "Well," he says, "I suppose they would have believed us over you. But you never know. There's a lot you don't know, and a lot I don't know. Who would have guessed that soul-eating is a disease? Or even that it's real —"

"You a gotdamn lie, boy. It ain't —"

"What does it matter now, eh? Just look at you, all twisted up together like this. You know, until I heard you speak, and until I saw him in your eyes, I didn't really think this was true. Of course, I would have still killed you any-way, Evan. But look at you. Who would have guessed that all these things work, the tere and all. Now I see why maybe I don't sell so many policies. Old Gueye is smart. I don't know if all he says is true, but it makes me think, anyway. It's kind of spooky, all this. Demm and jinni and — that reminds me, did you ever see your jinn? Well, not really yours, but that one they talked about? Was that real too?"

"Didn't see no gotdamn jinn," I tell him, but I am almost sure it is the boy with the peppercorn hair. And if it is not, I will always see it that way regardless of what Old Gueye or any drooling retarded boy sees. I must have something of my own here. Something for myself. It is what I came here for anyway. Lamont looks me up and down, still smil-ing. "But anyway, she's a beautiful girl, don't you think? Gull bi nerxna trop, Evan. Beautiful. In fact, Whitaker had his arm around her little waist when they left."

"You one cold dog, Lamont."

"I know —"

"Cold as ice."

"I know," he says, and he brings his face close to mine, till all its features blur and I see nothing but wallet black skin, and his eyes. "I am cold," he says, "but what do you expect? Do you think I can't guess how Aminata learned about your disease? She was perfectly fine before you came, and now . . ." He stands back and crosses his arms. "Listen, boy, you'd better lie down; you won't be able to move in just a few minutes."

I do lie down. Already my joints feel stiff. My skin tingles, my lips are numb. I feel very relaxed, all things considered. Lamont carefully peels the glove off his left hand, lifts up his khaftan, and removes a machete from a sheath. "All I can say now, Evan, is that I'm not doing this for bride-price. This is the price you yourself will pay." He takes my cigarettes and matches from my pocket. He diddles with a cigarette for a moment but decides not to light up. He slips all the cigarettes and the matches into his pocket.

"Did Aminata really wanna come see him tonight?"

"No. She left this morning."

"Decided she'd leave a few days early, huh?"

"No. She had planned to leave on this day a long time ago." He is silent for a while. He stares at me as though I am a museum piece. "I will marry her still, I suppose. She'll make a good living someday. And her father promises me I will be able to go to graduate school next year. In the U.S., maybe."

He runs his thumb along the blade and looks at me. He is trying to be cool, his brows raised, his bottom lip jutting, but he cannot hide his nervousness. He swallows almost every time he speaks; he trembles slightly. He places the blade at the foot of the bed and sits near my shoulder. His forehead shimmers with perspiration. He reaches down, feeling my face and neck. "Almost ready," he says. "You won't bleed as much if I wait long enough.

"You can still talk, can't you?"

"I can still talk, but I'm getting kinda cold."

"Tell me, where is the body of the crippled man?"

"Who you asking?"

"Why would I be asking you, Ford? Don't be stupid."

"Ain't no body. Wasn't no murder."

He knits his brow, looks down at a space somewhere between the end of his nose and the body that lies before him. His eyes move left and right, left and right. He clutches the shoulder. "I want him to tell me. It would be wrong to leave the man without a proper burial. He was a real Muslim. Not like you."

We do not answer him. We only smile. "OK. OK," he says, and he folds the blankets over the body, adjusts the pillow under the head. It makes no difference. We are cold deep, deep inside, so cold we cannot shiver. "You know I'm innocent, Lamont. You know I didn't kill her. Allah's my witness. Allah Akbar."

"I know," he says.

"Old One-Eye killed her."

"Sure he did. What else could he do?"

"Then why kill me?"

"Who's asking?" he says. He stands up and stretches. His forearm muscles ripple. He crosses the room and draws the curtains. He steps to the other side of the room and shuts out the light. The body feels suddenly warm, yet there seems to be no heartbeat. Everything feels as it did the night the body floated on the ocean. Free, soft, pure. It feels as though it could fly. *Its atoms will float upward and upward. Burst in the heat of the day. The consciousness will*

*rise up like vapor. Will steam. Will roll. Half-invisible. Far
into. The sky. Get caught up in. The clouds. Choke them.
Till they. Can hold. No more. The clouds will cast us down
in. A silent dry rain. We will hang in. The air. Between sky
and soil. Between sky and. Sea . . .* If we are not mistaken,
we are still smiling. We are smiling even though it is apparent that Lamont is actually going to go through with
this. He looks worried. We are not certain why it is Lamont
who is worried. We feel just fine. "Evan?" he says, his voice
as soft as smoke. "Evan?" We do not answer. "Evan," he
says, "What would you say if I told you that there was no
poison on that handkerchief, eh? What if I told you that, if
you wanted to, you could rise up from this bed, take this
blade from my hands, and cut me in half? It could be, boy.
It could be. Come on. Get up. It's true, my friend. You can
get up, my friend."

We do not answer.

"Do you give up that easy, boy? After all this? Come on,
boy, get up. Walk out of here. You can, if you want to. There
was no poison. None at all. See how it is? See how we teach
you? Another lesson, Evan. Come on . . . Come on."

We do not move. Lamont blows air from his nose, clucks
his tongue. "Come on . . . Come on. I'm not joking this time.
You can get up. Struggle a little. Fight me some more." No.
No. We do not move. We do not even try. Whatever he is
trying to do, it will not work. It has come to this. This is
what it will be. But there is something that must be said.
If the body will cooperate the words will come. We open the
mouth and can barely move the lips and tongue. "You know
something?" we say.

The moonlight, streetlights, headlights, taillights reflect
off his forehead, and his eyes, and the raised machete. "You
know something, homeboy?"

"What." He is shaking. His nostrils flare. There is something like terror in his eyes.

"Sometimes, you know, sometimes I really hate being black."

He grunts just once, and I am on the bus, and I am on the bus for good.